six month Rule

THE KINGSTON ALE HOUSE SERIES

A.J. PINE

Entangled Publishing, LLC
2614 South Timberline Road
Suite 109
Fort Collins, CO 80525
Visit our website at www.entangledpublishing.com.

Select Contemporary is an imprint of Entangled Publishing, LLC.

Edited by Karen Grove
Cover design by LJ Anderson
Cover art from Depositphotos
Kingston Ale House logo by Ashley @ BooksByMigs

Manufactured in the United States of America

First Edition July 2016

Journeys end in lovers meeting,
Every wise man's son doth know.

Twelfth Night
William Shakespeare

JUNE

Chapter One

Gemini: You are what you wear, so dress the part. Today more than any other day, make sure your clothes tell everyone who you are. Only when you show your true self can you truly be seen.

Holly's smile faltered. What the hell did that mean? No one was truer to herself than she was, and she had the clothes to prove it. Okay, well, she had last year's samples to prove it, but even on her worst day, Holly Chandler's designer wardrobe was a force to be reckoned with. And she kept *nothing* hidden, yet her app seemed to be accusing her of quite the opposite. Despite what seemed to be a disapproving horoscope—which she insisted to her sister she only read for fun—Holly felt like a million bucks. And there was no question—she looked like a million bucks, too. After pulling off Saturday night's fashion show as head assistant director, Holly knew her meeting with Andrea this morning was the one she'd been working toward for five years. Maybe all-black wasn't Holly Chandler's norm, but her sister said the dress made her look like Audrey

Hepburn, and paired with the perfect Jimmy Choo peep-toe booties, the vintage black frock was exactly what she needed to show her boss that she could be taken seriously as a partner rather than an employee. Holly was never one for business wear, but she was sure this look *meant* business, that it said she was ready to take on whatever Andrea threw at her. All she needed was her hazelnut soy latte, icing on the cake that she knew this day would be.

Yet just as the elevator doors were about to kiss, a polished, tan Cole Haan wingtip forced them back open. That would leave a scuff mark, which was why Holly was smiling when Charlie Tate, Trousseau's finance director, invaded her early-morning daydreams—and her private elevator ride.

"Morning, gorgeous," Charlie said.

Holly sighed. Conversations with him always seemed to circle back to when they'd been a *we*. But she wouldn't let herself get distracted. Not today. "Morning, Charlie."

She couldn't help but admire everything above the wingtips. The navy suit, one of the three buttons fastened over the periwinkle-and-white pin-striped button-down. Maybe the jacket could be taken in a notch at the shoulders, but who was she to judge? Charlie worked in finance, not in design. On any given day, he blew most suited men out of the water. And damn, she really did love a man who could dress.

"Everyone's talking about your home run Saturday night," he added, his grin spreading across his lightly tanned face.

"Really?" She innocently raised her brows while offering him a fuller response in her head. *I know, right? Andrea gave me the reins, so I worked my ass off for that show. And guess what? I nailed it, and now she's going to make me partner. Not bad for twenty-six, eh?*

Charlie nudged her shoulder with his.

"Celebrate later after Andrea makes it official?"

Holly's face erupted into the smile she'd been keeping at bay. Aw, screw it. Today was not the day for her poker face. Except her grin and Charlie's grin were probably not about the same things. So she dialed it back a few notches.

"Thanks, Charlie. But I don't think that's a good idea."

Ugh, why did he have to be all blond and designer suit wearing and, if memory served, pretty damned sexy out of the suit as well?

See? Distracting.

"Still on that six-month kick, huh?" he asked as the elevator made its first stop—*Charlie's* stop—on the fourth floor.

The doors opened.

"It's not a kick," she insisted, watching him back away. "You *liked* my rule eighteen months ago," she added, reminding him that he'd jumped at the chance for a six-months-or-less, no-strings-attached relationship.

Charlie was over the threshold now, and a handful of people pushed past him, again invading Holly's solo ride.

A sun-kissed wave flopped down over his forehead, and Charlie, laid-back as he was, let it hang there so Holly's fingers itched to push it out of the way. Jesus, it was like he knew that, rule or not, Holly was having a bit of a drought, which meant something as innocent as unruly hair could set her mind in directions it really shouldn't go on a Monday morning. The Monday morning when Holly would make partner.

There was a sobering thought. Work. Career. The reason for the rule in the first place. It wasn't that she didn't enjoy having someone to come home to at night. She quite liked that part. It was just that after the honeymoon phase—the part where everything was rainbows and puppy dogs and great sex all the time—then it became work. There were expectations that Holly couldn't meet. *Can you stop bringing work home with you? Do you have to work on the weekend?*

What comes first, work or me?

The answer was always the same. Holly's passion for Trousseau always trumped her passion for other people or things.

Charlie shrugged.

"And I'd like it again for another three to six," he added with a wink. "Don't I get a do-over after nearly two years?" he asked, but Charlie's face was lost in the sea of people who didn't care about Holly's life enough to wait for her to finish a conversation with a man she used to sleep with and with whom she was considering—maybe—sleeping again.

As the doors made their way toward kissing again, she leaned her head back against the elevator's wall, smiled, and reminded herself that after stopping for her latte on the fifth floor, she was riding up to ten, to where her life would be forever changed.

This time it was a black Ferragamo loafer that parted the doors. Yet it was as if the elevator knew not to mess with *this* shoe, that it was far too precious to carelessly scuff. Or, she decided as the wearer of said shoe entered the dwindling space, perhaps the elevator knew who was attached to it.

Holly's eyes trailed from the soft, black leather of the loafer to the cuff of the slate-colored pants expertly cut to fit these legs and these legs only. Of this she had no doubt. Then there was the jacket and vest, same color, each buttoned snug over a lean, taut torso. Holly thanked the stars, every last constellation, for perfectly tailored suits. And vests. What was it about a man in a vest?

"Thank you."

Holly's head shot up to see the words directed at an older woman whose finger depressed the door-open button. The voice was deep and buttercream smooth. And was that...an English accent?

Her ovaries might have just gone supernova, but she

could hold it together for one more floor. Holly Chandler wasn't a girl to lose it in an elevator, no matter how much those two words, spoken in that voice, with that *accent*, melted her insides.

This drought was going to kill her. Maybe another go with Charlie wasn't the worst idea.

When the circle of white light lit up the number five, Holly let out a long breath. The doors opened, and she exited with all the other folk who were on their way to a caffeine boost. As she did, she caught Mr. Ferragamo checking out her four-inch peep-toe booties, and a surge of confidence jolted her back to the Holly she knew she was.

"Like what you see?" she asked, stopping to glance down the length of her own legs to where his eyes still rested. This brought his head up with a snap, and a dark wave tumbled onto his forehead before he finger-combed it back into place. He cleared his throat.

"You pull off last season's design well enough, but I'd have gone for the red," he said, and *those* words, despite the velvet ribbon they were tied up in, pieced her insides right back together.

Holly smoothed out a nonexistent wrinkle from her dress as she brushed past him, ovaries once again intact.

"Ass," she muttered under her breath, and then let the promise of a hazelnut double pump patch up the tiny puncture in her bubble. *Of course* she could pull off last season's design. She could rock the hell out of last season's freaking design, because all she could afford right now were the free samples. But in less than an hour that would all change. The first thing she would buy with her new salary would be *next* season's Jimmy Choos. But they sure as hell would *not* be red.

• • •

Bloody well done, Will Evans thought as he rode the rest of the way to the tenth floor in perfect silence. First full day in the States and he was already letting the jet lag get the best of him. Or maybe it was that he loathed being across the Atlantic altogether.

He scrubbed a hand over the stubble he was sure made him look as travel weary as he felt, and then, because no one else was in the lift anymore, he took a picture of himself to document his transformation and then texted it to Sophie.

As promised, he wrote, *I've not shaved and won't until you see me again.*

Will checked his watch to make sure he'd calculated the time difference well enough and let out a sigh when he realized it was early afternoon back in London. Surely she'd be awake. He just hoped Tara would respond.

Seconds later the response came through. *Sophie says to remind you to send one each day. But I can't promise to respond each time.*

Despite his ex's evident irritation, Will relaxed just a bit. And again, because he was the only one in the lift, he let out a soft chuckle. His six-year-old daughter was the only one capable of making him laugh these days.

Tell her I haven't forgotten, he replied. *Each day.* That's what they'd agreed upon. Then he added, *Until your mum gets cross with me.*

He'd already hit send when he decided that maybe Tara would take that last bit with offense. It wouldn't matter that he'd meant it in good fun.

"You talk as if I'm some overbearing hag," she'd say, exasperated with him once again. Christ, he knew he asked a lot of her with all the travel, but she complied each time. For Sophie. She was a good mum, and someday soon, he'd be a good dad.

For now, all he could give Sophie was a photo — one a day

for the next six months. And he wouldn't shave until he saw her on his visits—as many as he could squeeze in before he was home for good. That's what she'd made him promise, so he'd think of her every time he looked in the mirror.

Sophie, Sophie. Didn't she know he didn't need a reminder to think of her? It wasn't Chicago's fault he could barely stomach stepping off the plane and into a city that would replace his home for half a year. He was sure it was a lovely place—as were New York, L.A., Milan, Paris—all the cities that served as surrogate homes for him in the past. But only the real thing—London—had what all the other cities lacked.

It had Sophie.

Right, then. He'd get through this meeting and head back to the hotel, where his suitcase sat still packed and the bed not yet unmade. It always took a day or two for his body to regulate to another country's time zone. He'd sleep tonight. Right now there was the matter at hand—his new client's account. If he pulled off this event without a hitch, he'd have enough time with the firm to take that yearlong sabbatical he'd promised himself. Time to spend with Sophie and be the father he should have been all along. But he had been too young and stupid when she was born to see past the money and the allure of travel, too afraid to step away from a competitive industry that would only replace him with the next up-and-coming young bloke.

Sophie had been an unexpected surprise, but it hadn't been enough to save their already failing relationship. Tara wanted stability, and Will had wanted the world. So she found Phillip, who loved Sophie as his own, and Will became a third wheel in his own daughter's life as the work kept piling on.

Give us another year, and we'll give you six months' leave.

Come on, Will. You're on fire. Another year and we'll up it to eight months.

Sign this contract, Evans. Five years, and you'll have

enough in the bank to retire before you're thirty-five, mate. We'll even hold your position for a full year.

And so, like an arsehole, he'd signed on the bloody line.

Before he knew it, time had gotten away from him. Tara was happy with Phillip. Sophie was happy with them.

The familiar *ding* of a lift reaching its destination sounded in his ears. Seemed like he knew lifts better than the stairs to his own front door.

The doors opened on the tenth floor, and Will Evans strode into the offices of Trousseau, *his* office for the next six months.

He hadn't realized until it vibrated that his phone was still clutched in his hand.

Love you, Sophie had written back.

Love you, too, Will replied, then slipped the phone into his suit jacket pocket.

One day started, 179 to go.

Chapter Two

When Holly got to her office at half past seven—okay, it was a cubicle—Andrea had left her an email saying she'd be a few minutes late and she'd email again when she was ready. Holly spun back and forth in her chair, refreshing her screen again…and again. Andrea was always punctual, and she had called their meeting for eight.

Refresh. Refresh.

Still no email, and it was twelve minutes after eight.

"Partner yet?"

Holly gasped as the Arts and Entertainment section of the *Tribune* dropped onto her keyboard.

"Shit, Charlie! You're going to kill me before I even have a chance!"

"Just thought you might want to see your name in a headline," he said, and Holly's eyes fell to the paper in front of her.

HOLLY CHANDLER: A FRESH NEW NAME ON THE CHICAGO FASHION SCENE.

"You beat out every concert, movie premiere, and even

that high-end boutique opening with all those celebrity guests. Holly Chandler can't be beat," he added.

Her heart swelled in her chest. Maybe she'd never played competitive sports, but it still felt good to win. Sure, she was fresh as far as the newspaper was concerned, but Holly had been on the fashion scene since she graduated college. She was already a five-year veteran, but the recognition was something new—and definitely welcome.

She stared at the picture of herself standing center stage, dwarfed by all the models from the show, but there she was nonetheless: Holly was used to the spotlight. She'd been a theater kid all throughout high school and college. But this was different. This was the rest of her life, seeing something she created come to fruition. And even before she entered Andrea's office, someone had already recognized what she had to offer—what she'd worked so hard for.

"Aren't you lonely putting your personal life second?" her sister, Brynn, had asked more than once. But she didn't get it. Personal…professional…it was all the same to Holly. Making a name for herself would bring her happiness in *all* aspects of her life. The proof was in the headline, because, without even reading the article, that tiny puncture in her bubble sealed itself right up. Nothing could burst it now.

And just like that, up popped the email from Andrea she'd been waiting for.

Ready for ya, rock star, was all it said, and it was enough to permanently affix the grin to Holly's face.

"Thank you, Charlie," she said, grabbing the paper to bring with her, in case Andrea hadn't seen it yet. She stood and curtsied, giving him a wink. After all, she *had* beaten out all the other Chicago entertainment that weekend. Nothing was going to stand in her way now.

"Still around if you want to celebrate tonight," he said. "Kingston Ale House?"

There would definitely be cause for celebration. Besides, no one liked to celebrate alone. Why not?

"Sure, Charlie. I can always go for a pint."

With that she rounded the corner to where the reception desk separated the cubes from the full-sized offices—Andrea's and a space that served as a conference room but was big enough to be split into a meeting room and another office. *Her* office.

Andrea's door was open, so Holly walked right in, permagrin in place, heart swelling, and the article with her name in bold letters folded in her hand.

And then her impenetrable bubble started to squeal as that small puncture began to leak. Because Holly was now face-to-face with not only her boss but with Mr. British Elevator Ass, too. Or, she supposed, for him it would be *arse*.

"There's my superstar!" Andrea said, and Holly should have been beaming right along with her. "So glad you're here. Holly, this is William Evans."

Holly's palm began to sweat against the inky paper it held, and she was happy for an excuse not to be able to shake hands, not that he was offering her one. He stood next to Andrea, a cup and saucer in his hand as he sipped her boss's beverage of choice, straight espresso. His blue-eyed gaze betrayed nothing of their meeting in the elevator, so she did the best she could to shutter hers.

"I wanted to wait until Mr. Evans got to town to tell you the good news," Andrea continued, all grace and poise as if she still walked the runways. "We've landed the Tallulah Chan account. Her debut American show will be with Trousseau. Mr. Evans is her publicist and will oversee the planning of the event, which means you and he will be working together from now through the new year."

Holly still hadn't said a word. Or had she? She wasn't sure. The only thing she was sure of was that so far Andrea hadn't said anything about converting the conference room into Holly's new office.

Andrea placed her own cup and saucer on her desk and moved closer to Holly. The woman's smile was giddy. Holly was supposed to see this as some gift sent down from the heavens. But what that smile was really saying was that she hadn't proved herself yet, not by a long shot.

"I'm giving you this show, from the ground up, your first international client. Will said he wanted my best director, and I told him you're it. Hands down. Pull this off, and you can kiss that cubicle good-bye."

Holly could feel the ink bleeding into her palm, the headline fading into her skin as the reopened puncture turned into an explosive *pop!* Shreds of that perfect bubble littered the office floor, but Holly was the only one who could see them.

"Holly?" Andrea asked, and Holly realized she had been staring at Will Evans the whole time Andrea had been speaking. The suit, the accent, the wavy hair perfectly situated on that beautiful, British head. The hint of a grin, like she was some form of amusement, tugged at one corner of his mouth. He was picture-perfect, yet that didn't stop her from wishing actual daggers would shoot from her eyes and into his chest.

"What? Oh, yes. An international show." She was looking at Andrea now. "Thank you for this opportunity," she said, her own voice sounding far away, though she knew she was no ventriloquist. "You know I won't let you down."

Then she brought her eyes back to meet *his*.

"And Mr. Evans will set up shop…"

"In the conference room, of course," Andrea said.

Of course. The room that would have replaced her cubicle. That *should* have replaced it after what she pulled off this past weekend.

"It's very nice to meet you, Mr. Evans." *Bubble burster.* "I look forward to working on Ms. Chan's show with you." *Office stealer.* "I'll start drawing up some initial ideas today." *So go back to your espresso and stay the hell out of my way.*

Andrea beamed. "See?" she said. "What did I tell you? She's the best of the best. My go-getter!"

He offered a slow nod, his grin never quite making it past the halfway point.

Holly started backing out of the office.

"I'll have a proposal for you by the end of the day," she said, so close to a clean getaway.

"Great!" Andrea said. "Wait, what are you holding?"

Holly looked down at the crumpled article in her hand and packed it even tighter into a ball.

"Oh," she said. "Just wanted to know if you saw the paper today." She straightened her posture, shoulders back and head held high.

Andrea smiled warmly. "I did. You should be really proud. Like I said, you're my best director. Just one more box to tick off—an international show—and you're in."

Funny. She'd thought all the boxes were already checked.

She pressed her lips together and forced one final smile.

"Thank you," she said. "I should get back to work. Good to meet you, Mr. Evans."

Then, along with the certainty of what today had meant, Holly dropped the article into the trash.

Maybe she'd been beaten, but only temporarily. If Andrea wanted her to prove herself one last time, then prove herself she would.

And nothing would distract her from what was rightfully hers.

Chapter Three

Will leaned back in the conference room chair and rubbed his temples. Andrea Ross, runway model turned entrepreneur, would hear nothing of him heading back to his hotel, not wanting him to work all day alone when she and her company were there for whatever he—and by extension Tallulah Chan—needed. He knew she meant well, offering up her conference room to him as his home away from home when he was at the office. But he didn't want to get comfortable here.

He'd filled the day well enough with phone calls and site surveys for where they would hold the show in December. But the morning's espresso had worn off hours ago, and the plush leather sofa beckoned him from his ergonomic chair. All he had to do was wait for the lift woman, Holly, to finish her proposal so he'd have reading material for the evening, and he could return to his hotel and finally unpack, shower, maybe even sleep. Hell, it was past midnight his time already. Where was this bloody proposal?

He rolled up his sleeves and loosened his tie, just enough

comfort that he could tilt his head back and close his eyes for no more than a minute or two.

"You know, Andrea did give you full rein of the *entire* room. There's a couch."

Looked like his proposal was on time after all—possibly a few minutes early.

Will opened one eye to take her in, and Christ if she wasn't still as crisp and polished as she had been in the lift this morning. Her silky brown hair hung in a long ponytail over her bare shoulder. Had he noticed her hair before? Or the vintage black dress that she *more* than pulled off, even with last season's shoes? No, he realized. What he remembered were the eyes. Those shining green eyes he'd noticed earlier now narrowed at him in slits, and he could feel her ire, lasers of it aimed at his head.

Right, well, this would be a lovely six months.

He crossed his arms over his chest.

"I quite like the chair," he said. "Excellent lower-back support."

Her expression remained impassive as she strode through the doorway and slapped a manila folder onto the table in front of him.

"I know Ms. Chan's designs," she said. "I own quite a few of her pieces. Even if they are *last season*. I've been following her progress since she launched her line in London a year ago, and I think I have a handle on what will give her the best exposure here in Chicago. We're honored your client has chosen our firm for her U.S. debut."

She was all business, which was what he wanted. No distractions, pull off this event, and get back home. Yet the sting in her words, *last season*, niggled at something inside. He had been honest, after all, even paid her a compliment, yet she somehow felt he had wronged her.

She had caught him off guard earlier. Maybe he had come

across a bit untoward. But Will wasn't in the habit of smoothing things over in a place he didn't want to be smoothed. The less he found pleasant about his time in Chicago, the better to remind him what waited at the end of his stay. Still, the way she pierced him with that stare—he should say *something*.

"About the lift," he began, placing his hand on the folder next to where her palm still lay. Her brows rose slightly, and he realized his mistake. "The elevator…about the elevator…"

She leaned down, close enough that he could smell a mixture of floral and citrus, and spoke, her head inches from his.

"I work hard, Mr. Evans. I may not have the bankroll to prove it…*yet*. You noticing what line my gorgeous peep-toes are from tells me you might know a thing or two about shoes, but you know nothing about me."

He didn't flinch. Never mind that each second she stood near him he grew closer and closer to losing focus, her scent mixed with her anger an intoxicating combination.

No, it was the bloody jet lag. And now that he had the proposal, he could finally head back to the hotel and regain his sanity.

"Well, Ms. Chandler," he began, sliding the chair behind him so he was standing along with her. "I work hard, too, and I don't rest until everything is as it should be." Will tugged the folder out from under her palm. "I'll review your proposal this evening and get back to you with any concerns in the morning."

She straightened. Even in those four-inch heels, he still towered over her, but that didn't overshadow her presence. She was beautiful, sure. And poised. And dammit, she wore the hell out of that dress. But her talent and work ethic preceded her. The article she'd brought up to Andrea was the same one he'd read on the car ride over. Maybe he should have recognized her in the lift, but the photo in the paper had been grainy, and it was a group shot.

There was no mistaking it. Holly Chandler had *presence*.

She chuckled, a playful sound. Her lips parted into a coy smile. "You won't have any concerns, Mr. Evans."

She was bloody confident as well, and he couldn't help but admire her more.

"Then I guess that will be all, Ms. Chandler. Thank you."

Will reached for his jacket that hung over the back of the chair, then spun back to drop the folder in his leather case. He strode down the side of the table toward the door, and Holly made her way down the opposite side, her pace matching his. When they met, she stood in the door frame, blocking his exit.

"Wait a minute," she said, and he nodded. "Did you just... dismiss me?"

Will sighed.

"Look, Ms. Chandler, I've been awake since yesterday. I've still not unpacked. It's..." He made a show of looking at his watch before his eyes met hers again. "...nearly midnight in London, and I still have to read what I'm sure is a lovely proposal for Tallulah Chan's U.S. debut, the one you're so honored to be working on. I may even be able to squeeze in room service and have a shower as well. So pardon me if it seems I've *dismissed* you, but it's been a long couple of days, and now I'd like to leave. Is that all right with you?"

Holly stepped aside.

"Quite," she said.

The set of her jaw was tight, and her gaze bored into him once again, lasers and all.

Will slid past her. Andrea was already gone for the evening, so all he had to do was make a beeline for the lift. Once inside, he let out a breath, only now realizing he'd been holding it so he wouldn't fall prey to her scent again.

Then he let his head fall back against the wall, and he laughed.

He had just dismissed her, hadn't he? Christ. He could tell himself it was the jet lag all he wanted, but Holly Chandler was a force to be reckoned with, one he wasn't prepared for.

Right, then. He'd get to the hotel, regroup, read her proposal, and finally—sleep. Everything would right itself in the morning.

Chapter Four

"Another," Holly said and slammed her pint glass down on the bar.

Jamie raised his brows, reprimanding her with no more than a look.

Holly's sister, Brynn, sneaked up behind him, wrapping her arms around his waist.

"Aw, go easy on her, James. She had a shit day."

Jamie tilted his head back and kissed Brynn on the cheek. Ugh. This was not what Holly needed. She *needed* another pint. Stat.

Holly's cell phone vibrated atop the wooden bar. When she glanced down, she groaned.

Still up for a celebratory drink?

"Charlie," she said, quietly, but not quietly enough.

Brynn's eyes went wide. "You're seeing Charlie again?" she asked. "I thought he was part of your little six-month experiment."

Holly rolled her eyes. "It's not an experiment. Not all of us have time for..." She waved her hand toward her sister and Brynn's longtime best friend...now boyfriend. "Plus," she added, shaking her empty glass in Jamie's general direction, "it always fizzles. Every time. I never make it past the honeymoon phase, so why bother trying? Fun and done. That's all there is to it."

Jamie refilled her glass with the newest addition to the Kingston Ale House tap, Chandler's Witbier. Sure, it was named for her sister, but Chandler belonged to her, too, so she could pretend. Also, it was a good brew.

Brynn came out from behind the bar and sat on the stool next to Holly.

"Holls—maybe if you put in the work with one of these relationships, you'd feel differently."

That was just it, though. If something was right—if it was meant to last—it shouldn't be so much effort. At the end of the day, after the hard stuff was over, Holly wanted *easy*. She wanted a neutral zone where she didn't have to prove herself or where her priorities lay. With the six-month deal up front, she could come right out with it. *Everything else comes first, but I'd sure like to enjoy you for a while.*

Holly took a long, slow sip of her fresh pint, giving herself one hell of a foam mustache, which she did *not* wipe away before responding to her sister.

"I work all the time," she said. "I don't want to have to work more after I leave the office. Besides, do you know how many guys have complained about our little part-time alliances?"

Brynn sighed. "And what does that say about a guy who's eager to sign up for such an *alliance*? You make dating sound like *The Hunger Games*."

Holly nodded. "*Exactly.* Except the odds are always in my favor."

Now her sister groaned. "I get that, sweetie, but aren't you—you know—lonely?"

Holly chuckled. "Nah. That's why I've got you, roomie."

Brynn's half smile fell, and Holly's gut sank.

"What?" she asked, and Brynn wiped Holly's upper lip with a beverage napkin.

"Lease is up next week," Brynn said. "Remember?"

Yes. Holly remembered. She'd just been trying to forget.

Jamie leaned across the bar and kissed Brynn again, this time on the temple. Once more, there was that sinking feeling.

"But she'll only be a couple blocks away," Jamie reminded her. Because as of next week, Brynn would no longer be Holly's roommate. She was moving in with Jamie.

Holly picked up her phone, still needing to respond to Charlie's text. *Sorry, Charlie. No celebration tonight.*

Then she drained the rest of her pint in four long gulps.

"I think I've had enough fun for a Monday," she said, hopping off her stool. Brynn stood to join her, linking their arms together.

"Jamie's closing the bar tonight, so I'll head home with you."

"Brynn, I'm fine. I don't need a chaperone."

But her sister wouldn't loosen her grip.

"Shame," Brynn said. "I was going to stop for ice cream."

Holly's eyes lit up. "Shooting Star Café?" she asked, and Brynn nodded.

"I'll even sit outside and won't complain more than twice about mosquitoes."

Holly bounced on her toes. "I think it's clear enough tonight to see Venus. I'll show you."

Jamie smiled at them both, and Brynn kissed him goodbye.

"Come over when you're done?" Brynn asked him, and he nodded. Jamie always spent the night at their place when he closed the bar. Then again, on those other nights when Jeremy or another employee stayed through last call, Brynn was usually out the door and at Jamie's before Holly even made it home. But for the next few hours, Brynn was Holly's. Brynn, a quadruple-scoop sundae between the two of them, and a clear night sky.

It was a small victory but one she was willing to celebrate.

· · ·

Holly checked her phone again. Yep. It really was two in the morning, and she really was still awake. She'd like to blame it on the beer. Or the ice cream. But the truth was, she had a stomach of steel, always had. Brynn had to swallow two lactose pills before feeling confident enough to dive into their sundae, but not Holly. No, it wasn't dairy belly keeping her up. It was her stupid, overactive, overanalytical brain.

Because what if this whole making partner thing was just a pipe dream? What if Andrea never had any intention of converting that conference room into an office? What if all she ever had was a cubicle with no windows and no name on her door and…

Holly was still staring at her phone's screen when an email notification popped up.

It was from Will Evans.

Holly's first instinct was to ignore it. After all, his presence at Trousseau had been the start of the domino effect that was this crappy day. Or, technically, she supposed *yesterday* was the crap day, but since she hadn't exactly gone to sleep yet, yesterday was still today. Whatever.

And why was he still up, anyway? Wasn't he complaining about jet lag when he freaking dismissed her? Not that she was still harping on that. He was probably writing to tell her all the things he hated about her proposal, most likely about how *last season* it was. Not that she was still harping on *that*, either.

Well, if he thought he could trash her ideas and then go off to la-la land, he had another think coming. Holly unlocked her phone and opened her email, readying herself for the worst and already planning her defense. Then she read.

Ms. Chandler—

I've had a chance to go over your proposal and wanted to let you know what I thought.

It's brilliant. You really do know Ms. Chan's line, and I believe what you've drawn up will capture her vision for this show. I actually had a good laugh that you chose the W Hotel for the top choice in venue, as that is where I'm staying. In my preliminary research, I'd had the W on my top list of locales to scout, so I figured why not get to know the place? I've not yet met the events coordinator, so how about we pay her a visit in the morning? Nine a.m. coffee at the hotel? I realize you may not get this email before then, as you're surely sleeping, in which case we can make it ten. I look forward to your response.

Good evening, Ms. Chandler.

Respectfully yours,
Will Evans

Holly giggled. And then she full-on snorted. He signed his emails. Will Evans, stuffy British arse, signed his emails like a business letter. Of course he did. And he'd also called her brilliant. She had *not* missed that. It wasn't as if she had anything to prove to him, but after this day—or this yesterday—it was nice to hear something *nice*.

She decided to respond, on the chance he still had his

laptop open, because surely Will Evans did not sit in bed tapping away on a phone. He was at a desk, in a chair, cup of tea next to him, most likely, drafting his most formal email in button-down pajamas and a silk robe.

She snorted again. He was probably still in that slate-gray suit. Then her mind went places it shouldn't, remembering the millisecond before she made her presence known in the conference room, Will sitting with his jacket off and sleeves rolled up. With his head tilted back and expression relaxed, he certainly was a sight.

She shook her head, freeing herself of the vision, and tapped out her response.

Mr. Evans—

Actually, can I call ya Billy? Nah. Scratch that. I think I should go the other way with the full William. You don't seem the nickname type. Anyhoo, I'm glad you enjoyed my proposal. Coffee at nine sounds lovely. I look forward to scouting the location and getting the planning underway.

I'm not always on email in the middle of the night. We're colleagues now, right? Please feel free to use my cell phone number if you need to reach me right away—773-555-0102.

Sleep well.
H

Holly set her phone on the nightstand and snuggled back into bed, her racing thoughts finally reaching the finish line. As she sank into the pillow, eyelids getting heavier, her phone vibrated with a text. She grabbed it once more to see who it was from, not recognizing what looked like a lottery ticket number rather than a phone number, so she opened up the text to read. *And now you have my mobile number, too. Sleep well. W*

"Well, Mr. Evans," Holly said aloud. "That wasn't so formal, was it? Maybe there's hope for the arse yet."

Then she programmed him in as a new contact, *Billy Evans*, and laughed. He didn't seem the type to enjoy being teased, but then again, he'd never know. It was her own private joke with herself. Brynn might say that was a little sad and lonely, but not Holly. Because Holly would always find Holly funny, and she'd never have to work to impress her.

As her eyes fell closed, she thought about how much better the next day would be. And in six months, Holly *would* impress the person who mattered most—Andrea—and she'd finally get what she'd always wanted, what she knew she deserved.

Chapter Five

Will stepped into the lift at forty minutes after eight. He'd only just fallen asleep at half past four and figured he could squeeze in a dose of caffeine before Holly arrived, but when the doors opened to the lobby, it wasn't the espresso bar he noticed first. It was the woman in the sleeveless red peplum dress and high brunette ponytail standing at said espresso bar ordering a drink. Will followed the hair to the bare shoulders and down the fitted bodice of the dress, the flare of the fabric at her narrow waist. He let his eyes dip to where the skirt hit just above the backs of her knees and then down, down to the black leather ankle boots with the stiletto heels. He waited a beat for the woman to finish her order and turn, telling himself that it was just another hotel patron. But Will Evans didn't have that kind of luck.

The woman in red spun on her spike of a heel, beverage in hand, and beamed when her eyes locked on his. Because of course Holly was early *and* the type who smiled to greet the morning. Will was so sleep deprived at this point, he only knew it was morning because he trusted his mobile not to lie to him.

Despite his irritation with—well, life in general—the corner of his mouth quirked up in response to her grin, enough that he returned the sentiment, but it was nothing compared to the warmth that radiated from Holly Chandler, and she was at least fifty feet away. What would it be like as he approached her? He had to move toward her now that she'd seen him. It would be quite odd if he didn't, yet there was this inexplicable hesitation—something that told him not to get too close to her or he'd get pulled into some kind of vortex that wouldn't spit him out.

This was ridiculous. Nothing had changed since she'd shot daggers at him yesterday afternoon, and he certainly wasn't swayed by the teasing nature of her email or the warmth he felt at her sign-off.

Sleep well.

Two words. And he imagined that if she'd spoken them, her voice would have been soft and dreamlike, sweet, even. Or maybe it was just that no one had said that to him in a long time. Sophie always said good night when she stayed with him, but something about those words, *Holly's* words, had tugged at him.

They were coworkers for the next six months. No, *Trousseau* had been hired by Tallulah Chan—against Will's urging. He'd suggested New York, a city tied more tightly to the fashion scene and one that would have provided easier travel between the States and London, the second reason the more selfish one. But Tallulah didn't want to do what everyone else did. That was the way she designed, and that was the way she went about promoting her career—unconventionally.

So here he was, smack-dab in the middle of a country that wasn't his, in a city that would force him to work harder to get out of it what he wanted for his client, with jet lag–induced delirium making him think a complete stranger wishing him a good night's sleep was anything other than a courtesy.

A complete stranger who was, for all intents and purposes, his employee—and Will's days of blurring the lines between work and play were over. So he would ignore that Holly looked stunning in that dress and that yesterday's narrowed eyes had been replaced by a smile that lit up the whole bloody room.

"Good morning, Ms. Chandler," he said when he was near enough, but Holly had closed her eyes, both hands wrapped around her disposable coffee cup as she inhaled the steam that seeped through the opening. Her lips, the exact shade of crimson to match her dress, pressed together in the most serene grin.

He cleared his throat, and she opened her eyes.

"Sorry," she said, though her tone was unapologetic. "But there is nothing like the scent of hazelnut in the morning." Her grin grew wide again. "Don't you think?"

He shook his head, pleased for a reason to disagree with her.

"I prefer the espresso as is," he countered, stepping past her to order a triple shot. Then he looked at her over his shoulder. "I do wish you would have waited and let me put your coffee on my room tab."

Holly barked out a laugh. "I may not be able to afford a pair of four-hundred-dollar shoes, Mr. Evans, but I can cover my own latte, thank you."

He turned back to the barista and gave him his order, upping it to a quadruple shot, and shook his head slowly. He'd need the extra jolt to keep up with her today.

"Your quadruple shot," the barista said moments later, handing Will his cup.

"Cheers," he said to the young man behind the counter, then dropped a few bills in the tip jar.

"Four shots?" she asked, eyes wide. "They should make

you sign a waiver for that or something."

There it was again, that involuntary twitch of his lip, but he never let the smile poke through. This was business. Four shots meant business.

Holly lifted a bright yellow bag—Will couldn't place the designer but knew he'd seen it on the runway somewhere—and slung it over her shoulder. She caught him staring.

"I like color," she said, then did a mini curtsy. "Like the dress? I went for the red."

She raised a brow at him, and he knew she still hadn't let go of the shoe comment from their first meeting.

She sat on one of the high-backed, white leather couches that curved like snakes through the W's ornate lobby. Then she patted the spot next to her.

Will unslung his leather case from over his shoulder and smoothed out his vest.

"You've got something against it, I can see," Holly said as he sat instead in a chair across from her. "Color, I mean."

He looked down at his beige linen vest and matching trousers, then back at her.

"Shirt's blue," he retorted, making sure not to sound defensive. "Tie's navy. I think I've got color taken care of."

She shrugged and took a sip of her hazelnut concoction. He removed the lid from his four shots, enjoying a larger swig of the rich yet bitter liquid.

Holly wrinkled her nose and leaned over the small coffee table between them, peering into his cup.

"You like that?" she asked. "Like, you really, truly enjoy it?"

Will sighed. "When it's brewed right," he admitted. "Yes, I quite like it. Right now I suppose I just need it."

Holly hummed and leaned back against the couch.

"Hard time falling asleep last night?" she asked, and Will straightened in his chair.

"Right. What are we doing chitchatting over coffee? I thought we were going to call on the hotel's events coordinator. I've looked her up. Marisa Gonzalez. She will be in her office at ten, so I thought we'd go over a game plan, talk about a couple of notes I have on the proposal."

Holly set her coffee down on the table and held up her hand, giving him a pointed look.

"Slow your roll, there, Prince Harry. I thought my proposal was — and I'm quoting you here, by the way — *brilliant*."

Will rolled his eyes. "Right. That doesn't mean I don't have a few notes. Mainly, it's the date you propose."

Holly clasped her hands in her lap. "Ms. Chan is busy on New Year's Eve?" she asked.

"No," he said firmly, "but hotels like this throw mammoth parties for the new year. It's June. I'm sure they've already got this year's planned."

"Riiiight," Holly said, drawing out the word with a tone Will knew was surely mocking him. "Why would the W want a high-profile event such as this on the same night ticket-buying partygoers will be deciding where to drop a load of cash on a celebration and a room to sleep in? I'm assuming we'll make the show invitation only, but imagine the classy crowd the hotel will draw for other concurrent events with this one on the docket as well?"

Will scrubbed a hand over his jaw and sighed, scratching at the itchy start of the beard-growing process.

"I'm right, aren't I?" she asked with a self-satisfied grin.

"You may be onto something," he allowed. "But we won't know until we speak to Ms. Gonzalez and get a quote. A holiday will up their fee, especially if *they* don't know who Ms. Chan is yet."

This wouldn't surprise him, but then again, that's why Tallulah had hired him in the first place. Will Evans made sure that those who were unknown to the public did not remain as such for long.

"I'd suggest we offer a few alternative dates, as my client has said she could do anything before January 15, which is when the new line launches officially in the U.S."

Holly nodded. "Challenge accepted," she said.

"Pardon?" Will asked.

"You propose your dates, and I'll propose mine," she added. "We'll see who wins."

Will leaned back in his chair and sipped his espresso. "It's not a competition."

They were meant to work together on this, so why the need to challenge him? Then he remembered their introduction yesterday, Andrea's mention of *this* event being the end of her sitting in one of those cubicle things.

After this account—once the calendar rolled over to the new year—Will's contract would be up, and he'd finally be free to be the father he should have been all along. This show meant amazing life changes for both of them. He could respect that.

Holly held up her cup in a gesture of cheers. "It is now."

• • •

Holly sat next to Will in a reception area outside a small set of offices on the W's lobby level. He was reading a newspaper on his iPad, so Holly decided to check today's horoscope. She thought back to yesterday's consideration that a person's clothes spoke the truth about them. Holly had gone to Andrea's office hoping for a promotion and instead felt like someone had told her that her cat died—and she didn't even have a pet. Maybe she gave off the wrong vibe by wearing all black. Maybe the app was onto something and she hadn't listened.

She chuckled softly. Holly knew her horoscope didn't

control her destiny or anything. She had free will, made her own decisions, and trusted herself to make the right ones. But she felt a certain comradery with the stars—the ability to shine so brightly from so far away. *That* was a powerful sort of magic. Okay, fine, it was science, but couldn't everyone use a little magic in their life? Maybe her little horoscope app was just that—still believing in magic.

> *Gemini: A strange visitor will come to you in search of a gift. He/she will offer you something in return. Professional obligations intensify. Prepare to bring the office home with you this week.*

This time she held in a snort. *Bring the office home.* Her whole life was her office, and that was just fine. She knew she was still young by industry standards. At twenty-six she was still four years younger than Andrea had been when she'd finally left modeling for the business side of things. But Holly had been with Andrea from the ground up, one of her first hires. For five years she'd learned the ins and outs of the business. She knew she was just as good as Andrea, and she also knew Andrea wanted to share the growing workload. The carrot still dangled, and Holly had not yet caught it. *This* show would be it, her ticket to the top. If that meant bringing work home this week, next week, next month, then that would be the plan. *Thanks, magic*, she thought. No need to hit her over the head with the obvious.

"Ms. Chandler and Mr. Evans?"

Holly's head snapped up to see a young woman in a chic, short-sleeved black pantsuit—and red pumps. Will cleared his throat and threw her a glance, and she threw him a mental *screw you*.

Holly stood to shake the woman's hand, but Will beat her to it.

"Ms. Gonzalez?" he asked, hand gripping hers, and the

woman nodded, soft brown curls bouncing on her shoulders as she did.

"I'm Will Evans, and this is Holly Chandler," he added, his smile broad, and Holly almost stumbled at the sight of it. She'd only known him for twenty-four hours, but she knew well enough that the Will Evans she met yesterday didn't smile like the guy standing next to her right now.

Wait a minute. Why hadn't he smiled like that when he met her? Holly considered herself smile inducing enough.

"Holly?"

She blinked at the sound of her name and realized that Marisa Gonzalez was now holding out her hand. How long had she zoned out? Was she staring at Will or Marisa? Because right now, both were staring at her.

"Sorry, right." Holly shook Marisa's hand. "Holly Chandler. But I guess Will already said that."

She waited for Marisa to usher her into an office or something, but the woman made no move to do so.

"My assistant tells me you are interested in booking a fashion show at the W?"

Okay, so it looked like they were going to have a meeting right here.

"Yes," Holly said. "Our client—Tallulah Chan—would like to do her American launch here in Chicago, and we thought the W on New Year's Eve would be perfect."

Will gave her a pointed glance, but he didn't interrupt or correct her on the date. It would be poor form for them to argue when they were trying to make a deal for the busiest party day of the year. Competition or not, Holly considered this a point for her team.

Marisa's smile faltered. "Look," she said. "I would never give an outright no to business for the hotel, but we don't need any business on New Year's Eve. Our party sells out every year, and we use the grand ballroom for the event, which would not leave you much space in the venue should you choose one of our other rooms. Plus, there's no way I could offer you any sort of a deal on a night when, six months out, most large venues in the city are already booked. It would cost your client a fortune. If there's any other night—"

Holly opened her mouth to speak, but Will cut her off.

"My client…" he said, then paused for a second. "*Our* client," he continued, his eyes on Marisa and Marisa only, "would love to ring in the new year at your hotel. Ms. Chandler and I have a few brilliant ideas for how this could benefit the W's turnout for the new year as well as Ms. Chan's launch. We'd love to put together a formal presentation for you and see if we can't come up with something that has as much to offer you as it does us."

She crossed her arms and sighed, pursing her lips.

"You two have my interest piqued. I'll give you that," she said. "Listen, I am absolutely swamped this week. If you really think this will work, I'd love to see your ideas, say, a week from Thursday? Nine a.m.?"

"Of course!" Holly said, knowing she sounded too eager but not caring one stinking bit, because the score was now Holly, two, and Will, zero. Although he had gone to bat for her instead of suggesting another date, so maybe she'd give him half a point.

But as she shook Marisa's hand for a second time, she glanced at her partner in crime. Gone was the smile he only put on for this occasion. His jaw was tight, yet somehow he managed to look charming even through what Holly saw as apparent disappointment.

"A week from Thursday at nine sounds lovely, Ms. Gonzalez. We look forward to seeing you then."

As he spoke, the charm and the smile returned, and Holly thought maybe she imagined Will's distress. She couldn't help but beam. She'd begin setting her ideas to slides as soon as they got back to the office. Will could draw up the publicity plan, and in less than two weeks, they'd be well on their way to planning what would be, for Holly, the event of the year.

Once back in the lobby, Holly bounced on her four-inch heels and smiled like the freaking Joker.

"This is so in the bag," she said. "I will put together the logistics of how it will all look and how we can piggyback off the party they already have set up. You draw up a publicity plan that will have them basically paying *us* to have our event here, and *bam*! We did it!"

Instead of joining in the enthusiasm, Will checked his watch.

"You're right," Holly said. "We should head to the office and get going on this. Want to share a ride? I have a car, but I only drive it if I have to. There's no assigned parking on my street, and I hate giving up my spot. Nine days may seem like plenty of time, but it'll go by quickly, and we definitely want time to coordinate and to edit the proposal and make sure we're on the same page and—"

"Holly." Will interrupted her rant with a quiet yet firm request, all wrapped up in the sound of her name.

"Will."

He rubbed his eyes with the heels of his hands.

"I need to take care of a few things before heading to the office. Do go on without me."

He was formal Will now. Maybe he had been the whole morning, but she'd thought they were starting to warm up to each other. Whatever. It's not like they needed to be fast friends. They just had to be able to work together, make decisions that affected each other's livelihood, and pull off her first-ever solo fashion show on a date when no hotels had openings at one of the most sought-after venues in the city. No big deal.

"Oh. Okay," she said. "I'll see you when you get in."

Will adjusted his bag on his shoulder, then stood straight as his eyes fell on hers.

"Actually," he said, "you're right. We're both working on opposite ends of the proposal. It's probably best you work on your bit, and I'll work on mine, and we can convene next Wednesday to put it all together."

Of course, that would be a smart tactic. Efficient, even. Yet she still found herself opening her mouth to protest, but Will cut her off.

"That will be all, then, I suppose. Have a good day, Holly."

Wait—did he? Was he dismissing her again? She wasn't going to get flustered. Nope. She was *not* going to let this guy throw her off-kilter.

It's a British thing, she told herself. *Like the Europeans kiss you on each cheek to say hello and good-bye. Except he simply tells you to take your leave.*

She fished in her purse for her phone.

"Come to think of it…" Holly spoke to the contents of her bag until she retrieved what she was looking for. Then she swiped at the screen and began organizing her ride back to the office. "I have a credit, so I'm gonna Uber instead of taxi."

Will shook his head. "Sorry. Did you say Uber?"

"Uber," Holly repeated. He stared. "You don't have it in England? It's like a taxi, but people drive their own cars, and you call for one on the Uber app, and the closest one comes to get you. Pretty convenient, right?"

Will's eyes narrowed. "We *have* Uber. I've never had the pleasure, though. But you let strangers pick you up in their cars and trust them to take you where you want to go? You're not worried about ending up like Gwyneth Paltrow in that David Fincher film?" he asked.

Will checked his watch again. Obviously he had to be somewhere, so why the third degree?

Holly rolled her eyes.

"Do you mean like the strangers who pick you up in those yellow cars and charge money for you to trust them not to put your head in a box?"

He shook his head at her, and there it was, the ghost of a smile. But it never went further than that. Holly realized that in twenty-four hours, she'd only seen this man smile when it was called for. He could turn it on at the drop of a hat, but it disappeared just as quickly.

She waved her phone at him.

"Uber's here," she said. "Gotta go."

She snagged her sunglasses from her bag, repositioned the bag on her shoulder, and held her hand out for Will to shake.

"Well, Mr. Evans. Until next Wednesday, I suppose."

"Right. Next Wednesday."

"You sure I can't call you Billy?" she asked.

"Quite," he answered.

He clasped her palm, his hand a bit firmer and rougher than she'd expected. Not that he wasn't—how would they say it in England?—a strapping lad or anything, but Holly had assumed the tailored suits meant that every piece of him was cut from some fine cloth. But the callused palm said otherwise.

It must have been that discrepancy between perception and reality that made the hairs on her arm stand on end. That or the air-conditioning was working overtime in this place. Those were the only logical explanations, and logical explanations were the kind Holly Chandler liked.

Horoscopes didn't count. Those were just for fun. Though, as she pulled her hand away and strode toward the exit, Holly thought about strangers and gifts and the unarguable fact that tonight she would be taking the office home with her.

But then again, she always did.

Chapter Six

Will stood in the queue for a taxi outside O'Hare's international terminal. He rubbed his eyes with his thumb and forefinger, but that did nothing to take away the sting of exhaustion.

So this was how it would be if he kept it up, weekend travel back to London. Perpetual jet lag. At least Sophie allowed him to have a shave Sunday evening before his early-morning flight back. An eight-and-a-half-hour flight plus the six-hour time difference meant he could leave London at five in the morning and land in Chicago by half past seven, plenty of time for a nine o'clock office arrival. It really only gave him two full days at home, but after missing so much of the past six years with her, forty-eight Sophie-filled hours were glorious compared to what he had taken for granted for too long. And the fact that Tara gave him those forty-eight hours, well, that showed she was starting to trust he was serious about the whole sabbatical idea—about being a permanent fixture in his daughter's life. Because it wasn't just an idea. It was what he had to do to get his own life back in order.

Will lowered himself into the taxi and gave the driver Trousseau's address. No sense going to the hotel when he'd barely have time for a coffee before having to turn around and leave. He'd go straight there, maybe try the café on the fifth floor Holly couldn't seem to get enough of.

Holly Chandler. Will had avoided one-on-one time with her for the rest of the week after they'd met with Marisa Gonzalez. He didn't need any distractions, and something about her was—distracting. The more he accomplished in a twenty-four-hour period, the longer he could start making his weekends.

He took a quick photo of himself and attached it to a text message. *Hi, love. Back in Chicago. See you in a week.*

Sophie's reply was immediate. *Pancakes on Saturday, Daddy?*

He chuckled and replied. *Of course.*

• • •

The fifth-floor café was actually a small cafeteria, something akin to an American mall's food court. Will was not a fan of either, but he was too tired to seek out a proper café, and he certainly wasn't going to stand in Andrea's office and brew himself shot after shot.

With his garment bag over his shoulder and leather case slung across his torso, he made his way to the espresso bar line.

"Ah. The mysterious Will Evans returns."

It had only been a week, but he already recognized the lilt of that voice, the way it always seemed to tease even when he gave no indication he was up for teasing.

"Ms. Chandler," he said, pivoting to greet her. "Good morning."

She crossed her arms and narrowed her gaze, giving him

an expectant look, but he had no idea *what* she was expecting. And she was really close to him—too close. Enough that he could see yellow flecks in her green eyes and again, that bloody scent—lavender and grapefruit maybe? Christ, she was too close. He didn't have it in him, mentally or physically, to resist the urge. So he breathed in deep through his nose, and despite the aroma of coffee brewing just behind him, all he noticed was her.

"You look like you want to say something else," he said. "But I'm too bloody exhausted to figure it out."

She huffed out a breath and pursed her pale lips. Unlike at their meeting the previous week, the last time they'd been in any sort of close proximity, she wore barely any makeup today, just some sort of gloss on her lips. He could even count the dusting of freckles on her nose. Seven, like a small constellation spilling just slightly onto her cheeks. He wasn't sure how old she was, but this close she seemed so young, fresh. Not world-weary like he felt at thirty-two.

"I called your hotel Friday. Had some questions about Ms. Chan's color scheme, and the woman at the desk said you were out for the weekend and had instructed her to take messages while you were away."

Will blinked. "You rang me at the hotel?"

"Yes, Will. I *rang* you. Your cell went right to voicemail, so I tried your room. Who pays to stay in a hotel for six months yet takes off for the weekend?" She paused for a few seconds but then spoke again before he could respond. "Sorry. That's none of my business. Can I ask why you're *too bloody exhausted*? As a concerned colleague, of course." She offered a conciliatory grin but then narrowed her eyes at him. "And can we please stop with the Ms. Chandler bullshit?"

He couldn't keep his lip from twitching into a half smile.

"What?" Holly asked, clearly not liking that she was the butt of some joke.

He raised a brow. "I don't know. You. Saying *bullshit* first thing in the morning. It's—funny."

Her eyes narrowed. "Funny? My irritation at your insistence on formality is *funny*?"

He glanced down at his office attire. "We're colleagues, Ms. Chandler," he said plainly. "Should we be anything other than formal?"

"*Holly*," she said, gritting her teeth.

He furrowed his brows, feigning confusion. "We should be *Holly*?" he said. "Is that American slang? I'm afraid I've not done my foreign language studies for this trip."

He bit back a smile. Something about this woman brought out a playfulness he thought he'd lost, or at least buried down deep where it couldn't interfere with this perfect version of himself he was trying so desperately to be.

"You're impossible," she said.

"You're quick to judge," he countered. "Some might even say you're a bit adorable when you're cross," he added, sure that comment crossed some sort of line, but the fact was irrefutable. Holly Chandler, all ruffled by his apparent Willness, was quite enjoyable, and it had been a long time since he found enjoyment being away from home. Despite the way he seemed to vex her, he had to admit that he liked being in her presence.

"Adorable," she said flatly. "I'm not a puppy, *Mr. Evans*."

He tapped his lips with his index finger.

"No. I supposed you're not." He paused and quirked his head to the side, sizing her up. "Perhaps a bunny, though."

Holly groaned and pushed past him. "You snooze, you lose," she said, and proceeded to order herself a hazelnut soy latte.

Will chuckled to himself. So he'd have to wait another couple of minutes for his beverage. It was worth it.

. . .

If Holly was a spiteful person, she'd have pressed the door-closed button when she saw Will Evans approaching. But she'd had a couple of days to cool off since what she liked to call *the bunny incident*. So instead of freezing him out, she sighed and stuck her foot between the doors so they wouldn't close in his face, mainly because she wanted to watch him approach in that blue-and-white-checked shirt and navy tie. No suit jacket today, which was a first. He was almost casual. Well, casual for Will Evans. She liked this look.

"Thank you, Ms. Cha—I mean, Holly. Thank you, Holly."

Ah, yes. You can take the formal out of the apparel, but you can't take the formal out of the uptight Englishman...or something like that. Because this was how it had been since Monday. After the aforementioned bunny incident at the café, which at first irritated her but then convinced her that Will Evans actually had a sense of humor, it had been nothing other than this—a stoic, distant, extremely well-dressed yet mildly scruffy man.

They would be partners for six months, but in the span of ten days, they'd barely made it past *Ms. Chandler* and *Mr. Evans*.

"You're welcome," Holly said, backing up to create a comfortable distance between them in the elevator. But when the doors closed, leaving just the two of them in the small space, it felt infinitely more intimate than when it was packed from wall to wall. So, with a latte in one hand, she fished her phone out of her bag with the other and tapped open her horoscope app.

Gemini: Expect news today that will chase away the clouds for sunny skies. Lots in store for Gemini. Take advantage of new opportunities even if they present

*themselves as what you see as obstacles. Appreciate
what you're given, and allow time for joy.*

Holly blew a lock of hair out of her face, a piece that had
escaped her ponytail. She'd been restless the first few nights
without Brynn in her apartment, so last night she'd decided it
would be a good idea to take a scissors to her own hair and
cut some long bangs.

She'd cut them too short. And for the record, it was *not* a
good idea.

"Your hair's different," Will said in that matter-of-fact
tone of his. Though Holly had to admit that British matter-of-
fact was preferable to the American version, at least to listen
to it. God, if he wasn't so *Will*. Her mind went back to their
first meeting in the elevator, to her ears first registering the
sound of his voice. That *accent*. And then his blunt and quite
unapologetic remark about her shoes. Still, maybe this was a
step up. The comment was neither a compliment nor an insult.
It just—was.

"Bangs," she said, blowing the rogue locks out of her way
again, but it was no use.

"Sorry?"

Holly's brows knit together, and then she held up the
loose hair between her fingers.

"Bangs?"

"Fringe," Will said.

"Excuse me?"

His lips broke into a half smile, and something inside
Holly fluttered—something she tried to ignore.

"In England we call it fringe. Your *bangs*."

"Oh."

After that came the awkward elevator silence. They
passed the fourth floor, the fifth, the sixth. Jeez, didn't *anyone*
have to use the elevator?

"So…" Holly needed to fill the void. She wasn't a woman of silence. "One o'clock today?" They were finally going to go over their separate pieces of the proposal and put them together in time for tomorrow's meeting with Marisa.

Will nodded. "I'm just about done with the publicity plan for the hotel. You?"

Holly nodded as well. "I finished last night. Couldn't sleep. Plus, it was clear enough to see Ursa Minor and Gemini, and I like to stay outside on nights like that. But then I kind of lose track of time. You know? So I didn't get to bed until two. Hence the extra shot in the latte."

She held up her cup.

Whoa, Chandler, she thought. *He doesn't care about your silly stars. I mean, they're not silly, but he would think they're silly, so yeah. Just stop with the elevator chitchat.*

She could ramble on with the best of them, but when her inner monologue started rambling, too, she knew she was in trouble. Apparently there was too much silence in her head as well.

Hands still full, she was shaking her head, trying to get the stupid *fringe* out of her eyes.

Will stepped toward her, and her breath hitched as his hand that wasn't holding his four to eight shots of espresso reached toward her face, tucking the bad-idea bangs behind her ear. And there it was again, that annoying flutter in her gut. What if she was catching Brynn's lactose intolerance?

"There we are," he said. "I was going to have to amend my original statement if you kept that up. Definitely more puppy than bunny."

He grinned, and though Holly wanted to summon anger at his teasing, she couldn't help but grin back. Great. Lactose intolerance and elusive-uptight-Englishman smiles were *both* contagious, and she'd succumbed to each.

Holly eyed her latte warily, wanting to test her lactose-intolerance theory with a quick sip, but she thought better of it. There were too many variables. She'd revisit the equation after she was alone in her cube.

"Yeah, well," she said, still wearing a half smile, "I'm not wagging my tail or anything, but thank you." She held up both hands, one holding a latte and the other a phone. "No free hands."

He stepped back, and the elevator finally reached the tenth floor.

"You like the stars?" he asked, eyeing her still-open app as he waited for her to exit.

She beamed, speaking as they lingered in the reception area.

"I love them," she admitted. "When I was little, when my mom first told me about the constellations, I wanted to be one, a star."

He chuckled. "Do you mean famous?"

She shook her head and bit her bottom lip. Why was she telling him this?

"Nope. A real star—in the sky. I wanted to be the brightest, shiniest one up there so that whenever anyone felt lost and looked up, they'd see me and feel better."

His smile fell, and Holly realized she'd said too much, gotten too personal with someone who was meant to be only a business acquaintance.

"Anyway, my parents put me in theater classes and said I could be the star of the stage instead, and now I can sing 'All That Jazz' like no one's business. The end."

She laughed and shrugged it off, just like she did anytime things got too personal, and made it a joke.

But Will Evans wasn't laughing.

"I'll see you in the conference room at one," he said, then turned toward his side of the reception desk, so Holly turned toward hers. There was no tone of dismissal, only a statement of fact.

She *would* see him in the conference room at one. And despite her involuntary sharing-is-caring moment, Will Evans would remain a mystery. For now.

But—mysteries were meant to be solved. She'd crack through that well-groomed exterior. She had to. Or else this would be one hell of a long six months.

Holly dropped her nearly full coffee cup in the garbage can by her desk as the fluttering in her belly continued. *Damn lactose.*

Never mind she only drank lattes made with soy.

Chapter Seven

"It's brilliant!" Holly exclaimed, swiping through Will's proposal on his tablet. "*We're* brilliant. This is exactly the direction I wanted to go, and—and I love it, Will. I really love it."

Will leaned back in his chair, arms crossed over his chest, and he grinned. Holly knew he wasn't playing a part. This wasn't the grin he wore when they'd met Marisa last week. It wasn't painted on to appease her. Those steely blue eyes that always gave her the notion that Will Evans was somewhere other than here—they were fully present and accounted for, crinkled at his temples.

If they'd both been standing and not had a table between them, Holly would have hugged him. Because they were going to get their venue, and Marisa Gonzalez was going to thank them for choosing her hotel.

"You seem right pleased with yourself," Will said. His sleeves were rolled, and the tension that usually tightened his shoulders was nonexistent.

Holly was looking through his slides again and nodding.

"A boho-chic party to tie in with Tallulah's line, and the VIP tickets getting them into the fashion show as well as the New Year's gig—I love it. There aren't enough themed parties. This one will stand out."

Holly rolled her chair closer to Will, sliding her own tablet in front of him. He stayed put and let her fly through slides of Tallulah's designs along with her mock-up of the set. The runway would be made of artificial grass and flowers, and the models would walk it barefoot, the polar opposite of the few European shows Tallulah had done already.

"I know this isn't Tallulah's norm, but then again neither is launching in Chicago with a small boutique firm. I want to capture the free spirit of her line, to make the show retro, or a throwback, you know? Like Woodstock…without the nudity and drugs."

Will stayed silent as Holly spoke a mile a minute. At first she didn't care, because she couldn't contain her excitement. But when she paused for a breath, she hesitated. Still nothing from Will. He sat with his elbow on the table, head resting in his hand as he watched the slides.

"Oh, shit," Holly said. "You *hate* it. I mean, I love it. I really do. But if you think Tallulah will say no, tell me now, okay? I still have until tomorrow morning to rework it for Marisa. It has to be right for the hotel *and* the client. I get that. I—"

He straightened to look at her, shaking his head, so Holly shut up.

"Tallulah's going to go mad for this." Will's voice was soft yet intent. He cleared his throat and stood. "Sorry, I just remembered I have to speak with Andrea about something."

"Did someone say my name?"

Holly and Will both turned toward the door, where Andrea stood in an ivory halter jumpsuit. Holly offered a silent *harrumph* to anyone in the fashion world who thought thirty-five was too old to walk the runway. Just look at Andrea Ross. It was more than what you saw on the outside that made her shine. It was her confidence, and Holly liked to think she had some of that in herself as well.

"Right, yes. I was on my way to see you," Will said. "If you have a minute."

Andrea strode to the table and pressed her palms to the dark wood.

"Actually," she said, but the smile she wore was tentative, and Holly was sure bad news was on the way. So much for her horoscope getting it right for once. "I just got off the phone with Marisa Gonzalez. Reception accidentally forwarded her to me rather than to the conference room."

This was it, Holly thought. They'd lost the venue before they even had a chance to do the proposal. She could feel the adrenaline from today already slipping away.

"Will, I'm sorry, but something came up, and she had to cancel your meeting tomorrow. She wants to meet Friday night instead." There was apology in Andrea's voice. "She said she'd love to buy you two dinner for canceling, that you could pick the place."

"Ooh! We could do Kingston Ale House, my sister's boyfriend's brewery. Friday nights are pitcher specials, and they have the *best* sweet potato fries in the city. Not that I've been thinking about them all week. And I could probably get Jamie—he's my sister's boyfriend—to do dinner on the house anyway, so that would sweeten the deal even more."

Holly paused. Why wasn't anyone joining in her enthusiasm? And why was Andrea only addressing Will? And why was Friday night over Thursday morning a big deal?

She couldn't see Will's face, only his stubbled jaw that was clenched with tension. He ran a hand through his dark waves and breathed out a long breath.

"I'll cancel my flight," he said. Andrea nodded slowly but

didn't say anything else before leaving the room. And then without looking at her, he spoke to Holly.

"It looks like we have all we need for Friday, then. Would you give Marisa the details, say we'll meet her there at seven?" His voice was even, but Holly could tell he was holding something back.

"Of course," she said. "Will, is everything okay?"

He faced her then, and gone were the crinkles at the corners of his eyes.

"Yes," he said. "Smashing." And then he stared for a few seconds at what looked like an overnight bag on the floor by the couch.

Why did this guy seem to have one foot out the door at all times?

"I guess that's it for today, then. Thank you...Holly," he added.

Well, he didn't call her Ms. Chandler, though it seemed he wanted to. And he'd most definitely just dismissed her for the third time in ten days. But this was different. She could tell. So Holly said nothing. This didn't seem to be the time to reeducate Will Evans on the social mores of an equal partnership in the workplace.

But she made a mental note to do so later.

• • •

Holly fidgeted with the Gemini charm that hung around her neck. She wasn't one for superstitions and good-luck charms...okay, so she had a thing for stars, and she maybe sometimes thought they navigated tiny aspects of her life. So sue her for wanting tonight to go perfectly. She was wearing her lucky necklace, dammit.

"You're doing it again," Brynn said.

"Huh? What?" Holly glanced down at the miniature

silver constellation in her hand. "Oh," she added. "I guess I am."

Her sister rested her palm over Holly's, and she stopped tugging at the necklace.

"You're Holly Chandler," Brynn said.

"Stating the obvious, are we?"

"I'm just saying I'm not used to seeing you like this, all nervous and stuff."

Brynn swiveled back and forth on the bar stool next to Holly, her wild curls bouncing on her shoulders as she did. Holly loved this new Brynn, who was really the old Brynn. It was the Brynn in the middle who'd gotten a little lost, thinking her unrequited high school crush was the one who got away when all along it was Jamie, her best friend. It just took them ten years to finally get it right. And now here her sister was, more glass-half-full than she'd ever been, and Holly had started moving in the other direction.

"Well, I've never wanted anything this badly. It might also be the first time I'm at risk of *not* getting what I want," Holly admitted.

Brynn barked out a laugh. "What about Eponine in *Les Mis* your freshman year of college? You called me after your audition, *sure* you'd never be allowed on stage again, and you stole the freaking show."

Holly shook her head. "It was in the bag. I was just a drama queen back then."

"So all those times you thought you wouldn't get a part, that was you crying wolf? I sent you a cookie bouquet and everything for that one!"

Holly shrugged. "I did enjoy those cookies. And it's not like it was any different than you losing your mind about some calculus exam and thinking your life was over."

Brynn groaned. "That was the AP exam, Holly. And it saved me a whole year of college math that would have been a repeat of what I'd already done."

Holly gave her sister a pointed look. "What's the highest score on the AP exam?" she asked.

"A five."

"And what score did my dear old sister get?" Holly continued.

Brynn mumbled something and looked down at the Sox T-shirt she'd promised Jamie she'd wear if she ever came into the bar on game night. In fact, game night was what sold Marisa on meeting at Kingston Ale House. A die-hard Sox fan herself, she'd jumped at the chance to go to a Northside bar that was playing a Southside game.

"I'm sorry," Holly said. "I couldn't hear you."

"A *five*," Brynn said at full volume. "Fine. We're both drama queens."

Holly smoothed out her own shirt, a vintage Woodstock tee she'd found at an upscale resale shop, and hoped she wasn't too casual for a meeting. But this was a bar where they'd be watching a baseball game. She'd told Will no suits allowed, and that was pretty much the extent of any conversation between the two of them since Andrea disrupted their meeting two days ago. Who knew which Will she'd see tonight—arrogant and dismissive? Counterfeit and putting on a show? Playful and teasing with a genuine smile? Or sullen and enigmatic, the only Will she'd seen for the past two days? Whatever flight he'd had to cancel, it hadn't agreed with him. But tonight she crossed her fingers for brilliant and determined—the man Marisa Gonzalez had met and the one she needed to see.

The brewery door swung open, and a gust of late-June heat cut through the air-conditioning. Holly's mouth fell open.

"What?" Brynn asked, but then she followed her sister's gaze. "Is that—is that *him*?"

And by him she meant the guy in the door frame, searching the bar most likely for a familiar face—Holly's face—because when his eyes found hers, his features relaxed into an almost smile. He took her in, and wait—no—now he was full-on grinning. But Holly was sure her chin was still resting on the floor. Because stalking toward her now was Will Evans in—denim.

It wasn't just the dark wash or the fact that his snug-in-all-the-right-places jeans ended at a pair of black-and-white Adidas sneakers—*worn* Adidas sneakers. Like, he hadn't just purchased them today. And it wasn't even the fitted forest green pocket tee that stretched over biceps she hadn't known existed under his suits. It was everything, from the loose waves of his hair to the five-day-old almost beard to that crinkly-eyed smile that was as elusive as a unicorn.

Something began to quiver and dance in her belly, like… like…a butterfly.

She tried to recount the last time she had dairy, but Holly never got her chance.

"Looks like we beat Marisa, yes?" he asked, and then Will's eyes bounced from Holly to Brynn. "You must be Brynn," he said, shaking her hand. "I'm Will. Holly talks about you quite a lot."

Brynn's face broke into a mischievous grin.

"Well, Will. I don't think I've heard nearly enough about *you.*"

• • •

Something was definitely in the air—or the brew—because not only was Marisa blown away by their ideas, enough to give them 20 percent off her original quote, but the White Sox were winning, and on more than one occasion, Holly caught Will Evans smiling. Like now, while he and Marisa played pool and she nursed her pint at a nearby high-top, he looked almost happy.

Not that Holly cared about his happiness.

Except that she kind of did, especially seeing how shaken he'd been when Andrea told them Marisa had to cancel Thursday's meeting and reschedule for tonight. He was meant to be going somewhere on a plane, somewhere he obviously wanted to be rather than here, and though she barely knew him, it had tugged at her heart the tiniest bit to see him full of disappointment. So yeah, it was nice to see him enjoying himself. Plus, she was going to be working with the guy for the next five and a half months putting this show together, and a happy Will was much easier to work with than that brooding guy she usually got to see. He did wear brooding well. There was no doubt about that. But when he smiled, like really smiled, Holly forgot about resenting that she had to wait another half a year before Andrea offered her partner.

"You've got your stargazing face."

Brynn was helping out behind the bar tonight, and she'd just brought the table another pitcher of Jamie's chocolate stout, even though Holly hadn't finished her second pint. Or was it her third?

"Huh?" Holly asked.

Brynn nudged her shoulder with her own.

"Not like I blame you," Brynn continued. "I mean, jeez, Holl. All I've heard you talk about is what a jerk this guy is, but you never said he looked like *that*. Not that *that*"—Brynn nodded toward Will and Marisa, the latter of whom seemed to be heckling the tall drink of British water as he scratched trying to sink the eight ball—"excuses jerky behavior, but tonight he's been nothing but super—"

"Charming?" Holly interrupted. "Delightful? Way too easy on the eyes when he smiles?"

Brynn hopped onto the stool next to her sister. "Like I said—stargazing face."

Holly waved off her sister's insinuations. "He's a

coworker." She cocked her head to the side. "Actually, since his client hired Trousseau for this event, you could consider him my boss."

Brynn chuckled. "His client also hired him, sweetie. So... level playing field, if you ask me."

Holly shrugged. "It's just a crush, and an intermittent one at that. This is not typical Will Evans. Plus, I'd like to restate the obvious—we work together. Conflict of interest."

This time Brynn threw back her head and laughed. She almost toppled her stool.

"If Andrea Ross had any sort of fraternizing-at-the-office rules, you never would have hooked up with Charlie for your little six-month experiment. You're just looking for excuses not to be..." Brynn slapped her hand over her mouth, but it was too late.

"Happy?" Holly asked, brows raised. "Is that what you were going to say? Because that's Mom's line, sis. And you know what it means when you start parroting your own mother, right?"

Brynn shook her head wildly. "You can *never* tell Mom I did that. I'll never hear the end of it, even if she might have a point."

Holly groaned. "I'm happy," she argued, though the statement would probably be more believable if she was smiling when she said it. "I love what I do, and I love living life on my terms. Add anyone else into the mix, and there's bound to be disappointment." Holly drained the pint she'd been nursing. Yeah, it had only been two. She could stand another, so she refilled her glass one more time. "Maybe it sounds selfish to you, Brynn, but the six-month thing? It's not an experiment. It's like my entire dating life since high school has been the experiment, and the only constant is the breaking point. Six months. The newness wears off, and either feelings fizzle or I get accused of not being present enough in the relationship anymore. So I pulled out the biggest variable in the equation—expectation. If we both know going in that whatever this is has an expiration date, then we let the thing run its course and go our separate ways without all the hurt. Honeymoon phase plus no broken heart. Win-win."

Brynn sighed. "Oh, honey. I want more than that for you."

Holly shook her head. "I don't. Not now. I've never been able to put a guy first, back then before theater and now before my career. I'm being fair to me and any guy I get involved with. And if Charlie taught me one thing, it's that six-month rule or not, it's best to keep work at work and other stuff, well, other places."

Both sisters watched Marisa finally sink the eight ball and win, so she and Will hung up their cues and gave the table to waiting patrons.

"Want a refill?" Holly asked as Marisa put her empty pint on the table.

"Thank you, but no," she said. "My husband just got off work, so I'm heading home. I've barely seen him all week."

"Must be hard with the two of you working long hours," Holly said, wondering if the statement was too personal, but Marisa just shrugged.

"It is," she admitted. "But we work at putting each other first even with all the long hours. Otherwise we never would have lasted our first year together."

Holly gave Brynn a look, and Brynn gave her a subtle eye roll. But Holly got what others didn't. *Work* was work. The other stuff should be easy. How else could one find any sort of balance?

Will said nothing and gave no indication of noticing the silent sisterly exchange. He just refilled his glass and took a long sip.

"Anyway," Marisa continued, "I'm really looking forward to working with both of you. And, Brynn, it was great meeting you and Jamie. Any future meetings will *have* to be here. I love this place. Excellent choice, Holly."

And somehow, Marisa's departure made Brynn remember something really important she had to do behind the bar. This time she was not so subtle.

Will held up his glass.

"Here's to a successful show."

And then he grinned.

"Cheers to that," Holly said, and they each brought their glasses to their lips.

As Holly swallowed the rich, smooth liquid, she willed it to douse the feeling in her gut, like she'd just tipped over the edge of a roller coaster's steepest drop.

It'll pass, she told herself. *It always does.*

Chapter Eight

Holly gave him a sidelong glance.

"I can walk home by myself," she said. "I do it all the time."

Will looked up and down the street. It was only eleven, early for a Friday evening in any big city, but letting her walk home alone didn't sit right with him. There was also the small part of him that, despite having to cancel his flight back to London for the weekend, had enjoyed himself this evening, and he didn't want that feeling to end. Walking Holly to her apartment meant he could hang on to that shred of happiness, but it also meant admitting to himself that spending time with her was the reason for it.

He shoved his hands in his front pockets as she kept pace beside him.

"I know you *can*," he said. "But maybe I don't want you to."

Music and laughter, at different volumes and combinations, poured from each pub's door they passed, a disharmonious sort of revelry that brought Will back to what his life had been before—weeks away from home, long days working and even longer nights *not* working—and he felt an uneasy longing. Not to live like that again but to be free enough from responsibility to do so if he wanted.

Hell, who was he kidding? He'd never been free of responsibility, not when it came to his career. And not when it came to Sophie. It had just taken him six years to get his priorities straight. That's where the longing came from. What Will really longed for was to be selfish again, just for a little while, but then he hated himself for even thinking it.

Holly smiled at him and fidgeted with the charm that hung at her neck, the Gemini constellation, and he had the oddest urge to grab that hand and lace his fingers through hers. She was beautiful. There was no argument there. But she was also brilliant and funny and adorably petulant when he frustrated her. She was too much for him *not* to notice every little thing about her. But the last thing he should be thinking about was touching her, even if it was simply her hand.

What the bloody hell was getting into him?

"Thank you," she said. "I mean, this is a pretty safe area, but I guess I appreciate the concern. That's usually my sister's job."

He nodded. "Does your sister let you walk home alone?"

Despite the darkness of the evening, the streetlights and taxi headlights gave the illusion of being inside a lit room, and he could see her cheeks turn pink at his question.

"Actually, I used to walk home with Brynn. But she lives with Jamie now, so…"

Will heard the ache in Holly's voice. He could tell at the brewery that she and her sister were close, and the sound of her voice confirmed what he knew too well. She was lonely, missing someone she loved even though she'd just been with her. Wasn't that his perpetual state of being these days—missing the person he loved most in the world?

Holly's pace began to slow. He hadn't noticed they'd

made their way into a more residential area of Lincoln Park, but it was suddenly quieter, the only sound coming from across the street, a small dog barking as its owner took it for a late-evening walk.

The street, canopied with trees that were likely decades upon decades old, was lined with parked cars. He and Holly came to a stop.

"This is me," she said.

He glanced up at the old building through a break in the trees that also let him see the stars peppering the clear night sky.

"You know," he said, face still turned toward the heavens, "you don't need a stage, Holly, whether you're on it or behind the scenes." Could she really not know how bright she shone, no matter where she was?

He was treading dangerous ground here, but this woman had stirred something in him the moment he saw her in that lift. She was beautiful, of course, but it was when she'd opened her mouth and called him an ass—yes, he'd heard—that he knew Holly Chandler was not to be trifled with. It had been ages since a woman had gotten under his skin enough on first meeting that he behaved like such a wanker. And try as he wanted since that initial meeting, he couldn't let himself enjoy her company for too long, because it only made him want more.

Christ, they worked together. But Holly had some sort of gravitational pull, like she *was* a star and he a helpless planet sucked into her orbit. And so he proceeded, as if he didn't have a choice in the matter. Gravity, proximity, and that stupid *L* word—longing—it had all won out over his free will.

He let his gaze fall on hers, and she stood there, head tilted as she considered him, but she waited for him to say more.

"You were a star with Marisa—in a pub with a tablet and a pitcher of stout. She saw it. I saw it. And you blew her away with your vision for Tallulah's show. You blew *me* away."

Not just tonight, though. That morning in the lift, when she stalked into the conference room ready to put him in his place, every time she refused to let him be formal with her, when she'd given him her mobile number even after he was an arse to her more than once that first day. And then she'd told him to sleep well. Each instance was nothing more than a small gesture, but added together they all brought him to where he was right now, walking a woman home who should remain nothing more than a coworker to him.

Yet he took a step closer, wondering what it would be like for a planet to collide with a star. He lifted a hand, intending to put it on her cheek, but reached for the pendant from where it rested below her neck, second-guessing himself for the hundredth time.

"It…it's Gemini. My sign."

She was nervous, too, so that at least cleared up whether or not what he'd been denying was one-sided.

"I know," he said. "Your stars. Your bloody stars."

She swallowed, and he watched the movement in her throat as she did so.

"Holly…" He didn't know what came next. All he knew was he wanted to kiss her, to have this one small moment for himself.

"Dammit," she said, and his brows rose. "It's just," she continued, "when you say my name like that, all soft and in that smooth, deep, dripping-with-a-gorgeous-accent voice of yours so it sounds like *Holy* instead of *Holly*, it makes me want to do things I shouldn't."

One corner of his mouth twitched into half a grin.

"What about other times I say your name?"

She let out a laugh, but he could hear the tremble in it, the excited, nervous tremble that mirrored what was going on inside his gut—a gut that should be telling him to back the fuck away before they both crossed a line, but Will wasn't moving. And neither was Holly.

"Do you think about me saying your name often?"

He was teasing her now, and it made her smile. And Holly's smile was magnetic, not that it mattered. He'd already been sucked into her orbit. Unless she asked him to, he wasn't leaving it, not tonight.

"I think about you being really good at your job," she said. "And being ridiculously well dressed, even tonight. Don't get me wrong, Evans. I love your suits, but this?" She looked him up and down, raking him over with her eyes, and he felt like her stare could strip away every last one of his defenses. "This takes the cake, because tonight, for the first time in almost two weeks, I think I've caught a glimpse of the real Will."

She put her hand over his, the one still fingering her pendant, and he felt the first jolt of that planetary collision. And when he didn't move or pull away from her touch, Holly did what he was too hesitant to do. She rested her palm on his jaw, and he couldn't stop himself from instinctively tilting his face into it.

"And what do you think of him, the real Will? He's a right prick, is he not?"

She shook her head. "He's charming and funny, wildly talented at what he does, and also decent at snooker."

She said the last word with an exaggerated British accent, and Will couldn't help but laugh.

"I also think he doesn't do that enough," she added. "Smile. I think he's sad, and I'd like to see him smile more."

Will let out a long breath. Jesus, she saw a lot. He wasn't sure he could handle more. But at this point he used Macbeth's logic: *Returning were as tedious as go o'er.* Fine, Macbeth might have been talking about murdering more people while Will was just contemplating a kiss, but otherwise the situation was the same. A line had already been crossed. She was touching him, and her necklace still rested in his palm. If they stepped away now, it wouldn't matter. This moment would always hang between them. But if they saw it through, well, then what? He had to find out.

"You, Holly. *You* make me smile."

She sucked in a sharp breath.

He knew Chicago summers were charged with heat, and despite the sun having set hours ago, the temperature probably still registered a good eighty degrees. But the air between him and Holly right now—it was damn near combustible.

"Whoa," she whispered, and Will dipped his head toward hers.

"May I kiss you?" he asked, and she responded by clasping her hands around his neck and pulling his lips to hers.

Holly was shorter without the four-inch heels she usually wore, and he smiled against her as her tongue swiped across his bottom lip.

"What?" she asked. "Is something funny?" And he pulled back for just a second to reassure her.

"The real Holly is much shorter than the one I see at the office. I think I like her best, too."

And with that his lips found hers again, sweet and soft as she explored him with her mouth and hands. Her fingers trailed down his back while he kept her face cradled in his palms. God, she felt good pressed up against him. With his eyes closed and her lips parting to invite him in, he could forget for a few minutes where he was meant to be, what leaving Chicago in January—for good—would mean.

His hands found their way to her hips as hers traveled up to his face, like they were part of some choreographed dance. Her T-shirt rose as she reached for him, and the tips of his fingers brushed soft skin.

Holly ground her hips into him as their tongues became part of the choreography as well, and Will thought he would lose his mind.

"Bloody, fucking hell, Holly."

She giggled, her fingers tracing his hairline from his forehead to just below his ears.

"Can I ask you a question?" She kissed his neck and then the line of his jaw.

"Yes, you're driving me fucking mad. Does that answer it?"

She laughed again, and it was a sound Will liked very much.

"No…" She teased his neck with more soft brushes of her lips before making her way to the other side of his face. "But I do enjoy doing that." She nipped at his earlobe, and Will decided that whatever she asked of him, he'd give it, no objections. "I want to know why you only shave once a week — and if it has anything to do with where you disappeared to last weekend…or where you were supposed to be tonight."

Holly's lips were on his again, but he froze against her. He was sure she felt his whole being go rigid. And then she stepped away.

"Shite." He growled under his breath, and Holly's eyes grew wide.

"Look," she said, regaining her composure. "It's not like I'm looking for anything big here, Will. But I'm not a home wrecker. If there's someone else back in London, I want no part of this." She motioned between them. "Do you understand? It doesn't matter that I can barely stand right now or that you taste better than ice cream—and that is saying *a lot* coming from me. I mean, you have *no* idea. But I don't condone cheating, okay? I won't be the girl—"

"I have a daughter," he interrupted. And there it was, out there. Despite their professional relationship and the bleeding Atlantic Ocean separating her world from his, there was also the small matter of Sophie, the six-year-old other woman in his life, the reason why someone like Holly would never be right for him and why he could never be right for her.

"That's it," he continued, knowing the short, lovely something that was between them was over. "That's my big secret. Her mum left me before she was born. Can't much blame her, but yeah. I have a daughter. Her name is Sophie, and she's six, and I should have been back in London squeezing in a few precious hours with her, but instead here I am."

"Will, I—I don't know what to say."

He shook his head. He needed to get out of here, and fast. Because he could still taste Holly on his lips, feel her on his skin, and if she asked—if she still wanted him now—he'd follow her right up to her apartment, but that wouldn't be good for either of them.

"It doesn't matter," he said. "I'm sorry. This was a mistake. I shouldn't have… You're home safe, yeah?"

She nodded and pulled her keys out of her pocket. She wasn't even carrying a purse. *This is the real Holly*, he thought. Stripped down to the bare essentials, and all he could think about was that he was already too bare in front of her.

"I'll stay to make sure you get in safe."

She took a step forward, and he used the last ounce of his willpower not to reach for her.

"Will, you don't have to go."

He shoved his hands in his pockets and took a step back.

"Yes, Holly. I do. I—this could only be temporary. At best," he said. "I'm only here because it's my last step in the fulfillment of a contract I never should have signed. I was an arse to even consider jeopardizing our professional relationship. I'm sorry."

She closed her eyes—a long, slow blink. And when she opened them, she nodded and walked to her door without another word. Will watched her enter her building, and then he turned and walked away.

Chapter Nine

Shit.

Holly let her head thud against the door after she kicked it closed behind her.

Shit.

He's—a dad. Will Evans—king of rude dismissals, enigmatic behavior, and kisses that had molten heat still pooling in her belly—was a father. That's where he took off to that first weekend and where he was supposed to be now. Home. With his daughter.

His *daughter*.

Part of Holly wanted to run after him, pull him close, and tell him she knew what it was like to miss someone. Not that Brynn moving out was even remotely close to what he must be feeling, but still. She got it, loving one person more than everything else and having to say good-bye. With their parents both retired and constantly traveling, Brynn was it for Holly, the one person who would always be there for her. Except now she wasn't.

Holly closed her eyes and started reliving the kiss, not able to shake the feeling of standing on her tiptoes and pressing her pelvis to his. She'd felt him hard against her. She *knew* he wanted exactly what she did. Okay, well, she couldn't confirm that he was going through a dry spell, too, but he wanted her. That much she knew.

Shit.

She stalked to the bathroom and turned on the faucet so that water rushed out in a loud, whirring splash. Then she stripped herself bare and adjusted the temperature before changing the water source from bath nozzle to showerhead. Holly stepped over the lip of the tub and pulled the curtain shut, letting out a resigned sigh.

The water hit her face, her neck, her breasts—nipples still sensitive and hard just from brushing up against him. She imagined Will's velvety voice asking, *May I kiss you? May I touch you? May I...*

Holly lifted the showerhead out of its cradle and adjusted the setting to her favorite combination of pulse and vibration. She gave it a pointed look.

"Do *you* have any secret children you'd like to tell me about before things go any further?"

The showerhead said nothing, but she knew what it was thinking. *I'm it for you, sweetheart. I'll always be here, and you'll always come back to me. We're meant to be.*

Well, they were meant to be for this evening, anyway.

She let her head fall against the cool, tiled wall and dropped the hand holding the showerhead between her legs. Eyes closed and shoulders finally relaxing, Holly let her hips pulse to the rhythm of the water, and she let the water do what she needed it to do.

Only, her H_2O lover wasn't doing his job. She shifted her stance, but it still wasn't right. Maybe it was placement? But no, adjusting placement did nothing to uncoil the tight heat from her core. Then, understanding the risks, she did the unthinkable. Desperate times called for desperate measures. With her thumb resting on the small lever at the base of the head, Holly swiveled it forward just a notch—and changed the setting.

"Shit!" she yelled, throwing the nozzle against the wall. It bounced and sprayed hot needles at her torso, her face, and then the shower curtain. She grabbed it before it nailed her in the face again, not wanting another aggressive facial.

Note to self—

Next time you want to change the showerhead setting, remove said showerhead from between your legs first!

Holly's much-needed release was going nowhere fast, so she nudged the dial back to where it was—or where she thought it was—and attempted to get back to business. But it was no use. The pulse was too weak, the water streams too thin. She tried again, and then again, prodding the dial just enough to enact the smallest change, but she couldn't get it back to her original setting.

Her greatest fear had been realized. Her showerhead setting had lost its sweet spot, which meant *her* sweet spot was to remain unsatisfied.

She groaned and slammed the water off altogether, feeling bad for the pint of Häagen-Dazs waiting in the freezer that only had moments left to live before she devoured it without mercy.

May I kiss you and leave you aching between your legs, reminding you that there is better out there than the six-speed Turbo Elite?

"Why, yes, Will Evans," she said aloud, wrapping herself in a towel. "It appears that you can."

Halfway through her pint of pure, untampered with chocolate

ice cream, Holly still couldn't find anything to watch on TV that would distract her from the crazy that was this evening, so she tightened the belt on her robe, grabbed her phone, the remainder of her ice cream, *and* a spoon, of course, and headed out to her balcony.

Will had called her a star. He'd called her a star, kissed her, and then walked away because he knew that whatever was between them couldn't go any further. And something was definitely between them. Holly could admit now as she sat in her small wooden chair, laying waste to the rest of her dairy savior, that she was *not*, in fact, lactose intolerant. She was Will Evans intolerant, and if this severe physical reaction was something she could control with an over-the-counter medication or sheer avoidance, she would. But there was no antidote for what was brewing between them—other than Holly's foolproof way to run a relationship into the ground: let it continue past six months.

But Will Evans wouldn't be in Chicago past the six-month marker. And he certainly didn't want anything long-term with her. Not that she wasn't great with kids—she *had* worked at a kids' theater camp throughout her high school and college summers. But Holly had never seriously considered having children, not while she was still so focused on her career. And trying at a real relationship for the first time since high school with a guy who lived on another continent? *Thanks, but no thanks.*

She and Will were so, so, *so* wrong for each other, which was why her idea might work. Because it was so right.

Holly squirmed in her seat. She obviously needed to get Will Evans out of her system. And the way things usually panned out for her, it might take a little longer than one or two times. What she knew for sure was that regardless of how long it took, whether it was two weeks or two months or the whole rest of his stay, if they agreed up front to what they were getting into, they could walk away unscathed.

She dipped her spoon into the pint only to hit the cardboard bottom, her ice cream reservoir depleted. So she licked the spoon clean and then tapped it against her chin as the wheels began to turn.

The smart thing to do would be to just give it another go with Charlie. They still saw each other on a daily basis, and while he clearly was not in love with her—nor she with him—it would be easy for them to fall into some sort of pattern, especially since Charlie hadn't been shy about letting her know he'd be up for another six months if she was. Charlie was comfortable. The sex was good. And he didn't expect anything more from her than what she was willing to give.

Pushing things any further with Will could complicate their work. After all, making partner was Holly's end game, so this show had to go off without a hitch. But she couldn't stop thinking about that kiss, how it awakened a need in her she'd thought was long dormant. How could she see him day in and day out without being distracted? Maybe she didn't want comfortable. Maybe she didn't want *good* sex. Maybe she wanted electricity. Didn't Will want it, too? Or else why kiss her at all?

Holly tapped open her horoscope app on her phone and backed up to the last one she'd read. *Take advantage of new opportunities even if they present themselves as what you see as obstacles. Appreciate what you're given, and allow time for joy.* A six-month fling with Will Evans would absolutely be an opportunity as well as a possible obstacle. But not seeing this through was an obstacle as well, because the tension between them might never dissipate. Totally valid argument.

Holly did love her job. It was everything to her. But that second sentence niggled at her brain. *Appreciate what you're given, and allow time for joy.* It had been a while since joy had come from anything other than work. And physical joy? Well, she could practically kiss that good-bye unless she solved the Rubik's Cube puzzle of the showerhead setting.

She tapped the arrow to move the horoscope forward to tomorrow. Well, today, since it was past midnight now.

Gemini: Congratulations. All your worries of yesterday will work themselves out today as long as you don't sit idly by. Wrongs will be righted, and Gemini will find happiness in taking action, in moving beyond stumbling blocks to get what she wants.

See? Even her horoscope app thought she should take action. If this wasn't giving destiny a nudge, she didn't know what was. For a minute Holly considered calling Brynn and talking this through with her, but as much as Brynn teased about her apparent attraction to Will—stupid stargazing face—once Holly told her sister about Will's whole being-a-dad situation, she knew Brynn would go all logical on her, tell her this wasn't a good idea.

What if you got attached? she'd ask. Holly wouldn't. *What if he got attached?* Will wouldn't, either. He couldn't. Holly was here. His daughter was there. He wouldn't say yes to Holly if he had any potential real feelings for her, right? This was all just attraction and sexual tension they needed to get out of their systems, let it run its course and then be on their merry way. Well, it looked like she'd survive without sisterly advice this time.

Holly leaned back and peered up at the sky, finding Ursa Minor staring back at her, though not as bright as it was last week. If she squinted the right way, she could make out Castor and Pollux just above, and she smiled up at the Gemini twins.

"You're onto something, guys," she said quietly.

Hopefully Will would think so, too.

Chapter Ten

Will scrubbed a hand over his jaw and scratched his neck. He'd shaved under his chin. *That*, at least, was allowed. Sophie's rules.

I still want you to look smart in your suits, Daddy, she'd said when he'd asked permission to maintain the beard without getting rid of it. God, he loved that sweet voice of hers, hated that he'd missed a weekend of her curled in his lap, reading *Madeline* to him.

Will you take me to Paris, Daddy, like Madeline?

That was the promise he'd made her—well, the second one. The first was that he'd come home as many weekends as he could while away, only shaving just before he returned to the States. The second was a trip to Paris. He still had to convince Sophie's mum to let him steal her away for a week once he was back for good. But he knew Tara and Phillip would enjoy some alone time. He could use that angle. And once he proved to her that he was back for good, that he was finally putting family first, then he'd bring up the idea of sharing custody.

He took advantage of the lift's solitude and snapped a photo of himself with his phone. Will had decided to come in a little later this morning, hoping to avoid any awkward one-on-one time with Holly, even though she had been on his mind all weekend. He was a right prick for doing what he'd done Friday night. But since the morning he met her, she'd burrowed under his skin. Holly Chandler was maddening. She didn't back down from him when he was a prick. She was good at her job. No, she was brilliant. She didn't need him to pull off this show, yet they worked so well as a team. But it wasn't just what Holly could do for his client. It was what she did to him. She made Will smile when happiness was thousands of miles away. She made him think these next five and a half months could be bearable if walking into Trousseau every weekday morning meant he'd see her. And the sight of her in jeans and a T-shirt drinking a pint in a pub, well it damn near floored him. She was a whirlwind in the office, alight with a frenetic energy that energized him as well. But Friday night's Holly, after they'd sealed the deal with Marisa—she was a sort of Holly unplugged. A glimpse into a side of her she didn't unveil when they were working. For a tiny pocket of time that evening, he'd let himself imagine what it would be like to have someone like that in his life. But that Holly was a fantasy. The woman he worked with, the one who knew her partnership at Trousseau rode on this show being a success, that was the real Holly. A woman with the freedom to put her career first.

And he'd nearly fucked it all up by kissing her. Holly's job was important to her, and he'd put that in jeopardy the second he said, "May I kiss you?" Perhaps he *was* the bastard Tara claimed he was when she'd finally had enough and had left before Sophie was even born. He hadn't put her first, so he'd lost them both. What was he thinking being so selfish with Holly? He certainly wasn't putting her best interest first, and wanting anything from her at all—*enjoying* himself while he was away from his daughter—that wasn't putting Sophie first, either.

Will tapped the icon on the photo of himself that allowed him to send the picture, and then he typed in Tara's name. She'd agreed to him texting Sophie on her phone as often as he liked.

Love you, Soph, he typed under the attached photo as the lift came to a halt. Will was ready to step out when he glanced at the lit-up number above the door. It was five, not ten. *No worries,* he thought. Just another straggler grabbing a coffee and heading in late. So he stepped back against the wall and waited for the doors to part. When they did, the first thing he noticed were the red peep-toe booties, the heel at least four inches.

Holly might have been petite, but in shoes like that, her legs went on for miles, and his eyes traveled up their length covered in sheer, black stockings speckled with tiny polka dots—polka dots that made him think of those freckles on her nose.

Will cleared his throat, hoping it would clear his head, but when he saw that the stockings disappeared into a pair of fitted black shorts—oh good God, it was one of those short suits, bloody sexy as hell—he half considered bolting out the doors as she stepped in.

"Guess we're both running a bit late this morning, huh?" Holly asked with a pleasant, red-lipped smile. Her hair fell over her left shoulder in a loose plait, the soft look framing her vibrant features. "Purposefully, maybe?" She shrugged. "Actually drank my latte in the cafeteria."

She *shrugged*?

But that wasn't the fiery, take-no-shite Holly who stormed into his office or called him out on something as simple as being dismissed. Not that he'd meant to dismiss her.

Why wasn't she yelling at him? Why wasn't she giving him hell for not bringing up Sophie before he'd tried to kiss her? No. She was taking the piss, making him squirm. That must be it. Holly knew fashion. There was no doubt about that. But walking into work today looking like that, with…with those shoes. His first words to her echoed in his head. *I'd have gone for the red.*

He was ever the bastard, and she was most definitely taking the piss. He deserved it.

"Holly," he said once the doors closed, giving them a possible five stories of privacy before they'd have to get on with their day. "I never should have — "

She waved him off as if he was apologizing for knocking her bag off her shoulder, not for falling into his old habit of thinking of himself before anyone else.

"I have a meeting with the runway designer at ten thirty," she said. "And then I was thinking of a lunch meeting."

His brows furrowed.

"A lunch meeting?"

Holly nodded. "Yes. You liked Jamie's bar, right? Kingston Ale House? Well, they have a fabulous beer garden, and it's only in the seventies today. I thought we'd hop in a taxi, enjoy the sunshine, and have a meeting."

She bit her lower lip, only for a second, but it was enough to crack the facade, for Will to see she was nervous — and also bloody adorable. Christ, he had to stop looking at her like this. A lunch meeting would do them good. They could relax, clear the air, and set new parameters from this day forth. Their relationship would be nothing but professional. It had to be, because she was already driving him mad. He could take the first part of the morning to regroup, make a few phone calls to potential sponsors for the fashion show, and then — lunch. He could keep it together for lunch.

"Lunch sounds lovely," he said, and Holly's shoulders

relaxed. He was glad to know she was just as nervous about seeing him today as he was to see her. And even better that she wanted to get things back on track, with her as the show's director, him as the publicist, and that would be that.

"Good," Holly said. "That settles it. Oh, and make sure your afternoon is clear, too." The lift stopped at the tenth floor, and the doors opened into Trousseau's lobby, so they both stepped out.

"My afternoon?" Will was lost again.

Holly nodded, all confidence back in her stance, and Will had to force himself not to let his eyes dip to those legs again.

"Yes. I told Andrea I'm going to show you a few window displays on Michigan Avenue to give you an idea of what I'm aiming at for the show. Since the show will be Ms. Chan's spring line, I thought it couldn't hurt to check out what draws the Chicago fashionista's eye."

She had already taken a step toward her side of the office while he was poised in the direction of his.

"Yes. Of course. I had a phone call scheduled, but I think I can ring them tomorrow."

Lunch he could handle. But an afternoon walking the streets of the city with Holly? It sounded wonderful and terrifying all at the same time.

Her lips dipped into a small frown as he watched her give him the once-over.

"What?" He glanced down the line of his body. "Did I spill coffee on my tie? What is it?"

Her concern quickly changed to a giggle as she shook her head.

"No, it's not that. It's just, I didn't plan this very well. I always have a change of clothes at my desk, just in case, but I don't think you'll be comfortable walking for hours in a three-piece suit and wingtips."

His lips curved in a grin. He had a secret stash, too,

his weekend bag, just in case he needed to jet home in an emergency or if there was an opportunity to fly home early to surprise Sophie. His bag had been there, packed and ready to go last Wednesday when Andrea broke the news he'd have to stay in Chicago for the weekend. The memory of that set his mind straight, and although he knew he'd need a lot more than a simple reminder to keep his thoughts on home rather than here, it was a start.

"I'll be fine," was all he said. She didn't need a long, drawn-out explanation. "Meet here around noon."

"Noon it is, Mr. Evans." And there was a tease in the lilt of her voice. But then her face grew serious for a second as she said, "And Will?" Her hand fidgeted with the zipper of the small red bag slung across her torso.

"Yeah?"

"I'm sorry you missed the weekend with your daughter." There was genuine sadness in her voice, and his breath caught at the sound of it. Without waiting for a response, Holly spun on her heel and headed toward her desk.

A throat cleared to his right, startling Will from the stupor Holly had just put him in. When he spun toward the sound, he was greeted by Jackie, the front desk assistant, and her toothy grin.

"Good morning, Jackie," Will said, straightening his already straight tie before heading toward his office.

"Good morning, *Mr. Evans*," she said, parroting Holly teasing him with use of his surname.

She said nothing else, and he didn't let the assuming tone bother him, whatever it was she was thinking. Because nothing was going on between him and Holly Chandler.

Nothing other than a kiss and the image of her stepping into that lift burned into his brain—along with the memory of Holly unplugged, the one who loved the stars as much as Sophie did, who could relax and enjoy a pitcher of stout at a neighborhood pub. The one he'd love to know better if she lived a little closer and maybe worked a little less.

No, nothing was going on between them. Nothing at all. Will just had to keep repeating that to himself. Hopefully by lunch he'd believe it.

Chapter Eleven

Holly hid behind her menu, wishing Kingston Ale House was fancy enough for daily specials, a reason for her to have to study the text more carefully. But the food menu only changed if something wasn't selling. All Jamie cared about were his brews. Still, Holly kept reading, just in case she wasn't sure if there really was parmesan cheese on the truffle fries—or if the cheese fondue for the hot pretzels was a beer fondue. Of course it was.

Holly practically lived here. She knew the menu by heart, and having her meeting with Will here was supposed to lessen the anxiety. But every time she peeked over the top, she saw him genuinely studying the beer list, eyebrows raised as he moved a palm back and forth across his jaw. Add to that the short-sleeved navy henley and dark-wash jeans he just happened to have in his office, and well, Holly's mouth went dry.

"Business or pleasure?" a familiar voice asked, and Holly looked up to see Jeremy Denning, her friend Annie's brother and Jamie's assistant manager—and apparently also a sometime server. He stood poised in a Kingston Ale House tee and jeans, either squinting from the sun or smirking directly at Holly. She guessed it was the latter.

"Excuse me?" Holly asked, immediately regretting giving him the opening to repeat the question.

"Just making small talk with the customers," he said, and Will set his drink menu down to give Jeremy the once-over. "Middle of the day on a Monday," he continued. "Figured either it's a business lunch or you kids are calling in sick to enjoy the weather."

And then he had the nerve to freaking wink at her.

Ugh. Jeremy wasn't even working Friday night, which meant Brynn had already blabbed to Annie about Holly's *stargazing face*, and Annie must have filled her brother in. Jamie was the only one who stayed out of the rumor mill. He had his beer, and he had Brynn. Nothing else mattered. But jeez, start a game of telephone with Brynn, Annie, and Jeremy, and the message reached the end of the party line in seconds flat. If there was one thing Holly hated, it was gossip.

Okay, that was a lie. Holly loved gossip, but if she was the subject of said gossip, then she turned her hypocritical nose up at it in a heartbeat.

"You're the only kid around here, Jeremy. And I thought you gave up waiting tables when Jamie made you manager."

Will leaned back in his chair and regarded the two of them, arms crossed over his chest and lips in a tight line. But he said nothing.

Jeremy shrugged. "You got one year on me, Holls. That only counts in high school years, and we've been done with that long enough for it not to hold any weight. As for waiting tables? Only when it's a beautiful day like today and I get to do the beer garden." He looked back and forth between Holly and Will, his grin widening. "Casual dress with an air of uncertainty—I'm calling it business with potential."

Holly coughed just as she was about to sip her water.

"Sorry," Will finally interrupted. "But do you two know each other?"

Holly groaned.

"Just my friend Annie's annoying little brother," she said.

Jeremy brought a hand to his heart with an exaggerated gasp. Then he held a hand out to Will.

"Jeremy Denning," he said. "Annoying little brother at your service."

Will shook his hand but still eyed Jeremy warily.

"Jeremy, Will is in Chicago for a bit while he and I work together on a project for Trousseau."

Jeremy nodded.

"Business it is, then. Can I start you two with an appetizer?"

Holly wasn't sure if she had the stomach for food any longer.

"I'll have a pint of the Kingston IPA," Holly blurted—not exactly an hors d'oeuvre—and smiled, sure Jeremy could see right through her.

"Right," Will said, clearing his throat. "Make that two."

Jeremy raised a brow.

"Like I said." He smiled. "Business with potential." He winked again, and Holly wanted to crawl under the table. Then she realized hiding out with Will's legs in those great-fitting jeans would not ease the situation, so she thought better of it. After all, Jeremy was right. If things went according to plan, Holly and Will would be on their way to potential.

• • •

"Here we go!" Jeremy set a plate down in front of Holly. "Fish and chips for the lady. And..." Doing the same for Will, he added, "Fish and chips for the gentleman. Malt vinegar, ketchup, salt and pepper—it's all on the table. Anything else I can get for you?"

As much as Holly did not want to be under Jeremy's watchful eyes, she kind of didn't want him to leave. Because that would mean she'd have to start talking to Will instead of insisting she had to answer phantom emails from Andrea or bringing her pint to her lips every time it seemed like Will was going to ask her something. After all, Holly had set up this meeting. She'd been so sure of herself when she saw him in the elevator this morning, but now?

What if he said no? Charlie had jumped at the chance for six months of fun, no broken hearts at the end. And it had worked out perfectly. They didn't have to see each other every day if things got awkward, but things never did. Charlie was just as committed to not committing as Holly was. It was kind of a win-win other than Holly really not being into him anymore.

"Can I ask you something?" Will reached for the malt vinegar and doused his whole plate as he spoke. "Or do you have another email to respond to?"

Holly's eyes darted from her phone to Will's, then she instinctively put a french fry in her mouth and held up a finger since she couldn't possibly speak while chewing.

"Did you order fish and chips because I'm English?"

The corner of his mouth quirked up into a teasing, lopsided grin.

Holly swallowed her fry—and her hesitation.

"Did *you* order fish and chips because you're English?" she asked with small chuckle.

Now Will sprinkled salt over his vinegar-doused plate. "When it's done proper, and when I ache for home, sure." He picked up a fry soaked with vinegar and dropped it in his mouth, his tongue reaching below his bottom lip to catch a rogue drip.

Holly's mouth watered, so she ate another of her own fries to occupy her needy taste buds.

"That's not how you eat yours, is it?" he asked, and her eyes widened. Will shook the bottle of vinegar. "Either you do it proper or—I'm sorry. I can't let you eat that."

Holly washed the fry down with a sip of her IPA.

"You can't *let* me? You're kidding, right?"

Will's expression was impassive.

"I don't kid about fish and chips."

Yeah, he didn't kid about much at all, come to think of it.

"If you call them chips, then what do you call *real* chips?" she asked and popped another fry.

"You're just stalling now," Will said, grinning as he leaned toward her. "You think if you distract me, I'll let you continue this mockery you've made of my country."

She snorted. "Mockery? You're joking, right? Will Evans knows how to make a joke?"

"Crisps," he continued. "We call chips crisps. And fries are chips. Trucks are lorries, cookies, biscuits, and elevators, lifts. There's your American-to-English dictionary, love. Now you have a choice, Ms. Chandler. You can try a proper chip…" He lifted one off his plate and pointed it at her. "Or you can tell me why you asked me here for a meeting that seems on the verge of never actually starting."

"Both!" Holly blurted, not giving herself time to think. Nope, it was time to dive in. She watched him waver for a second, could see the wheels turning. He could drop the fry and let her call his bluff, or he could keep right on leaning closer, sliding his elbow across the table until his fingers met her mouth.

She watched him swallow, his Adam's apple bobbing as a sort of nod—a decision.

Will went with option number one.

First Holly tasted the salt as the fry—or perhaps the

chip—hit the tip of her tongue. Not a big fan of pickles, she had always thought the vinegar was to blame. But as Will's fingers came closer to her mouth, pushing the fry farther back on her tongue, she felt the tang on her taste buds and couldn't help the sigh that escaped her parted lips.

"Mmm," she said softly, closing her lips over the edge of the fry, Will's fingers escaping, but not before the tip of one brushed her chin. "I stand corrected." Holly licked her lips. "Thank you for showing me the error of my ways, Mr. Evans."

Will cleared his throat. "Come on, Holly," he said. "What's this about? Lunch—the afternoon? So far it doesn't feel quite like a meeting, and I thought—"

"I don't date," Holly interrupted.

There. She'd put it out there. Now all she had to do was follow through.

Will's brows pulled together, and his mouth hung open as he stopped midbite. So she continued.

"Friday night was—a lot of things. I wasn't expecting the evening to go in the direction it did. I mean, we work together. I'm from here. You're from there. I have career advancement to worry about and you have a—a—"

"A Sophie." Will filled in the blank.

"Right. A Sophie. And I *get* it, Will. I do. You're a father, and I'm certainly not in any position to impose on that when… Family? Holly progeny, Batman. Not even on my radar."

"Holly progeny—?"

Nope. She couldn't let him take the wheel. Not now. Holly had to steer this baby home.

"What's your sign?" she asked.

Will seemed to have lost interest in his food and drink altogether as he leaned back in his chair and ran a hand through his already breeze-tousled hair.

"Taurus. I don't understand—"

"See?" She bounced in her seat. "See? A Gemini and a

Taurus?" She scoffed. "We're so completely wrong for each other. If we dated it would *never* work out."

His eyes narrowed. "Do you really believe in all that? That the stars decide who's right for whom?"

She groaned. "No. I mean…I don't know. I'm just saying that the odds are stacked against our compatibility, which is *actually* in our favor."

She felt like they were speaking two languages. She had to get to the good part so he'd understand.

Holly huffed out a breath. "We kissed."

He nodded. "We kissed."

Will wasn't stopping her, so she was going to soldier on, see how far they'd get.

"And it was good, right? Like *really* good."

Another slow nod. "Christ, Holly." His voice was soft and rough. If she closed her eyes, she could swear they were in the middle of that kiss again, because she knew Will was replaying it in his head just as she was in hers. "It was bloody spectacular."

His words came out like a confession.

"I don't date," Holly repeated. "Not seriously, anyway. Because it always seems to fall apart around six months. And you?" She smiled softly, waiting for him to catch on. "You're only here—"

"For six months." He blew out a breath. He was up to speed, but she could still sense his hesitation. "Holly. We work together."

"I know. Good thing we both have the same goal—the best show possible for Tallulah Chan."

"And I go home to London every weekend I can. For Sophie. Sophie *always* comes first."

"I know." She nodded, then offered him a teasing grin. "And work comes first for me. But there are all those weekday evenings—and days like today."

Their food was growing cold, and Holly didn't think either of them cared.

Will leaned forward on his elbows. "What are you proposing, Ms. Chandler?"

He wasn't smiling. Not yet. But he was interested, and that was all she needed.

Holly leaned forward as well, palms flat on the table. Her fingertips brushed his.

"Do you think about that kiss?" she asked, her lips so close to his.

"I do."

"Do you think about what could have come *after* that kiss?"

Holly fought not to squirm in her seat as her core burned with the memory of Friday night.

"I do," he said again, and his warm breath ghosted across her lips.

"What if you didn't have to worry about what this meant for you and for Sophie? What if while you're here, we work during the day, and at night—when we're both up for it—we take advantage of spectacular? Everything runs its course by the time you leave, and we end up with a lovely half a year spent putting together a brilliant fashion show and getting all that kissing stuff out of our system."

Will shook his head. "You've got this all figured out, don't you?"

She shrugged. "It's *like* dating, but without all the expectations and heartache. We enjoy the honeymoon phase and call it a day."

"Just like that?" he asked, and she nodded, her lips so close to brushing against his.

"Just. Like. That."

He reached a hand toward the back of her head. "I've got one condition," he said. This was it. He was going to kiss her, and they'd take this thing between them as far as it would go. But instead she felt a soft tug. Then another. And another after that until her brown hair fell in soft waves over her shoulders. "I want to know when we're off the clock, when we're no longer office Holly and office Will. Because this show is just as important to me. I can't cock things up because you smell good or you drive me bloody mad by wearing red shoes."

She giggled. "I knew you'd like those."

His hand rested on her neck now, under her hair. And despite the heat of the sun overhead, goose bumps broke out all over Holly's skin.

"How will I know you're off the clock?" she asked, feeling bold. "I don't want to pick the wrong time to do this." Holly flicked her tongue against his lips, and Will sucked in a sharp breath. She'd caught him off guard, but he didn't back down.

"I'll take off my tie."

Her eyes took him in—head, shoulders, torso, and the denim she knew was under the table.

"You're not wearing a tie now."

Will shook his head.

"Holly Chandler—whatever happened to your plait?" He tangled his fingers in her hair. "You're sure about this?" he asked, and she could feel him so close to letting go.

"I'm sure."

His lips tickled hers.

"Then, Holly Chandler—may I kiss you again?"

Chapter Twelve

"God, I love it when you say *May I?*"

And again she answered him without words, just with her lips on his, outside in a beer garden—over two plates of fish and chips.

What was he doing? This wasn't okay. This wasn't what he'd come to the States for. He was here for Sophie. All he had to do was make it through the first of the year and he was a free man, free to be the father he should have been since day one, to put his daughter first.

But hell if Holly Chandler wasn't breathing new life into him with every brush of her lips, that tease of her tongue.

"We shouldn't do this here," he said gently against her mouth.

"I know." She laughed softly, pulling away, and Christ, he'd have let her keep kissing him despite the public display, because it had been too long since he'd felt anything other than guilt or disappointment at the choices he'd made.

"I'm not really hungry anymore," she said. "For pub fare, I mean."

As if the kiss wasn't enough to bring him back to life, the insinuation in Holly's tone sent Will reeling—and straining against his goddamn jeans.

"Can't say I am, either." He pulled his wallet from his back pocket, but she put her hand on his before he could retrieve his bank card.

"Oh, no, you don't," she said. "I set up this *meeting*, which means lunch is on me. Ask me to dinner sometime, and maybe I'll let you take care of the bill."

Dinner. Would he take her to dinner? What, exactly, had they just agreed to? Will couldn't think clearly, not with thoughts of his lips on hers again. But they were supposed to be doing something other than kissing, right? There was a reason she'd had him clear his schedule for the rest of the afternoon.

"Windows!" he blurted as Holly left cash on the table next to their uneaten food. "You were going to show me windows, right? For design ideas."

Holly stood and grabbed his hand, urging him to join her.

"My apartment has windows," she said. "Can I show you those first?"

Will swallowed hard. They were really going to do this. Now. This was mad. Holly Chandler and her six-month plan were just plain mad. But he wanted her more than logic could argue, and he knew if he didn't get this wanting out of his system, this job would be fucked, and his superiors would find a way to take that sabbatical from him. As it stood now, if he fulfilled the terms of his contract, he'd have a year off with job security. But fuck it all up, and he'd lose the job completely. Sure, there was enough money to live leisurely for a year, to take care of Sophie, and even to put away for her. But he wasn't set for life. Far from it. He had to wade into these waters with care.

But right now, he couldn't think past the next three

minutes. He just needed to see those windows.

"Yes," he answered, letting her pull him from the table, passing Jeremy on the way.

Holly paused for a moment as Jeremy looked toward their table and then back at them, grinning like the damn Cheshire Cat.

"Enjoy your potential," Jeremy said, and Holly backhanded him on the shoulder while Will stayed quiet. Not like he could disagree about what lay ahead for them.

We will, he thought instead, as Holly led him through the beer garden's gate and out onto the sidewalk.

He remembered their walk Friday night, how they'd lingered with each step, the feeling that neither of them wanted to reach their destination because that would mean the night would end. Now they practically raced to Holly's flat, Will barely remembering the journey until his back was against the door she'd disappeared into only three days ago.

Hidden from the street under the door's small overhang, Holly whispered to him, "May I kiss you, Will Evans?"

He was dizzy with need, but he was with it enough to remember that he didn't live his life like this anymore. When he'd come home from that Paris trip six and a half years ago to find Tara had left him for Phillip while he was gone, Will had felt a sense of relief. He'd been only twenty-six, on fire at Spotlight PR. Being single would give him the freedom to do what he loved, what he was damn good at, without anything or anyone holding him back.

Until Tara told him she was pregnant, and tests confirmed the baby was his.

"Holly, wait."

She stopped, and he rested a palm lightly on her cheek while his other hand fisted at his side.

"You're having second thoughts," she said, and the light in her green eyes dimmed. "It's okay," she added. "I knew there was a chance this would be too much. I mean, we barely know each other, but *God*, the heat between us, right? Maybe it's that whole opposites-attract thing. I don't know. I just thought if I could get it out of my system—let my little crush run its course—by the time we were ready for the show, we'd be past all this...this...*need*."

She ducked under his arm, and Will instinctively moved out of the way as she stuck her key in the lock. She turned back as she pushed the door open and shrugged.

"Meeting adjourned, I guess?"

Oh, for fuck's sake. He kissed her again, and Holly's eyes grew wide, but she melted into him nonetheless. When he felt her relax, he pulled away to speak.

"Do you ever stop talking?" he asked, and she opened her mouth to respond but then, he assumed, thought better of it. "Right," he continued. "I just wanted to set some parameters before we go inside. Is that all right?"

She nodded and leaned against the door, backing it open into her flat.

"I'm not some prick who's going to just walk in there for a one-off shag and be on my way. I don't know exactly how the next five or so months are supposed to go, but I—I'm—quite fond of you, Holly. And maybe we are wrong for each other outside this next half a year, but that doesn't mean I can't do *some* things right before I go."

She nodded again.

"Dinner. Tonight. My turn to choose the place."

Her lips were pressed together, but she was grinning. She liked the idea.

"And after—theater. I'll speak to the concierge at my hotel."

She bit her bottom lip. "Okay, but Will?"

"Yeah?"

She wiped away the smile for an exaggerated somber

look.

"I'm sorry, Mr. Evans. Permission to speak, sir?"

He rolled his eyes.

"Look, this is all really sweet, and gentlemanly, and very chivalrous and all, and I'm very much looking forward to a proper date with you this evening. But I have to tell you one thing."

He licked his lips, suddenly parched.

"Yes?"

Holly sighed. "I'm a sure thing. Right here. Right now. I know you don't want me to think you came here *just* to shag me, but good Lord, please tell me that you *are* going to shag me, because I so want to shag you."

His resistance crumbled, and he couldn't help himself. He laughed.

Holly exhaled and grabbed him by the arm, pulling him the rest of the way into her place so she could shut the door. He half expected her to push him up against a wall and start kissing him again, taking the speed train to Shagville. But instead she just stared at him, arms crossed.

"You can be moody," she said. "And rude."

"I'm sorry, what?" Will interrupted, but she put a finger to his lips.

"And also funny, intelligent, and ridiculously handsome in both a three-piece suit and a T-shirt and jeans."

Okay, then. At least he wasn't simply moody and rude.

"And I'm quite fond of you, too, Will Evans. But we are on a ticking clock here."

Holly removed the small bag that was slung across her midsection and took a step back from him, placing it on a table against the wall.

"And I don't want to waste any part of our six months that could be used for activities other than quibbling over who is fond of whom or whether or not your intention was to shag me."

She took another step back and pulled her tank top over her head so she stood before him in just her jeans and a bra.

If Will's resistance had already crumbled, now it was blown to dust. If she took off her bra, he'd be powerless against her. Who was he kidding? He'd been in trouble since day one. Only now was he able to admit it.

"Because intent doesn't matter as long as right now, in this moment, we both want the same thing."

Holly leaned against the back of her sofa now, her fingers resting on the front clasp of her bra. And just like that, she flicked it open, and just as quickly let the straps drop to her elbows before she shook it to the floor. Her hair spilled over her shoulders, and Will's gaze traveled to where the locks rested against her milky-white skin, then lower to where the flesh pinked around the hard peaks at the tips of her breasts.

She blew the fringe out of her eyes, losing her footing for a second. Will stifled a laugh as she righted herself, taking comfort in the fact that maybe Holly wasn't seasoned in the art of seduction, that perhaps this was all for him. Plus, she was adorably sexy when she was just being herself.

He strode toward her, careful and deliberate, stopping when the tips of his shoes met hers, and he grinned at her small feet covered by Nike trainers. She'd worn practical shoes in case they'd gone walking, he supposed, and damn if that wasn't adorable, too.

"May I...?" he asked, his voice hoarse and expectant as he raised a palm toward one of her breasts.

She half smiled while biting her lip, then nodded, and Will brought his hand to her skin. As he made contact, they each drew in a sharp breath.

"God, Holly..."

"Say it again," she whispered, her hands clasping around his neck.

"God, Holly?" he asked, teasing, because he knew what she meant, but he wanted her to say it one more time.

She shook her head, grinning, and gently tugged his head toward hers.

"I want you to ask permission in that sexy accent of yours."

He brought his lips to hers, not yet in a kiss, but close enough to feel her breath on his skin. One hand was still on her breast, and the other had found its way to her back. Will was barely hanging on, but he wanted to do this right, put someone else's needs first, give her what she wanted.

So he asked, "May I do this?"

He kissed her, featherlight, and she spoke softly against him.

"Yes."

His lips moved to her jaw and her neck, and all the while he spoke sweetly against her.

"And this? May I kiss you here?"

He felt her swallow as he peppered her skin with tiny kisses, and again he heard her voice, faint yet insistent.

"Yes."

Her breast was still cupped in his hand, and he lightly pinched the hard peak while asking, "What about this, Holly? May I do this?"

She gasped and rocked her hips against him, and he took that as a yes. God, it had been so long since he'd been with anyone like this, and the way she responded to him was enough to drive him mad. He knew this was dangerous ground, that he wasn't just attracted to Holly physically. He should be logical here, weigh the pros and cons, but her hands had left his neck and found the button of his jeans, and that was it. Will finally put his overactive brain to rest. It was all instinct from here, because Holly Chandler responded to his impulses, and he to hers.

"May *I* have the pleasure, Mr. Evans?" She undid the button. "Or can I call you Billy now?"

Will scooped her into his arms and dropped her over the side of the sofa so she now lay on her back. Holly yelped with laughter as he stepped around to meet her, sitting on the edge of a cushion.

"No to Billy," he said. Then, "You first," returning the favor, unbuttoning and unzipping her jeans. "If I *may*."

Holly responded by nodding and kicking off her trainers, so he slid the snug denim down over her legs, fingers skimming the flesh of her inner thigh as he did, and watched her stomach contract with each breath.

And then she was there, in nothing but a pair of red lace knickers—damn Holly with the red shoes this morning and now this. *She* wasn't the sure thing. *He* was, and she bloody well knew it.

He slid his palms up her thighs, slow and controlled, even though he was coming undone with each inch of her skin she let him touch. He reached the place where thigh met hip, where his thumbs could sneak underneath the bottom hem of those drive-him-insane knickers, and he asked a final question.

"I want to touch you everywhere, Holly. I want my hands all over your beautiful skin." He watched her hands fist the material of the sofa cushion, and he knew what her answer was. But damn if he didn't love how she loved those words.

"May I?"

He tugged at the material that would bare her to him completely, and she squirmed.

"Yes."

Something in his gut lurched at the sweet insistence in her voice.

Will shook his head and, with it, shook away the last of his logical thought. He would not let the past keep him from enjoying this moment, and he would not think ahead to what it would be like to have a woman like Holly and then give her up. So he closed his eyes for a moment, did a mental regroup, slid Holly Chandler's knickers to her ankles, and then dropped them to the floor.

"Blimey," he said under his breath, and Holly relaxed, placing her hands behind her head.

"Like what you see?" she asked, and he grinned at the echo of her first words to him in the lift. So much about today—seeing each other in the lift for the first time since Friday, the red shoes, her words—it all mirrored their first meeting two weeks ago, yet with a twist. It was a redo of sorts, if they'd met under different circumstances and entertained possibilities such as this.

"Very much," he answered. He liked everything about the way he saw things between them today, right here, in this moment. Will leaned down to kiss her stomach, then raised his head again, eyeing a line of three birthmarks on her hip. He traced his finger across the tiny dots.

"Orion," he said. "You've got Orion's belt, haven't you?"

Holly's eyes were closed as she spoke. "Uh-huh. It's how I first learned about the stars." Her voice was dreamy and far away. "When I was little and asked my mom why I had three spots where my sister had none, she told me it was my very own constellation. And when she showed me Orion's belt in the sky, and so many other constellations over my head that told all these stories, I wanted to be a part of something like that."

"You wanted to be a star," he said quietly, remembering what she'd told him, and she nodded.

"It's silly," she said, opening her eyes to meet his. "Less talking? I've given you permission for just about everything. I just have one more request."

Will recognized a subject change when he heard one, so

he let the star thing go. He wouldn't tell her that he could already tell she burned brighter than anything in the sky. That would be too much for where they were headed. So he grinned and gave her his full attention.

"What is your request?"

"Lose the shirt."

He did as she asked and watched her take him in. It had been so long since he'd bared himself to someone like this, and he wondered how deep her eyes could see. Because it felt as though she saw through every barrier he could construct. But that wasn't possible, was it? They were still practically strangers. So he let it go, choosing to stay in the moment. He could worry about the rest later.

"Like what you see?" he teased, and she nodded. He nudged her over on the sofa so he could lie next to her, head propped on his hand, allowing him to watch her every reaction. Then Will took advantage of Holly's full permission, sliding his hand between her legs and dipping a finger into her warmth. Her muscles clenched around him. He was so hard, aching for release, but he could exercise restraint. He wanted to watch her, pleasure her, let that sweet and agonizing ache build.

Holly reached for his face, pulled him to her, and kissed him hard as he exited her in a long, slow stroke up her center, swirling his finger over her swollenness. Just as slowly he slid back down, adding a second finger this time, and she writhed against his hand, bucking into his palm.

He thrust his tongue into her mouth, and she rode him harder, her legs falling open as far as they could with him lying next to her.

His fingers pulsed inside her, and hell if he wasn't about to come right with her just from watching her reactions.

"God, Will, I don't think—oh my God…"

She couldn't articulate the thought. He knew she was

close, but he didn't want her to finish just yet.

He kissed her again, then slid off the sofa and to his knees as Holly squirmed. He sprinkled kisses down her shoulder, her breast, her torso, and then her hip. He gave his fingers a slow pump, and she gasped. Still inside her, he lifted his palm to give himself room, then flicked his tongue against her clit, and Holly cried out.

Will worked her, inside and out, savoring the sweet tang of her in his mouth. He slid his fingers out and spread her legs wide, giving her one long, slow lick up the center, and she went mad.

"Inside me, Will." She grabbed his hair. "God, please, get inside me. I don't want to do this alone."

He was ready to protest, tell her that today, for their first time, it was only about her. But that word, *alone*, it rocked him to his core. How well did he know that word? How much did he hate it, the loneliness of travel, of going home to an empty flat, of nothing more than weekend visits with his daughter?

If Holly knew half the heartache of such solitude, he wouldn't be the one to perpetuate it.

"I don't have a—"

"In my purse," she said between breaths. "There are condoms in my purse."

He wasted no time retrieving the foil packet, dropping his jeans and boxers to the floor, and rolling it down his length.

"You're beautiful," she said as he stood before her, and he didn't want her to say any more. No words to deepen the connection he already felt for this woman. Just their bodies.

Together.

Will lowered himself to the sofa, his knees at her hips. He didn't need to say *May I?* again, and Holly didn't have to say *please*. He nudged her open, and she welcomed him as he sank deep—all the way—and rocked inside her.

"The thing is," she said, her voice soft and her breath

warm against his skin. "I don't need a proper dinner or a trip to the theater." She pulled him closer, deeper, and whispered, "If it's all the same to you, we could just order in and not worry about putting our clothes back on so soon."

He'd wanted to do this right, whatever *this* was. And if that meant being with her like this for a while longer, he wasn't going to protest.

He closed his eyes and kissed her as the tension coiled in his gut. In another time, another place, if the circumstances were different, Will Evans would fall for a woman like this. Instead, as their bodies found a blissful rhythm, and as she came only seconds before him, he resigned himself to six months of happiness, six months of selfishness, six months of wanting something that was only for him.

And then, when the new year arrived, he'd say good-bye.

JULY

Chapter Thirteen

Gemini: Arguments abound today. Everyone has an opinion on Gemini's decisions. Take heed of useful advice, but hold strong and resolute to what you believe, even if you find opposition coming at you from every angle.

Holly dropped her phone next to her on the chair and pulled her hair into a ponytail. Even though the sun had set, sweat trickled down her neck.

"The air's on inside," Brynn said, poking her head out from Jamie's balcony door. *Her* balcony door. Holly still wasn't used to this being her sister's place.

"I'm looking at the stars," Holly told her.

Brynn crossed her arms. "There is no way you can see anything but smoke right now. That was one hell of a fireworks display. If there are any stars out tonight, they're going to be hidden for at least the next half hour."

"What's up, Holls?" This time it was their friend Annie at the door, her boyfriend Brett's arms wrapped around her waist as he stood behind her. She looked past them to where Jamie sat on a stool at his breakfast bar sipping a beer. Two plus two plus Holly.

"She's looking at the stars," Brynn told Annie.

"What stars?" Brett asked.

Holly growled and pulled the door shut. Maybe she wanted to imagine where the stars were. They'd be out to keep her company soon enough. She leaned back in her chair but barely had enough time to relax when she heard the door slide open again. She didn't bother looking, because she knew it was her sister.

Brynn dropped into the chair next to her, and for a few long moments she said nothing, just sipped the bottle of beer that bore their name, Chandler's Witbier.

"You know," Brynn said, "it's kind of funny if you think about it."

Holly kept her eyes trained on the hazy sky above, knowing her stars were out there.

"You're going to make me ask what, aren't you?"

She could see Brynn nod in her peripheral vision.

Holly sighed. "What?"

Brynn grabbed her sister's hand and squeezed.

"*You*, moping during the celebration of your country's independence because you're pining for someone back in Mother England." Brynn chuckled. "Like I said—funny."

Holly rolled her eyes and finally turned to face Brynn.

"So what if I am? This is the fun part, B. The honeymoon phase. The part I actually like…and I'm *missing* it."

She wasn't fooling herself, though. Or her sister. She was missing *him*.

Holly missed Will.

This wasn't unusual. The beginning of a relationship was always the best—the time of butterflies in the belly and sex all the time. With Will, the butterflies were most certainly there, amplified by his weekends away, this one being the second. Last week he had taken the red-eye home and hadn't even had enough time to go to the hotel before meeting Holly at the office with samples she needed from Ms. Chan. In order to hire the right models, Holly needed to see some of the show pieces in person to gauge the fit. Then she'd spent the week visiting various local agencies, recruiting her top choices and seeing how their fees would fit into the show's budget. She and Will had worked tirelessly all week, cramming in as much as they could before the long holiday weekend, and they'd only seen each other twice outside the office.

And now he was gone until Tuesday morning.

Stupid butterflies.

Stupid other happy couples surrounding her.

And stupid, stupid holiday weekend.

Cue toddler tantrum.

"You ever think that maybe it's different, the intensity of your emotions?" Brynn asked. "Knowing not only that it's going to end but that *poof*, he'll be gone?"

Holly's stomach tightened.

"It might have occurred to me," she said. "It just heightens the excitement, you know? Ticking clock—got to get it all in before the buzzer rings."

Brynn shook her head.

"No, honey. I guess—I don't know. What I meant was, do you think the whole situation might be making you…" Brynn hesitated.

"Just say it," Holly said.

Brynn blew out a breath and squeezed her eyes shut. "Okay. I think the ticking clock scenario is heightening your emotions—making you feel things quicker and possibly deeper, and I don't know. It's early. Like, you've only known him a month, but I think maybe you could fall for this guy, and I don't want to see you get hurt by your own devices."

Brynn peeked at her out of one eye, keeping the other one closed. When Holly didn't jump down her throat, which was what she assumed her sister was waiting for, Brynn opened the other eye.

Holly pulled her hand free and cupped her sister's cheeks. "Are you done?"

Brynn nodded.

"I am not falling faster or harder," she said. "I'm not *falling*, period. You know me, B. I'm defective that way, remember? You always think the next guy I date is going to be *the* guy, and he never is. You even had your fingers crossed for Charlie! Smarmy Charlie!"

Brynn shrugged. "I want you to be happy," she said.

Holly looked past her sister and into the apartment. "I'm fine. It's just fifth-wheel syndrome."

"Fine isn't happy."

She kissed her big sister on the cheek and stood up.

"In five months Andrea is going to make me partner, and I will have everything I've ever wanted before I'm twenty-eight," she told her. "I'm happy. And tired. I'm gonna head out."

Brynn opened her mouth to say something, but Holly cut her off with an exaggerated grin.

"See?" she said, slipping through the sliding glass door. "Happy."

"You don't need to leave," Brynn said, following her into the apartment.

"Don't go," Annie added, but Holly already had her shoes on and her purse slung across her body.

"Everyone enjoy the day off tomorrow," she said, blowing a kiss with her plastered-on smile. "As always, thanks for the brew, James."

He offered her a salute, and Holly silently thanked him for not joining the chorus that asked her to stay. Maybe this was what her horoscope had meant. The sky was against her. Her sister was against her. And even Annie tried to make her stay and keep her from doing what she wanted, which was to go home, take a hot bath, and eat a pint or two of ice cream with a rom-com cued up on the DVR.

She stepped out onto the street and gave herself a mental pat on the back for holding firm to her beliefs, even if said beliefs were to try to get friendly with her showerhead again followed by eating her feelings. Scratch that. These were not feelings. It was just the euphoria of the honeymoon phase coupled with the longing that absence created. Nothing self-pleasure and ice cream couldn't cure.

At home, Holly peeled off her clothes as she made her way to her bedroom, her skin sticky with the humidity. Once the air-conditioning hit her, though, goose bumps dotted her flesh, and she craved the cleansing heat of the bath. She threw on her robe and started the water running, poured in a generous helping of her eucalyptus-spearmint bubble bath, then took a detour to the kitchen for a couple spoonfuls of pure, ice-cold chocolate.

There was a soft knock at her door as she cleaned off the spoon for a second time, and Holly rolled her eyes.

"I told you to keep your key," she called, throwing the door open to assure Brynn once again that she was, in fact, fine.

"I didn't know we were exchanging keys already."

Will stared at her through tired-looking eyes. But they were beautiful and blue and here at her front door instead of an ocean and a bunch of time zones away. His weekend bag sat at his feet, and Holly realized he must have come straight from the airport.

"You're here," she said, trying to contain her complete and utter elation.

"And you're holding a spoon," he said. "If we're stating

the obvious."

She let out a nervous laugh.

"Ice cream." Then she noticed what was different from when she'd seen him Friday. "You shaved. I'm still getting used to you looking like a new person at the beginning of every week."

Will scrubbed a hand across his jaw and grinned.

"And the robe?" he asked.

"Oh, shit!" Holly ran, leaving him standing in the opened door, and made it to the bathroom just in time to turn off the tub before the bubbles overflowed onto the tile. She gave herself a once-over in the mirror and groaned. Her face was flushed. And her hair, up in a messy bun now, showed off the tendrils still damp with sweat from her walk home. Still, she couldn't stop smiling because Will at her door was so much better than what she originally had planned.

Crap. Will was still standing at the door. She scurried back through the kitchen toward her entryway, noticed the spoon still gripped tightly in her hand, and backtracked to the sink to throw it in. When she finally stood in front of him again, she found it difficult to calm her nerves, hands fidgeting with the belt on her robe.

"Is everything all right?" he asked, and she nodded. "May I come in?" he added.

"Ohmygodyes," she said, all in one word. "Shit! Yes. Come in."

She backed up as he grabbed his bag and stepped through the door, closing it behind him.

"Do you always shout so much profanity when you're about to have a bath?"

He smiled, and her shoulders relaxed.

"You caught me off guard," she admitted.

Will ran a hand through his hair, which was charmingly disheveled, and Holly imagined him sleeping on the plane.

"I apologize. I should have called, but it's the holiday, and I wasn't even sure I could change my flight, but I forgot that England doesn't exactly shut down for July the Fourth, and Tara has Sophie in this art class on Mondays, and—"

"Will," Holly interrupted, and he ended his seemingly nervous rant, which only made him more charming.

"Yes?"

She took his bag from his hand and dropped it on the floor.

"You are going to kiss me, right?"

He let out a long breath and nodded.

"God, yes," he said, and in seconds his palms cupped her cheeks and his lips found hers with a sweet, gentle yearning she could practically taste.

Holly wrapped her arms around his waist.

"I missed…this," she said as she moved backward, leading him toward the bathroom. She wouldn't say what she was thinking, that it was the man himself she missed, because she knew that part would pass. For now all she knew was that what she had told Brynn wasn't a lie. Holly *was* happy, right here, in this moment.

"I missed *this*, too," Will said, kissing her again as they reached her bathroom door.

She stepped back and untied her robe, and his eyes seemed to darken at the sight of her.

"Join me?" she asked, and Will responded by parting her robe so his hands rested on her bare hips. One slid up her left side until his hand found her breast while the other dropped behind her, cupping her ass.

"You're bloody gorgeous."

"I'm a bloody mess," Holly told him, and she breathed in sharply as he rubbed his thumb over her pebbled nipple.

"Gorgeous," he said again, the word insistent, and he kissed her hard, his need seeming to multiply as it mingled with hers. "And you taste like chocolate."

"Is that good?" she asked, her words coming out in pants.

Will tugged the robe from her shoulders, and she stood bared to him now.

"It's a dangerous combination, actually." He dipped his head, swirled his tongue over the nipple he'd already begun teasing, and Holly's knees buckled. "I might devour you, body and soul," he added.

Holly pushed his head from her before she collapsed and knocked her head on the tub. Then she stepped over the short wall and into the steaming water, lowering herself under the foam of the bubbles.

Will chuckled. "That's quite cruel, taking away my view."

Holly shrugged as she submerged herself up to her neck.

"Maybe I want a little show first," she said. "Take off your shirt."

Will leaned against the counter and crossed his arms.

"Say please," he said, grinning, and she had to restrain herself from climbing right

back out and tearing his clothes from his body.

Play it cool, Chandler. Don't show your hand too early.

"*Please* take off your shirt."

He pulled the black T-shirt over his head. The one thing Holly liked even more than Will Evans in a T-shirt and jeans was Will Evans in no shirt at all.

"Lose the jeans, too," she told him, then added, "*please.*"

Will kicked off his shoes and socks, obliging without protest, and Holly squirmed beneath the bubbles as heat pooled in her core. There he stood, his long, lean, beautiful body a sight she hadn't expected to see for at least another day. He must do something to stay so toned, but Holly realized she had no idea what it was Will Evans did when he wasn't at Trousseau or in her bed. Speaking of which, those boxers did nothing to hide his erection, and she swallowed at the thought of her hand gliding over his rigid length.

"Are you a runner?" she asked, and he shook his head. "Weight lifter?" His shoulders and upper arms were cut but not thick, so she expected the head shake again.

Will lowered his boxers, and Holly's eyes widened when her memory of what lay beneath was confirmed. He stepped into the tub, lowering himself to face her, but she turned him around, pulling his back to her torso, his head resting on her shoulder.

He let out a long breath, and Holly realized how exhausted he must be after a day's worth of travel and the fact that for his body's clock, it was now the middle of the night.

"Rowing," he said softly. "I rowed at university. Still do whenever I get the chance."

She kissed his shoulder. That explained the rough palms, the ones she thought about now, touching all parts of her wet body.

"I think I need to tell you that I find that ridiculously sexy."

Will smiled as his eyes closed.

"The bubbles," he said dreamily. "They smell nice."

He relaxed against her, and Holly grabbed the washcloth she had folded over the ledge, soaking it and drizzling it over his shoulders and chest. She continued with this, and it turned into a slow pattern—kiss his shoulder or cheek, resoak the cloth, and let the water trickle over his skin. When his breathing slowed, she could tell he was falling asleep, so she convinced him to get out and dry off, leading him by the hand to her bed, where he collapsed on top of the covers wearing nothing but a towel slung over his hips.

Holly tucked him in, sliding the towel free and pulling the sheet up over his waist. Then she sneaked into the kitchen for a couple more spoonfuls of ice cream before collecting Will's clothes from the bathroom. She glanced at her showerhead, so sure she needed some sort of physical intimacy tonight, but something in her had shifted, and she wasn't sure what it was.

On the way back to her room, she turned off all the lights and double locked her front door, a sense of safety ebbing through her. Standing over Will in her bed, she watched him for several long moments, the rhythm of his breaths calming the frenetic energy that was there less than an hour ago when she found him at her door.

She climbed in next to him, her forehead against his, both of them naked under the sheet. And though she wanted him—always wanted him, it seemed—for tonight this would be enough. She'd slept with Will three times already, but he never stayed the night, always claiming he had calls to make or emails to send to his English business associates, the time change necessitating the late-night work.

She brushed his damp hair off his forehead and kissed it, breathing in the soothing scent of the eucalyptus and spearmint mixed with what could only be described as essentially Will.

"Do you ever sleep?" she whispered, only now starting to grasp the toll the frequent intercontinental travel must be taking on him. Will said nothing, and she kissed him softly on the mouth. "Looks like tonight you will."

Both their heads rested on one pillow, and she closed her eyes, heart thumping in her chest, and let the cadence of his breaths lull her to sleep.

When she woke the next morning, Will was gone, a note lying where his head once was.

Ran back to the hotel to shower and make a few calls. But I'd love to take you to breakfast. I'll be by in a taxi at ten.

Holly let out a breath. She didn't know what they'd say to each other this morning after what happened—and didn't happen—last night, but one thing was for sure. She hadn't expected Will to be gone or for her to feel what she felt right now once she realized he was.

Relief.

Whatever happened last night, Will was avoiding it, too. They wouldn't have to talk about feelings and where this was going and whether or not she'd miss him when he was gone. If they didn't discuss all that—*stuff*—then it wouldn't become real.

Maybe they weren't as opposite as she thought.

AUGUST

Chapter Fourteen

Will was sure Holly had been awake when he'd left this morning, but she never let on, just played her part in this dance they did, never sure who was leading.

He tilted his head back and let the shower spray pelt him in the face. This had become the routine. Ever since he'd pulled that bastard move, showing up at Holly's on the Fourth and falling asleep in her bed, this was how the morning after went: slip out of bed before she woke, head back to the hotel to shower, show up to Trousseau separately, and go about their days as if they hadn't slept naked and tangled together the night before. Holly never asked him to laze away the morning, and he never considered it.

He couldn't explain why he could sleep through the night in Holly's bed but not in his own...or why he needed to come back here for a reboot before getting on with his day instead of waking with a beautiful woman in his arms and seeing where those early bits of sunlight took them. Without discussion, they'd fallen into a routine of what worked for them—for their *arrangement*.

Will stepped out onto the cool ceramic tile of the hotel's bathroom floor. He couldn't see his unshaven self in the fogged mirror and was happy, for the moment, not to have any reminders of home, which was where he'd be heading this evening.

A buzz sounded from his phone on the counter, and he had to wipe the condensation off his screen before seeing whom the text was from. *Hot out today. Pick you up six shots on ice for the fittings this morning?*

Will smiled at how well Holly knew what he liked, and it was immediate for him to respond with *Ta. I'd like that.*

But his finger hovered above the word "send." This wasn't part of the routine. It had been a month since he came back on the Fourth, and in all of those weeks, they'd avoided this kind of familiarity. Shite, it was just a text, but the fact he was overanalyzing an offer for a coffee was enough to tell him that continued avoidance was the safer route.

He erased the response and typed a new one instead. *Already had a coffee at the hotel. Ta. See you at nine.*

The first part was a lie, but Will hit send anyway.

. . .

Andrea was heading past the elevator when Will arrived, so she showed him straight back to the fitting room.

"Holly's the best I've got, you know," she said as they weaved through the cubicles on the side of the office opposite his.

Will nodded. He had no reason to argue that.

"She's young and focused, a few years younger than I was when I started Trousseau, and I know she's going to make a great partner *if* she doesn't lose that focus."

They stood outside the fitting room now, but Andrea wasn't opening the door. Will realized she wasn't making idle chitchat. She was warning him.

"Is there something you'd like to say to me, Andrea?"

She crossed her arms and narrowed her gaze at him.

"Yes, Mr. Evans. There's *much* I want to say, but for now I'll be brief. I know what it's like to have to prove yourself. I had to prove I was more than someone who'd walked off a runway and into an office. And I've been making Holly prove herself since day one because I know she's a natural, but I need my clients to believe it, too. I want to expand Trousseau's business overseas, and I need potential clients to trust me *and* my staff. That's why I haven't handed her the partnership yet, and that's why her first international venture has to go off without a hitch. Without distraction. Without *you* playing any part in ruining what could be a career-making event for her." She let out a long breath but never broke her stare. "I want it to be clear that Ms. Chan is a very valued client, but if there is a conflict of interest between any of the parties involved, I hope you'll remember what this job means to Holly." Andrea nodded toward the closed door. "Am I clear?"

Will kept his tone even but felt remnants of a younger, more reckless self itching to break free and put Andrea in her place for assuming he was a threat. This job wasn't important to just Holly. His future rode on it as well. It had taken him six weeks to relax into the idea of what he and Holly were doing, to be okay with having something to look forward to each day instead of just sleepwalking his way through to the Fridays he flew back to London. Hell, he was just starting to think he might even deserve the time he spent with Holly.

He let all of this swirl in his mind, a tornado of outrage and indignation, until he remembered one very important detail. "I do appreciate your concern, Ms. Ross, but would like to remind you that Trousseau is under the employ of my client, and I assure you there have been no complaints from her thus far. She thinks Holly's ideas are brilliant—as do I. We all have the same goal here."

"I hope you do," she said.

He opened the door, prepared to leave it at that, but Andrea put a hand on his forearm.

"Be careful, Will." Her voice was gentle but still held that air of warning. "Your client may employ my company, but I still run it. If whatever is going on between you and Holly—and don't think for a second I don't see the way you look at her when you think no one is looking—compromises this show in any way, I'll pull her off it. I want Holly to succeed, but Trousseau comes first."

His jaw clenched.

"Are we done, then?" he asked, and Andrea offered him one slow nod.

"I do believe we are," she said, brows raised, and then she walked away.

Will Evans had just been dismissed.

He pushed through the door to the fitting room and found Holly in a floral halter dress surrounded by half-naked models while a couple of Trousseau's seamstresses measured, cut, pinned, and draped Tallulah Chan's pieces over the women who would wear next year's spring line on the runway.

Holly beamed as she buzzed about the room, snapping photos for her plan book, and for a few moments he let himself get caught up in the frenzy…and in the pull of her orbit.

She made her way back to his side of the room and stopped in front of him, her radiant grin fading as her brows pulled together.

"What?"

She glanced at his right hand, the one that held a to-go cup from the fifth-floor café.

Oh. Right.

"I thought you'd already had a coffee at the hotel."

Holly parroted his accent, something he usually found charming and even a little sexy—especially when she was straddling him naked. But this was different. She was...hurt. And he'd done that. He'd hurt her.

Will ran down the morning's tally. He'd sneaked out on Holly after another amazing and surprisingly restful night. He'd lied to her, gotten skewered by Andrea, and then been caught in his lie.

And it was only nine o'clock. Brilliant.

Holly blinked, and her grin returned.

"Not my business," she said. "You're entitled to all the caffeine you need."

But he knew Holly's smiles now, and this one wasn't real. Her disappointment, that was genuine, but she was trying to hide that now.

She flitted off to the next model to take photos of Tallulah's freshly tailored piece.

It had all seemed so simple when he'd agreed to her proposal. Regardless of how much he knew he could fall for her, he also knew he shouldn't. It was impractical in every way.

The white lie shouldn't have mattered as much as it did. It was the emotional reaction from Holly that he wasn't expecting, and from the looks of it, neither was she. A deep ache settled in his chest. Because, shite, he cared that it mattered, and he had no idea what to do with that.

Whatever game they were playing, the rules had just changed.

· · ·

Will double-checked his calendar app to make sure he'd made all his phone calls and crossed any necessary appointments off his list. He knew he hadn't missed anything, but his conversation with Andrea had eaten away at him the entire day.

He pulled his weekend bag out from next to the sofa and tossed it onto the conference table. So it had come to this—everything necessary in his life fitting into a bag that could be stowed in an airplane's overhead bin.

He dropped down onto the soft cushion, closed his eyes, and tilted his head back. After a few moments of quiet, he'd regroup and head to the airport a bit early, have a drink in the airline's VIP lounge.

"Knock, knock."

His office door was open, so Holly spoke the words as she hovered in the frame of the entryway.

"Since when do you knock?" he asked, attempting a teasing smile, but it didn't feel natural today.

Holly entered the room and pulled the door shut behind her. Will sat up straight and watched as she locked it, as she'd done several times before, then sauntered over to him.

"Holly, wait." But she was already on his lap, knees hooked over his as the skirt of her dress pooled over them. She draped her arms around his neck and kissed him—soft and sweet, but something else lay beneath the surface. He kissed her back, realizing that despite Andrea's words, he needed this—reassurance from Holly that what they were doing was still okay.

He pulled her hands gently from his neck and laid them against his chest.

"Uh-oh," she said. "It's serious, humorless Will. I thought he was on holiday. When's fun Billy coming back?"

She said *holiday* with her improving English accent, and Will couldn't help but smile.

He sighed. "Holly, Andrea knows. About us."

She shrugged. "Andrea's not here. You know she leaves early on Fridays."

He did know this. It was the only reason he hadn't rushed

to throw his door back open when Holly entered. They were always careful not to let what they were doing as a couple make a mockery of what they were doing as business associates, but apparently they hadn't been careful enough.

He tucked her fringe behind her ear, finding it hard to breathe as she leaned into his palm.

"Holly," he said, his voice firm this time, and she dropped her hands from his chest.

"Okay. You're freaking me out a little. Is this about the coffee earlier? Because it's totally cool. I get that you—that *we*—need our space in the morning, and maybe I overreacted a teensy bit."

"No, it's not that. Really," he said. "But she said—" He paused. If he continued that sentence—*But she said if she thinks you're becoming distracted, she'll take you off this show*—Holly would choose the show one hundred times over. And while he didn't want to jeopardize her career, he also wasn't ready to say good-bye to whatever they had started. Maybe it would end before their six months were up, but he needed time to gear up to that, not let it happen spontaneously. Because one thing was for sure. This would end. It had to. Outside the show he and Holly were planning together, their lives ran in two parallel lines. These six months were their only intersection.

So he let self-preservation kick in, believing he could protect her from losing this job while still getting what he wanted, what he knew she wanted, too.

"She said she doesn't want me to distract you," he told Holly, assuaging his guilt by at least offering half the truth. "*I* don't want to distract you. This job is important to you, and I don't want to be responsible for anything getting in the way of that."

Holly rolled her eyes.

"Do you know anyone more focused on her career than

me?" she asked, and he shook his head. "I've never once let *this...*" She kissed the line of his jaw, and he groaned. This only propelled her to do more, traveling toward his ear and then down the length of his neck, all the while brushing her lips across the short, soon-to-be shaved beard. "...distract me," she added as her lips navigated their way to the other side of his face.

She was right. Holly never ceased to dazzle him with how good she was at what she did. She could wow investors with proposals, come up with a brilliant theme to tie the show into the hotel's New Year's Eve festivities, and direct the tailors and seamstresses into making Tallulah Chan's pieces look exquisite on the models they'd hired for the show, never once faltering in her confidence that she could do any of it.

"No," he said, his voice hoarse. "You haven't. But if that starts to happen before our six months are up, then we stop. All right?"

She straightened and met his gaze, her eyes now devoid of the playfulness that sparkled in them moments ago.

"All right," she told him. No argument. Instead she turned to face him, her legs straddling him under her dress. "I just stopped in to give you a proper good-bye before you leave for London," she added, a small smile lighting up her features, one she had to know he was powerless against.

Will kissed her with abandon and ignored that word, "good-bye." He pushed up her skirt and slid his fingers beneath her knickers, his thumb pressing against her clit. Neither spoke another word as she unbuttoned the jeans he'd already changed into for his trip and helped him wriggle free, taking his boxers with them. She pulled a condom from a pocket hidden in the full skirt of her dress, tore it open, and slid it down his length. Then she guided his hands as they removed the knickers.

Dress still on, the floral pattern covering them like a

blanket, she lowered herself onto him, burying his erection to the hilt. Will breathed in sharply, a small growl vibrating over his vocal cords, and Holly let a soft moan slip from her parted lips. They'd made love in the office before, knew the unspoken rule to keep things—well—unspoken. But something about today felt different to him. Even though the show was four-plus months away, this afternoon was the first they'd spoken of what their future held, which was nothing beyond the new year.

Holly rose on her knees and descended upon him again and again in slow, measured movements, enough that Will pushed any thoughts of the future back to where they couldn't interrupt the present. Because, good God, what this woman did to him.

He untied the halter from behind her neck, and as she writhed on top of him, the bodice of her dress fell. He laid his hands back on her hips, moving with her and simply admiring the view.

"You're breathtaking," he said in a rough whisper, and her heavy eyes opened to catch him staring, but she didn't stop moving.

"And you're going to get us in trouble," she teased quietly, "if you don't shut that mouth of yours."

Will grinned.

"I'm quite aware of the volume of my voice, and I assure you it is well within the safe range, Ms. Chandler," he said. "Besides, I'd be a daft bloke to risk not receiving a proper good-bye again."

And before she could chastise him again, he sneaked a hand underneath her skirt and pressed his thumb back into her center. Holly bucked against him, back arching, and then gasped much louder than any of his whispering.

"Careful," he warned. "*You're* going to get us in trouble."

But it *was* Friday afternoon, and the two of them knew

that no one was within earshot other than Jackie at the front desk. But Will took a bet on the constantly ringing phones and decided that Jackie was no threat to his need to finish Holly with a flourish.

He swirled his thumb between them, and Holly's knees gripped his thighs.

She braced her hands against his shoulders and held still as he rotated his hips and did his best to drive this woman half as mad as she'd already driven him. He fought against the building pressure between his legs, rubbing his thumb against her until she cried out so loud she had to straighten in order to clasp a palm over her mouth. Then it was game over as she gripped the sofa behind his shoulders and rode him hard and fast until he exploded inside her, silencing his own threat of giving them away by crushing his lips against hers.

The orgasm ebbed as Holly slowed to a stop. She kissed him one more time, straightened to tie her dress back around her neck, and then slid off him without another word. She picked up her knickers from the floor and shoved them in the pocket where the condom once was. Not until she was at the door did she turn to him one last time.

"Have a good trip, Billy. I'm putting in some extra hours at the office this weekend, so I look forward to a proper hello upon your return."

Will opened his mouth to respond, but he still couldn't articulate a coherent sound. So he watched her slip through the door, latching it once she was out, and he sat there half naked on the sofa trying to collect himself.

He chuckled. Holly was a single-minded woman when she needed to be, at work *and* at play. Andrea had nothing to worry about from her. It was Will who was beginning to forget why he despised Chicago in the first place. Never mind he still hadn't seen any of the sights.

SEPTEMBER

Chapter Fifteen

Gemini: You're great at seeing all angles of the story, which is Gemini's advantage. But that also makes you confused, especially when the other angles don't align with your own. Put yourself in other people's shoes for greater understanding.

Holly spun her phone around on the small outside table.

"Is your job laborious? Is that why you have the day off tomorrow?"

She grinned at the sound of Will's voice. She couldn't imagine getting tired of it, though she knew one day she would.

"Say that again," she commanded.

"Is your job—"

She waved her hand. "No, no. Not the whole sentence. Just that *L* word."

Will flipped the burgers on Holly's grill, then glanced over his shoulder at her.

"Laborious."

Damn she loved that accent, even more so when the word was polysyllabic. *Laborious* was now her most favorite word. Ooh, maybe she could get him to say *planetarium*. Or the way he said *aluminium*. There were so many polysyllabic words he could make infinitely more gorgeous with nothing more than that accent.

"Again," she insisted, and he dropped the tongs on the grill's small table and bent down to give her a kiss on the cheek.

"Laborious," he whispered.

His breath against her skin and the sound of her new favorite word sent waves of goose bumps up and down her spine.

"Now," he said, grabbing the veggie kabobs Holly had prepared this morning, "tell me more about your American holiday that gives *us* a three-day weekend."

Holly didn't ignore that emphasis on *us*. Will had been moody all week when he realized one of the weekends he was staying in the States was a holiday weekend, one where he could have had extra time with Sophie. But Sophie's mom had already planned a trip to the country to see Sophie's grandmother, a trip where Will was obviously not invited along. Plus, on Tuesday afternoon, Tallulah Chan was going to join them via Skype for a meeting with the set designer, which meant it was best for him to stay here anyway in case any last-minute details had to be ironed out before they met. So here he was on her balcony on a Sunday afternoon. An Englishman preparing a Labor Day barbecue for a party of eight.

Holly stood and wrapped her arms around his middle, careful not to bump into the grill. She pressed a kiss to the back of his neck and felt him let out a soft sigh.

"I know you'd rather be home this weekend. So thank you for doing this."

He backed her away from the cooking food and turned quickly enough to surprise her with his kiss.

"It's not a matter of where I'd rather be."

He held her tight, kissing her again, and despite the lingering heat of late summer, she melted into his warmth, not caring if he felt the beads of sweat at the nape of her neck.

"I've messed up these past six years," he added. "I've been everywhere except where I should have been—with my daughter. I made her a promise that after Chicago I wouldn't be going anywhere, not for a long time." He rested his chin on her head, and she sank into his chest. "It's not that I *don't* want to be here with you. Because I do. It's just that I'm *meant* to be there."

That made sense. She couldn't question that. But she also couldn't ignore that annoying, niggling part of her brain that thought, *Wouldn't you love it if he said he'd rather be with you?* She shuddered and stepped back.

"I'm going to go make sure the table's all set. I think I forgot salad forks."

Holly ducked back into her apartment before he could remind her that they weren't eating salad tonight. She just needed a minute to think and to remind herself that Will would always prefer his daughter over her—over *any* woman—as he should. Holly wasn't in a competition. She already knew she'd lost, which was why she'd proposed their arrangement in the first place. It was the perfect setup. She just wasn't out of the phase where she couldn't get enough of him.

Soon, she thought. *Soon he'll be gone, and you'll be yourself again, just like you always are.*

She uncorked the bottle of pinot noir Will had brought and poured herself a glass. The beer crew would be there soon enough, but she needed a little something to relax her now. She cleared her throat, ignoring the dry scratchiness she felt as she did, and took a long sip of the burgundy liquid. The warmth soothed her from her lips to her belly, and she leaned her elbows on the counter, letting her head fall forward in a moment of quiet.

Well, it was a short moment before her phone and Will's, both next to each other on the counter, buzzed at the same time. Not a good sign.

Holly unlocked her screen to read the text. It was from Andrea. *Break-in in our building this afternoon. Everything's all right. Insurance will cover what's missing, but I need you to come by as soon as possible to examine your work area and fill out a report. It looks like it's mostly electronics, but I can't be sure until everyone has come in.*

Holly froze, her body rigid as she squeezed her eyes shut and tried to remember. Had she brought her tablet home or left it at work for their Tuesday meeting? Because if it was at Trousseau—and now wasn't—*shit.*

Will stepped in from the balcony carrying a platter laden with burgers and vegetables, but his proud smile fell as soon as he looked at her.

"Holly, what's wrong? Are you okay?"

She could feel the color draining from her face, like all the blood was rushing out of her body. Her head pounded, and she wondered if she wasn't overreacting just a bit.

She slid his phone across the counter so he could read. He deposited the food on the table and read Andrea's text just as Brynn, Jamie, Annie, Brett, Jeremy, and a girl she hadn't met yet piled through her front door.

"Shite," Will said. "I take everything back with me to the hotel each night. Thank goodness for international relations, aye? Forces me to work odd hours from my room."

Holly's eyes welled. "I think my tablet's there, with the presentation for Tuesday's meeting."

"Happy almost Labor Day!" Brynn yelled as the group barreled into the kitchen and dining area. "We come prepared!" She set a mini keg on Holly's counter, but Brynn's brows drew together when her eyes finally met her sister's.

"Shit, honey. What happened?"

"A break-in at the office," Will said. "We need to head down to see what's missing and file a report."

His voice was so calm. How did he stay so calm?

Holly didn't form attachments to electronics. But she'd been so busy this week, preparing the presentation for the set designer, overseeing another round of fittings, and trying to coordinate with the W's New Year's Eve DJ, that she'd worked right up until the last minute on Friday, when she'd thrown the tablet in the drawer and rushed out to buy not only the food for this evening but something special to wear under her clothes for Will. She'd thrown her tablet in her drawer and not plugged it in, which meant it wasn't backed up. If it was gone, so was her presentation.

Brynn wrapped her arms around her sister and squeezed.

"You've got important stuff there, huh?" she asked.

Holly nodded, then pulled herself from her sister's embrace and dusted off her perfectly clean maxi skirt and took a deep breath. Holly Chandler could be calm, too. And positive. And—and this was *not* going to break her, because she was a professional, and professionals don't fall apart. They find a solution.

"It's fine," she said, forcing a smile. "Everything will be fine. I'll figure this out. You guys just start without us, and we'll be back soon!"

There was a little too much pep in her voice, but Holly wasn't exaggerating for her guests. It was for herself. She had to believe that all her hard work and planning for the past few months had not been so she could hit a roadblock now.

"Take your car, Holls," Brynn said.

"She's right," Jamie added while he tapped the keg and started filling glasses. "It's a ghost town out there. You'll wait forever for a cab."

"Right," Holly said. "The car. I'll take my car. Of course."

Brynn crossed her arms. "You did renew your license, right?"

Holly bit her lip.

"They let me do that sticker for the extension thingy because of my safe driving record."

Brynn groaned. "When did the sticker expire?"

"My last birthday?"

Brynn kissed Jamie on the cheek then grabbed her bag. "I'll drive you, honey."

A throat cleared.

"I have an American license. An Illinois one, I mean."

Everyone turned to look at Will.

"I don't have much in my office there, but I should still head down to check it out."

"Have you driven in the city before?" This question came from Jeremy.

Will shook his head. "Not exactly."

"But you've driven in the States before, right?" Annie asked.

Another head shake. "Technically, I don't need an international permit, but I applied for one anyway. I have a valid license in England, so that makes me eligible to drive here." His gaze narrowed on Holly. "Where are your keys?"

Holly pulled out the kitchen drawer that was a catchall for everything she didn't use but thought she'd need someday—like her car keys—and tossed them to him.

Brynn's eyes moved back and forth between the two of them.

"Are you sure it's safe? You know, other side of the street and car and all that?"

Will opened his mouth to say something, but Holly beat him to it.

"I trust you," she said, specifically to him, and he beamed. She wondered what this night would have been like, Will cooking for the people she loved most while they laughed and drank and whiled away the evening with nowhere they needed to be in the morning. She wondered if he'd stay once he woke. Not that any of that mattered, since Holly had a pretty good idea tonight would be spent working, doing her best to recreate a presentation that most likely didn't exist anymore. She'd have all of Monday as well.

Labor Day would be anything but a day off from work, but at least she had that cushion to prepare. That's what she told herself as they walked around the corner to her car, a compact hybrid that hadn't left its primo parking spot in months. Brynn made her start it every now and then just to make sure the thing still ran, but Holly saw the car as more of an in-case-of-emergency device, and tonight definitely qualified.

"Right," Will said, sidling up next to her at the passenger door. "This is where I get in, yes?"

Holly's eyes widened, and his face broke into a roguish grin.

"Joking, Holly. I'm joking." Then he opened the door and ushered her inside.

"You're lucky I like you," she told him as he settled into the driver's seat.

He put a hand on her cheek. "I *am*," he told her. "Are you all right?"

She nodded, then pressed her palm against the damp skin at her neck. "The heat's not helping."

Holly showed him how to start the car with the button rather than the key, and Will maneuvered out of the spot with expert precision. He gave her a look before continuing down the street.

"Still trust me?" he asked.

"I do," she answered. "Do you know where you're going?"

"Yes, Holly."

Will stepped gently on the gas and drove slowly to the intersection. He put on his left turn signal and began to accelerate when Holly grabbed his wrist.

"You can't turn here. It's one way for the next few blocks. Go up one more street, make a left. Go five blocks, and then double back over, and—"

"I've got it," he said, his jaw tight. So she tried to relax, crossing her fingers not only that they'd get there but get there in one piece. Jamie was right. The streets were empty, so the odds were in their favor. Still, when Will did make that left turn—into oncoming traffic—she couldn't help but slam on the invisible brake in the passenger seat.

He swerved into the correct lane, and she blew out a long breath.

"I've got it," he repeated, but she heard the slight falter in his voice. She bit her tongue, wanting to prove that she meant what she'd said. She trusted him. And after a few minutes, his grip on the steering wheel loosened. When he made the next left, he turned into the proper lane. And when he merged onto the expressway for the short ride to the office, his right hand let go of the wheel completely and reached for hers.

"See?" he said. "Give me the keys, trust me not to kill us, and Bob's your uncle. We're here."

He had already exited onto Trousseau's street, and she could see the building, two police cars parked out front.

"Bob's your uncle?" she asked.

"Means everything's going to be all right."

He squeezed her hand, and she squeezed back.

"Let's hope Uncle Bob is still waiting for us upstairs."

Will laughed quietly as he parked on a nearby side street.

"If he's not," he told her, "I am."

Chapter Sixteen

Will bypassed his own office, knowing there was nothing of import there if electronics were the target of the break-in. Instead he followed Holly to her desk. Andrea was there with police officers, going from cubicle to cubicle as employees arrived to assess the damage and fill out reports.

Holly's desktop computer was gone.

"It's okay," she said, her voice shaky. "I back up that one pretty regularly with cloud storage. I can probably find most of what I need." But she didn't need her desktop files right now.

The tablet was the issue. Holly had been so excited about this 3-D presentation application she was using to do a virtual set design. She'd shown a bit of it to him, and he'd been fascinated. She had an eye for the visual that he admired. He could set up appearances and interviews. He could wrangle high-profile sponsors. And he could stay in the loop on Holly's side of things to make sure her visual plan worked in harmony with Tallulah Chan's vision as well as *his* vision to put his client and her line of clothing in the best position when it came to the public eye. Though he couldn't do what Holly did. They were a good team, but she was a unique talent.

"It may have been well enough hidden," she said as she put her bag down on the chair. "I charge it in the drawer because I can feed the cord through the back. So maybe it's still there."

Will smiled and nodded, offering the best encouragement he could. Holly wrapped her fingers around the drawer handle, her hand unsteady. He laid his palm over hers. Out of the corner of his eye, he saw Andrea approaching from the other side of the room.

"Whatever happens when you open the drawer, Holly, stay calm. Okay? Can you do that for me?"

She turned to him, eyes wide in question.

"You know how stressed Andrea must be," he continued. "If the tablet's gone, don't let her know you've lost the presentation. We'll figure something out. Together. I won't let you go to that meeting unprepared. Just promise me."

His throat grew tight. He was digging himself in deeper by not telling her about Andrea's threat, but this wasn't the time. Holly had enough on her plate if she had to put together a brand-new presentation in less than two days' time. If she thought she'd lose not only the account but her chance at partnership? He didn't want to be the one to put that pressure on her. She put enough on herself as it was.

Andrea was steps away now. She'd be there when Holly opened the drawer, so he needed her to promise.

"Holly," he pleaded. "Did you hear me?"

She nodded. "Yeah, okay. Whatever. I promise."

Together they pulled the drawer open, Andrea there in time to catch Will's hand on hers before giving him a knowing look. He kept his poker face and waited for Holly to react.

"Hey," Andrea said softly. "How are things looking over here?"

Holly let her eyes rest on the empty drawer for a beat before she tilted her head up to meet Andrea's gaze. He held his breath.

Holly cleared her throat. "I'm sure you already saw that my desktop was gone," she said. Their hands no longer held the drawer handle, but they somehow still held each other's. And as Holly spoke her next words, she squeezed his hand, and he knew she was using him as her lifeline to keep it together.

"My tablet's gone, too," she added, her voice flat.

Andrea sighed. "We're doing laptops this time around. No more desktops. And I'm going to make it mandatory that everyone take their electronics home daily. Assholes found a way to get in here once. They'll find a way to do it again."

Holly nodded. "Sounds like a good plan."

"Your meeting on Tuesday," Andrea said, scanning the room absently and then turning back to Holly. "I can give you the company card to replace your tablet. It looks like they weren't able to unlock the conference room, so the projector and conference camera are still there. You'll be prepared to stick to the deadline?"

She stated it as a question, but Will was sure Holly heard exactly what he did—a command.

"Of course," Holly said.

"Good," Andrea said. "Tallulah Chan is our biggest account right now, and we can't afford for anything not to go absolutely perfectly at this point. So, thank you. Both of you." She held her hand up to her forehead like she was about to salute. "I am *this* close to losing it, so knowing we're still on track with this event will save me from a stroke, at least for this week."

"Ms. Ross?" A police officer approached. "Are these two ready to add their list of damages to the report?"

Andrea squeezed Holly's shoulder and nodded.

"You're my lifesaver, Holly." She turned to Will. "Thank you both for coming."

Then she was off to the next occupied cubicle.

Will stood by in stoic silence while Holly went over her missing items with the officer. Desktop, tablet, an external battery charger, power cords. It only took a couple of minutes to go through the contents. Her desk files were, thankfully, untouched.

They rode the elevator back downstairs in silence. The same went for the walk to the car. Once inside, Will let out a deep breath.

"You were brilliant in there, Holly. Just brilliant."

She swallowed hard, then nodded.

"It's gone," she told him. "The presentation. My image files. All of it. I worked on it the whole weekend while you were gone and finished it up during the week. Now I have to replicate all that in a day?" Her breathing sped up as she spoke. "I...I have to start now. I have to go home and kick everyone out of the apartment and start now."

Will blinked and tried to clear his head. "Do you always work when I'm gone?" he asked.

She waved him off like it was no big deal.

"Yeah. I mean, we spend so much time together during the week, so I sometimes play catch-up or get a little extra work in while you're gone."

He put a hand on her cheek, prepared to tell her that everything would be okay and that she needed to slow down and breathe. But when his skin met hers, he took a sharp breath.

"Jesus, Holly. You're burning up."

Her right hand flew to her other cheek.

"I am? I thought it was just hot out. Isn't it hot out?"

Will shook his head.

"It's down to the low seventies this evening. You're ill," he said. "You've got a fever."

She rubbed a hand over her neck.

"My throat's been a little scratchy, but I thought I just needed to hydrate. So I had some wine—I know, not the best for *actual* hydration purposes—and I thought that plus the heat… I don't get *ill*."

He started the car and pulled out of the spot.

"Call your sister and tell her they can finish the evening without us. She used to live there, so she can clean the place and lock up when they're done, aye?"

She nodded. "Where are you taking me?"

He tried to pay attention to the speed limit, not wanting his singular focus to earn him a speeding fine.

"You're exerting yourself too much." His stomach twisted. "If I'd known you were working weekends to make time for me—" He trailed off. Now wasn't the time to lecture her on a lifestyle he knew all too well. "I'm taking you to my hotel…if that's all right with you, I mean. You don't need to go home to a flat full of people, and you don't need to worry about the presentation. Not tonight, at least. We'll take care of everything tomorrow."

"But," she said, "we never go to your place."

She was right on that point. He'd always preferred hers. The privacy, her bed, the way they could pretend that whatever this was between them wasn't fleeting—that only existed at Holly's flat. Tonight things needed to change.

He shook his head.

"You're ill. Even if you work tonight—though I'll see to it that you don't—it's going to be shite if you're feeling like shite."

Holly let her head fall back against the seat and sighed.

"I *do* feel like shite. Can I pull that word off?"

He grabbed her hand and kissed the top of it, laughing softly.

"Come home with me and let me take care of you. Let me give you one quiet night away."

She dug in her bag for her phone and held it in her lap. He could see her warring with herself.

"It's okay to let someone take care of you."

She blew out a breath, and he didn't say anything else. It had to be her decision.

He saw her swipe the lock on her phone and then tap a couple of buttons before bringing it to her ear.

"B?" she said a few seconds later, and he listened to the one-sided conversation. "Yeah, no. It was gone. My computer and my tablet. I'll be okay...but...I'm sort of sick? Will says I have a fever." She glanced at him after saying this, and he could hear Brynn on the other end speaking a mile a minute. "No. It's okay. You guys finish dinner. If you're okay turning off the grill and locking up, I think I'm going to stay at Will's tonight." Brynn was speaking again, but it was quieter, and he couldn't tell if it was muted approval or disapproval. He guessed Holly *did* have someone to take care of her, and he wondered if that someone was okay with letting him step in for the evening. "Yes, I'm sure. Okay. Love you, too. 'Bye."

She ended the call and dropped the phone back into her bag.

"All right?" he asked, and Holly nodded.

"All right."

They stopped in the hotel shop before heading to his room and picked up a thermometer. She rested her head on his shoulder, and he felt the heat from her through his shirt.

"What else can I get you?" he asked.

Holly shrugged as he wrapped an arm around her shoulders.

"Ice cream, maybe? Anything cool for my throat."

She sniffled, congestion setting in, and he hoped it was nothing more than the common cold, something that could be combated with rest—and ice cream. He grabbed a bottle of NyQuil from the shelf, which would hopefully help with the fever as well as let her get some rest.

"I think room service can take care of that," he said.

Holly smiled.

Will charged the medical supplies to his room, waiting for Holly to balk at the gesture, but she must have felt too awful to care. Whatever they'd been doing these past few months, she insisted on their relationship being an equal partnership—no one owing the other any sort of obligation.

"It gets too messy in the end," she'd said. "Especially if one party doesn't *want* it to end and the other does. I know that won't be an issue for us, but still. On dates we go dutch, or else we take turns. No gifts and no financial commitments."

He hardly considered cold medicine a gift or financial obligation, but he was sure if Holly was up for an argument about it, she'd give him one. What was funny was this urge to take care of her. He knew he could chalk it up to logic, that he owed her this since she was running herself ragged making extra time in her schedule for the hours she spent with him. But that wasn't it. He was sure if he let her go home that Brynn would have stayed the night, made sure her sister was okay. She didn't *need* him. But the thought of letting someone else tend to her tonight was out of the question. That person had to be him.

Holly popped the thermometer into her mouth as soon as they entered his room. Will led her right to his bed, pulled off her shoes, then swung her legs onto the mattress. He checked her temperature when the thermometer beeped.

"How bad is it, Doc?" she asked. "Can I keep my leg?"

He couldn't help laughing.

"You're quite adorable with a fever of one hundred and one."

She pouted.

"I really am ill, aren't I?" she asked in an English accent, an increasingly nasally one, and he laughed softly again, then kissed her burning forehead.

"You're working too many hours," he told her, thinking of how he'd felt those first two weeks he was here, unable to unwind until that July Fourth night in Holly's bed. The travel, the anxiety of being one place when he wanted to be in another—it tore at him until he was barely functioning. Now he was the one sleeping like a hibernating bear while she was pushing herself beyond her limits. "You need to slow down," he added.

She lowered and rested her head on the pillow, curling into herself as she did.

"I don't know how."

He stroked the hair out of her eyes, tucking it behind her ear.

"Well, tonight you have no choice. I'm going to get you some water and medicine." He strode to the small dresser across from his bed and pulled a T-shirt from the drawer. "You can wear this if you'd like to change into something more comfortable to sleep." He handed her his Warwick Uni shirt, and she snuggled into it like it was a blanket.

"Mmm," she said, breathing in the fabric. "Even clean it still smells a bit like you."

He closed his eyes for a second.

Focus, Will. She's got a bloody fever.

But it wasn't like he wanted to lay her out and shag her. He just wanted to kiss her and mold her body to his, to be the one who could make her well again. But this wasn't about him.

"I'll be right back."

He left the room and wandered out into the suite, where he made a quick call to room service. He grabbed the bottle of NyQuil and brought it to her just as there was a knock on the door.

"Right," he said. "I'll be back…again."

A few seconds later he wheeled in a small cart.

"I should have asked what you liked. Instead I panicked and ordered everything they had."

On the cart sat dishes of chocolate, vanilla, strawberry, and mint chocolate chip ice cream.

Holly was sitting up now, wearing only his T-shirt and possibly a pair of knickers underneath. Not that he was thinking about her knickers.

She beamed at him, and he considered it a job well done.

"If it's ice cream," she said, "it's my favorite." She tapped a finger to her lips. "But tonight I think I'll take strawberry."

Will handed her the bowl along with a spoon.

"Are you going to join me?" she asked, and he nodded.

"Just one more thing, though," he said.

He headed toward the window on the wall next to the bed and pulled up the shade to reveal a dazzling view of the city as well as the clear night sky.

Holly drew in a breath as he crawled into bed next to her, still in his white oxford and cargo shorts. He slid an arm behind her and pulled her back to his chest.

"You didn't tell me you could see the stars from here."

"Now you know," he said. "Did you take the NyQuil?"

She nodded, then yawned before she closed her lips over a mound of strawberry ice cream on her spoon, a smile spreading across her face as she swallowed.

"Will?"

"Yeah?"

"This was the worst night in the history of nights," she said.

"Yeah."

"But it's also kind of the best," she added, her eyes growing heavy.

"Yeah," he said, taking the bowl from her hands and depositing it on his nightstand.

"Thank you." The words came out dreamily. "I love everything you did for me tonight."

She burrowed into him, her furnace-like body making him perspire, but he didn't care. Not one bit.

"You're welcome." He buried his face in her hair and kissed her head.

Then Holly was snoring like his old university roommate after a weekend bender. He laughed softly. It didn't matter.

Will loved everything he did for her tonight, too.

Chapter Seventeen

Someone knocked on the door, and Holly woke with a start, sitting bolt upright in bed. In *a* bed, but it wasn't *her* bed. She peeked under the blanket. Not naked. She was *not* naked and *not* in her own bed.

Her nose was a little stuffy, and her head was a lot foggy, but that didn't stop her from recognizing two of her favorite scents—coffee and bacon. *Room service.* It all came flooding back to her now. The break-in at Trousseau, her fever, ice cream, and a healthy dose of NyQuil.

She was in Will's bed, the morning after sleeping together. Well, not *sleeping* together, but they'd slept in the same bed. Hadn't they? And when Holly and Will slept in a bed together, the morning after did not include bacon and coffee.

Her first instinct was to clamber for her clothes and hightail it on out of this ridiculously comfy bed. Were these down pillows? She sank back into hers to test it, and instinct made her close her eyes and snuggle against the plushness. She wondered if she'd brought a purse big enough to smuggle it home, because there was no way she was laying her head on anything else again. Except maybe Will Evans's chest, but that was another story.

"How's our girl this morning?"

She couldn't help but smile when she heard that voice, one almost as luxurious as the pillow beneath her head.

"She's in love," Holly said dreamily. Then her eyes opened wide. "I mean, with the pillow. I'm in love with the pillow." She sat up and pulled her downy lover into her lap, cradling it against her body. "In love with a pillow and still a bit groggy on NyQuil. Please don't hold me responsible for any verbal vomit for at least another six hours. I forgot how that stuff knocks me out."

Okay, floor. Open up and swallow me, please.

But Will placed a covered plate on her nightstand along with a to-go coffee cup she would bet contained a hazelnut soy latte, and she decided there were better, more delicious ways to contain her befuddled speech.

She lifted the dome off the plate—eggs, crisp bacon, and a toasted bagel—and inhaled the steam, which not only helped to clear her sinuses but also convinced her that there was no way she was leaving this bed until she ate her breakfast. This might go against protocol, but then again, it would be rude to bail on someone who simply wanted to feed you.

Will sat down on the edge of the bed and laid a palm on her cheek.

"Your fever's gone down," he said. "When's the last time you slept past ten o'clock?"

Holly gasped. "What? *Ten o'clock?* What time is it? I—I have to get a new tablet and redo the presentation." She scrambled to get up, but he placed a firm grip on each shoulder and settled her back against the headboard.

"*Holly.*" His voice was gentle yet full of authority, so she stopped resisting and let herself relax.

"What?"

"Eat."

"But I—" She tried to protest, but he shut her up by sticking a piece of bacon in her mouth, and she let out a soft moan as she began to chew. "You aren't playing fair," she said after swallowing, and he laughed.

"I didn't know the way to your heart was through bacon."

She grabbed a second piece and devoured it before responding.

"It's not, Billy." She lifted piece number three to her lips. "It's the way to my soul." She was about to take a bite when she realized her gracious host wasn't eating anything at all.

"Where's your breakfast?" she asked. "I'm sitting here stuffing my face, and you're just watching me."

He kissed her on the forehead, and she realized that other than falling asleep in his arms last night, nothing at all had happened between them since he arrived at her apartment for the Labor Day barbecue. She felt a pang in her gut, a longing for something that was right in front of her. How could she miss something she still had? Will's response interrupted her thoughts, and she was grateful for the distraction.

"I've been working since seven. Tallulah Chan is my biggest client at the moment, but she's not my only one. I had a conference call, answered some emails, and then I called Andrea to get the corporate account number and sent the concierge to get your new tablet. Somewhere in the middle of that I had my own breakfast and an espresso. So eat up, and then we'll get your presentation sorted out."

Was this guy for real? Holly blinked at him a few times, but he was still there.

"You got my tablet?" she asked, bacon still dangling between her thumb and forefinger. She dropped it back on the plate.

Will nodded. "Yes, but I couldn't download the presentation app without your log-in. It's charged and ready to go, though. You can use my laptop for anything you need to retrieve from your online storage and, well—I'm at your disposal."

Her heart leapt, and she silently ordered it back to its proper resting place, because, frankly, Holly Chandler wasn't a leaping-heart kind of girl. She assured herself that this was the effect of the fever and the NyQuil—and the freaking bacon. It had all caught her off guard. Yet she couldn't let his damn chivalry go unnoticed without some sort of a thank-you.

"You did all that for me?" she asked. "And you want to help with the presentation, too?"

"Of course." The sincerity in his voice, his crinkled brow—it was more than she could handle in her vulnerable state.

"I don't know how to thank you."

He pressed his lips together in a thin line, like he was about to say something weighty. But then he grinned. Holly knew this grin. It was the same one he'd given Marisa Gonzalez the day they met and told her they wanted to piggyback off the W's New Year's Eve celebration. It was a gorgeous smile, as all of Will Evans's smiles were. But it was also 100 percent fake. He had just given her his *I'm charming, so don't you want to work with me?* grin.

"I'm sure you'll think of something when you're feeling well again," he said, then stood.

Holly finally noticed that she was in a T-shirt and he was fully clothed in a fitted navy polo shirt and khaki pants that hugged his shape in all the right places. She shook her head and collected herself.

"What's with the business casual?"

Will shrugged. "My call this morning was a video conference. We're going to be working today. Seemed appropriate."

Fine. He wanted to give her business smile and business

wear? She could be all business, too.

"Give me a few minutes to finish eating and freshen up, then," she said. "I'll be out in a bit."

"Of course." And Will exited the room.

Holly found her phone plugged in and charging on the nightstand. Jeez, he'd even found a charger for her.

Gemini: It's okay to be vulnerable today. You don't always have to put on a show. Let others see a new side of you, one you're not always willing to share. You may be surprised at the reaction you receive.

She blew out a breath. How was she supposed to stop performing when Will was putting on an act of his own?

She tossed the phone on the bed and picked up where she left off with her breakfast, allowing herself a few more minutes of bacon-induced ecstasy. Then it would be business as usual.

• • •

As soon as the screen went black, Holly let out a long breath. They'd done it. They'd freaking done it.

"Well," Andrea said. "That presentation seemed... rushed." She glanced at Holly, then at Will. "Don't get me wrong," she added. "You pulled it off, but only just. It's because I've known you for five years, Holly, that I also know that you're usually much more polished than this. What's going on?"

She and Will had worked tirelessly yesterday. Once they started piecing the presentation back together, she'd forgotten the weirdness between them that morning. But the process that had taken Holly nearly a week the first time had to be replicated in less than twenty-four hours while she felt like crap and with a partner who didn't know the application like she did. Will had kept her fed and medicated when her fever spiked again. He'd made her take needed breaks she would have ignored on her own, and when at midnight they'd had the bare bones of a presentation—compared to the original—he drove her home in her car and wished her a good night's sleep before catching a cab back to his hotel.

"I can explain," Will said, and Holly shook her head at him. She had no idea what he was about to say but knew this was her responsibility. Not his.

"I didn't back up my work for the weekend," Holly admitted. "It was a long week, and I was looking forward to weekend plans when I left on Friday. It was careless, and I'm sorry. But believe me, Andrea. It won't happen again." She didn't bother adding that she'd put everything together while fighting a fever. She didn't make excuses. Plain and simple, she'd dropped the ball.

Andrea tapped a pencil on the conference table and sighed.

"I know it won't," she said. "Because you know how important this account is, even more so after what happened Sunday afternoon." She let out a long breath and pinched the bridge of her nose. "Look, Holly. I'm not putting this all on you. The break-in certainly wasn't your fault, and I know that you are capable of doing great things. But please understand the added pressure this puts on Trousseau—on all of us. My insurance payments just skyrocketed, and we can't afford any other kind of loss this year. I hope this makes you understand how much I depend on you—how much *more* I'll depend on you to stay focused if you're going to be my partner."

Okay, so maybe Holly didn't make excuses, and while on the outside she kept it together, a considerate smile plastered on her face, inside she flinched at that word "if." She'd owned up to her shortcomings, but it still seemed as if Andrea was giving her a warning. After five years, was she still testing her? Yes, if she totally blew it with this event, she would completely understand if Andrea changed her mind. But Holly had worked her ass off to right this wrong, and even if her boss had noticed it wasn't her best work, the extenuating circumstances went further than a lack of freaking focus.

That last thought urged her to look at Will, but he wouldn't meet her gaze.

"Of course, Andrea," she said. "I understand."

Andrea pushed her chair back and stood from the table. "Good. I'm off to the insurance office to fill out some claims paperwork. I'll see you both tomorrow."

Once Andrea was out of the room, Will finally looked at her across the table, his blue eyes dark and contemplative.

"Well," Holly said, infusing pep into her voice in the hopes of lightening the mood. "We won that one by a nose, didn't we?" She smiled, but he didn't return the gesture.

"We didn't *win* anything, Holly. And Andrea's tone? She shouldn't have spoken to you that way, not without some bloody privacy."

She cleared her throat. "So you're embarrassed for me? Is that it? Because I can handle Andrea. I don't need your pity, and I certainly don't need your rescuing. What was that with you and your *I can explain*? This was *my* presentation, *my* mistake in not backing up, and *my* responsibility to clear the air with my boss."

She was standing now. She knew her adrenaline was fueled more by Andrea's treatment of her than Will's, but she couldn't unleash on her, so she'd dish it out to him.

"I appreciate everything you did for me yesterday," she told him. "I really do. But I'm good at my job, Will. Hell, I'm great at it. And if I make a mistake here and there, it's because I'm human, not incompetent. I don't need you to go all chivalrous on me in the office and try to fight my battles."

"Are you finished?" he asked.

She nodded.

"May I say something?"

Ugh, those words. *May I?* They brought her back to the first night they kissed and then to that night of other firsts. But this *May I?* didn't sound the same. It wasn't flirtatious or sexy. His even tone made it sound anxious. Or maybe that's just how hearing it made her feel.

She nodded again.

"I'm sorry," he said. "I was out of line."

She let out a breath.

"That's not what I thought you were going to say," she admitted, then realized how unfounded her fear was. Because she had sat there waiting for the blow, for him to say whatever this was needed to end. But how could she be afraid of the inevitable? How could she anticipate missing what she'd never wanted in the first place?

"What were you expecting?" he asked, but she just shook her head.

"Nothing. Apology accepted."

Will's shoulders relaxed, and she wondered where his relief stemmed from. But she didn't ask.

"Good," he said, a grin taking over his features.

"Good," she echoed, and the subject was dismissed.

OCTOBER

Chapter Eighteen

"Back up so I can see you," Will said as Holly grinned at him through his laptop screen. With her hair parted down the center and woven into two long plaits, the ends curled into long corkscrews, she looked ten years younger, and he knew the teen version of himself would have followed her to the ends of the earth. But he wasn't a teen, and she might have been dressed like Dorothy Gale, but Dorothy sure as hell didn't have a sexy smile like that. And now that he could see her costume from head to toe, ruby stilettos and all, more than just his Tin Man mouth was stiff.

"Like what you see?" she asked, and he bit his lip. He liked.

"Very…*very* much," he told her, and she beamed.

"Your turn," Holly said. "Lemme see my sexy Tin Man."

He adjusted himself in his now too-tight trousers and mumbled "Bugger" under his breath. Only she could motivate him enough to wake at half past three in the morning, put his costume back on, and wait for her to Skype him from a party. She hadn't even asked. *He'd* suggested it. Will had done his best to make the request sound like an opportunity for them to have a good laugh. She could walk around the party with him on her phone screen as her date. But the truth was, he simply missed her. Not that he'd tell her that.

"What's the matter?" Despite her question, she was still grinning, not concerned at all.

Will stood, which actually gave him some relief, and backed up so his laptop camera could capture his full height.

She giggled.

"Only you could figure out a way to dress up for Halloween and wear a three-piece suit." Then she brought her palm to her chest. "But I'll be the first to admit you are the sexiest Tin Man I've ever seen."

He grinned at this, then removed the gray-and-white pinstripe jacket and loosened his silver tie.

"It was a last-minute costume. If you recall, I was ready to take Sophie for tricks and treats in plain clothes. *You* insisted we spend Halloween together despite being an ocean apart."

Holly tapped her ruby stiletto–covered foot. Good god, those shoes. She was going to have to wear those when he returned. She narrowed her eyes at him.

"I wonder if *you* recall a certain tall, dark, and British someone who insisted he virtually accompany me to Jamie's Halloween party."

He did recall. It wasn't as if Halloween was particularly important to him. Sophie enjoyed it, and he was happy to celebrate the holiday with his daughter, especially since Tara and Phillip had their own party to attend, so he had Sophie all to himself for the entire evening and Sunday morning, which he guessed was *this* morning. But Holly loved it, and as much as he was happy to be where he was, this was one of those weekends he wished he could be two places at once.

"Where are you at the moment?" he asked, noting what looked like a whiteboard behind her.

"Jamie's office," she said. "It's the only place quiet enough for me to hear you. Once I bring you out there, we won't be able to talk anymore."

He yawned, and Holly's expression morphed into a pout.

"This is ridiculous," she told him. "You need your sleep. You're jet-lagged, and now you're up in the middle of the night, and if I know you, you'll go do some work or something after this and not go back to sleep and be a wreck for work on Monday."

Will chuckled. "Thanks, Mum. How about you take me on a tour of the party, and then I promise not only to go right back to bed but also to have a lie-in as long as Sophie lets me."

"God, I love it when you talk British."

He rolled his eyes. "Show me everyone's costumes already. I'll say good-bye now so you can just close out the app when you're done."

"Good-bye, Billy."

She blew him a kiss, and he shook his head.

"Good-bye, Dorothy."

With that she exited the office and aimed her phone at every patron she passed, then gave him a reaction shot for each. She beamed when she showed him a couple dressed as Fred and Wilma from *The Flintstones*. Then she offered him a thumbs-down after she passed a girl wearing a T-shirt that said THIS IS MY COSTUME. When she found a guy dressed as the Wilson volleyball from *Castaway*, she took a screen shot since she couldn't access her camera while still connected to Skype. Finally, she made her way to the bar, where Brynn and Jamie were both serving patrons pints that looked more like witch's brew than lager.

"Food coloring!" Holly yelled over the din, and Will could tell she was loving this. He was, too. This was the first time they'd done this—spent time together while they were apart. The time difference had always negated such a thing, but for some reason he didn't want to miss this, and now that he was "here" with her, he was glad he hadn't.

"Who's your sister supposed to be?" he asked, and Holly's brows furrowed.

"Let me put the phone by my ear!" she yelled again, and he chuckled.

"I asked who your sister's supposed to be!"

He could tell Jamie was a superhero, the Green Arrow. His costume was minimal, but the green hood and mask over his eyes were enough to evoke the Robin Hood–esque comic book figure. But Brynn simply wore a dress with her curly hair pulled back into a tight ponytail, a pair of black-framed glasses, and bright lipstick.

"They're Oliver Queen and Felicity Smoak!" she yelled. When he showed no sign of recognition, she added, "It's from an American television show!"

He nodded. If there was one thing he hadn't taken an interest in since coming to the States, it was television. His hotel offered plenty of channels, but the little free time he had he spent with Holly, and so far they had not watched any telly.

He nodded, not bothering to try responding with a comment, as he knew she couldn't hear a word he said. She sipped a pint of glowing green brew, alternating where she pointed the phone — at a costumed patron or at herself for her reaction. And only because the noise of the pub would drown him out, he decided it was a good idea to say what he never said when he left for a weekend.

"I miss you, Holly."

Only when he said the words, there was suddenly no party to drown him out. Instead he heard Holly ask, "What?"

Shite. He didn't catch that she'd turned back the way she came once she made it to the end of the bar. Will could see now that she was back in Jamie's office. It wasn't like she didn't know how he felt. He'd woken before the bloody crack of dawn to "attend" the party with her.

I love this. I love the way you touch me. I love how you taste.

They'd both spoken many sentences that used that *L* word, but no real *feelings* were ever expressed. But missing Holly when he was away from her—that was an emotional reaction. And he'd said it. And fuck it if he wasn't going to say it again.

"I said I miss you."

His voice was steady, and he spoke with conviction. They were four months in and eight weeks from the end of this thing, and dammit if he was going to head back to London in January without letting her know she meant *something* to him.

Holly sat in Jamie's desk chair and set the phone down in front of her. She sipped her beer.

"You miss me."

She wasn't asking, just repeating what he'd already said twice.

He rolled his eyes.

"Yes, I bloody miss you. I *always* miss you when I'm here. I'm grateful I get to see Sophie, but it's getting more difficult to leave each time I do."

Holly's eyes widened, and she hiccupped as she sipped from her pint, a dribble of green liquid dripping off her chin and onto her white top.

"Shit!" she said, rubbing at the green stain with her index finger.

Will chuckled. "You're in a pub. Go ask Jamie for some soda water."

But her eyes remained on the task at hand. She licked her thumb and rubbed at the spot.

"*Holly.*" He didn't yell, but he spoke with enough force to convince her to meet his gaze.

"What?" she asked. The effervescent party girl he was with minutes ago had disappeared. Though she smiled when she looked at him, her eyes were anything but happy.

"Is it not okay that I miss you?" he asked. "Do you not miss me? I mean, what are we doing right now? Why am I awake and fully clothed?"

"You offered!" she blurted, and he nodded.

"And you accepted. Christ, Holly. Why can't you just admit this one little detail? Look at me, for fuck's sake. I'm in a suit before six o'clock on a Sunday morning."

This made her laugh.

"You *do* look pretty spectacular in a suit," she said.

He raised a brow.

"What about *out* of a suit?"

Holly's teeth grazed her bottom lip, and she grinned.

"Yeah. I like that, too," she admitted. "But we don't say things like that, Will. I kind of thought it was an unwritten rule, you know? Because what would be the point when we know where this leads?"

He blew out a long breath.

"Maybe I'm changing the rules," he said and watched her suck in a breath. "Not entirely," he assured her. He knew she wasn't in it for the long haul, especially since with him that meant not only England but Sophie, too. He was one hell of a package deal, and the wrong package for someone who didn't do long term and wasn't looking to become a parent any time soon.

"How, then?" she asked, and he shrugged.

"If it doesn't matter," he said, "then why not say whatever we want *whenever* we want to say it? If we wipe the slate clean on the first of the year, then anything between now and then doesn't have to mean anything other than what it means in the moment. And right now, Holly Chandler, in this moment — or six hours into the future for you — I miss your smile."

As soon as he said the words, she tried to suppress the one that teased at her lips.

"I miss your eyes," he added. "Especially when you look at me with your brow all furrowed thinking I'm crazy." She was laughing now. "I miss eating ice cream with you, looking at the stars with you, and hearing what kind of prediction your horoscope has for you and the way you claim it's utter bullshit when I know you buy into it just a little bit."

She narrowed her gaze at him, but she didn't protest.

"I miss *you*, Holly. And when I get home tonight—tomorrow for you—I'm taking a taxi straight to your place because I refuse to miss you any longer than is necessary. Are we clear on this?"

"You said *home*." Holly spoke as she nodded, and this time Will was the one with the furrowed brow. "You said, *when I get home tonight*."

He swallowed hard at the realization. England was home, as was Sophie. He knew that, and it would never change. But maybe Holly Chandler was beginning to feel a bit like home as well.

"My mistake," he told her. "Jet lag."

But they both knew that was a lie. Will might have modified the rules, but he wasn't ready to change them completely.

"Of course," she said, then painted on a cheery smile. "So tell me, Mr. Evans, since you're six hours ahead, what will I say when you turn up at my doorstep tomorrow evening?"

If she believed in horoscopes, maybe she'd believe him as well.

"You're going to tell me that you missed me, too," he said.

"Good night, Tin Man."

He nodded.

"Good morning, Dorothy."

Chapter Nineteen

"*What* are you doing?"

Brynn's tone was more accusatory than inquisitive, and Holly was reconsidering letting her sister keep a key. Only because she *had* locked herself out more than once in the past year did she let it go for now, but sometimes a girl wasn't up for an unannounced visit. Especially if she was about to get reprimanded.

Holly looked up from her laptop and winced at the crick in her neck. She did a slow roll of her head from shoulder to shoulder, trying to loosen it up, because she knew this only gave her sister more ammunition.

Brynn plopped down on the couch beside her, and Holly sighed.

"I'm working."

She'd stayed at the party long past when it ended, helping Brynn and Jamie close up the bar. Holly had even let herself *have a lie-in*. Yes, she was thinking in Will's Britishisms because she adored them, and they made her conjure up his voice. She missed that voice even though they'd spoken only hours ago. She missed the *voice*. That's what she told herself. A voice could be missed independent of the man.

She was a terrible liar, even to herself. But the alternative was to try to rationalize what missing *him* would mean. It hadn't been six months yet. Would she still miss him after the new year? Holly wished *she* was in England at the moment, in the *future*. Maybe then she'd know.

Brynn crossed her arms. "I thought you weren't going to do this anymore—work straight through the weekends. You were sick for days last month because you're pushing yourself too hard with this Fallulah Chan person's account."

Holly placed the laptop on the coffee table and stood up to stretch. When her gaze fell on the kitchen clock, she did a double take. How was it already four o'clock? Will was taking an early evening flight out of London. He'd be landing in three hours, and she still had to read a revised contract from the W that would allow the hotel and Trousseau to share the DJ that had already been hired for the New Year's Eve party. That would take her at least another hour. Then she had to shower, because she'd collapsed in bed last night without even washing her face, and she'd slept in her Dorothy braids that now looked like two mangled nests. And he'd be hungry, right? She could make something quick or order in. He did like that Thai place around the corner. And since *today* was actually the thirty-first, trick-or-treating would be underway. Holly loved handing out the candy, but maybe tonight she should just place the bowl outside the door.

She grabbed Brynn by both wrists and pulled her up.

"It's *Tallulah* Chan, and you need to go."

"But I just got here," she said, wrenching herself free from her sister's grasp.

Holly nodded and tried this time to drag her sister toward the door. "I know. Thanks for stopping by, but I'm really swamped. Call you tomorrow?"

Again Brynn freed herself. She spun toward Holly and braced her hands on her sister's shoulders.

"Chill the fuck out, lady. *What* is going on?"

Holly worried her lip between her teeth then blew her growing-out bangs from her forehead.

"I've been good the past several weeks," she said. "I really have, balancing work and—outside of work *stuff*. But I don't know. He's coming home earlier tonight than he normally does, and I just got this new contract on Friday, and I *didn't* work all weekend. I was at *your* party last night. If…if I get sick again, maybe I'll blame it on you."

Brynn let go of her, and Holly tugged her rogue bangs behind her ear.

"Sweetie, you *can* balance it all, work and a relationship."

Holly laughed quietly. "It's not a *real* relationship. I mean, it's over in eight weeks, so I don't have to balance anything. We just need to enjoy the time we have until Will rows himself back across the pond for good."

Brynn's mouth fell open. "I *knew* it! He's a rower. God, that's sexy."

"I know, right?" Holly said.

Brynn waved the thought away. "Wait. That's beside the point. The issue here is you taking on too much and not admitting that if you slowed down, eased up on the deadlines you create for yourself, you'd be happier, healthier, and have more time for the relationship you're not really in. When does that contract need to be signed?"

Holly mumbled something, and Brynn raised her brows.

"I'm sorry. What was that?"

Holly huffed out a breath. "I have the week to review it."

Brynn narrowed her gaze. "Then what's the rush?"

"Because. I don't have a job like you, where I can go into my best friend's quiet little bookstore and hide in my office and add up debits and credits. I'm not perfect, organized

Brynn, who always knows what's coming next. I have *no* idea what new project will hit on Monday or what fire I'll have to put out—*literally*. Once, one of the models tried to sneak a smoke in the breakroom. When Jackie from the front desk caught her, she thought it would be a good idea to dispose of her cigarette butt in the pot of a fake plant...before extinguishing it."

Brynn shook her head.

"*Perfect* Brynn? You think all I do is calculate totals?" she asked.

"That's not what I meant," Holly said.

Brynn took the last several steps to the door.

"That's exactly what you meant, Holly. God, you know, some days I'm so proud of you, and others—like today—I think you just don't get it."

She was standing in the open doorway now, and Holly wasn't sure how this had gone from Brynn showing up uninvited to Holly hurting the person she loved most.

"What don't I get?" she asked.

Brynn leaned forward and kissed her on the cheek.

"I really hope you figure it out," she told her. "I hope Will has a nice flight *home*. Did you know you said that? That Will was coming *home*? He doesn't live here, Holly. No matter what you think you're going to feel in eight weeks, think about how you feel now and the fact that he really is leaving in January. You're so good at playing pretend. What happens when what you feel is real? I'm not sure you'll even know."

Then she closed the door behind her.

What didn't she get? What was she supposed to figure out? She loved her big sister, but sometimes she was just so... big sistery.

Pretend. Holly didn't pretend. If anything, she was the most up-front person she knew. She and Will had an agreement. Nothing more, because both of them knew that more was not a possibility. Which was a good thing. Holly Chandler's life was full. There wasn't room for *more*.

She went back to the coffee table and picked up her phone. At least she had her damn horoscope.

"You just don't get it," she mumbled, parroting her sister's voice.

Gemini: No matter the question, you always have the answer. It's just a matter of recognizing what that answer is. You can be headstrong, Gemini, your best and worst feature. Once you open yourself up to possibilities other than those you envision, you'll have that which you seek.

She sank back onto the couch. *Great.* Her freaking app was suddenly more of an enigma than her sister, just like Glinda was to Dorothy. Well, she was still dressed like Dorothy if you counted the hair, so she knocked her bare heels together three times. *Nothing.*

What possibilities were there other than saying good-bye to Will and hello to her career?

Holly had just finished setting the table when a knock sounded on the door. She'd decided to just keep things simple and order pizza. She'd given the delivery guy enough time to make it before Will arrived so she could keep the pizza warm in the oven, and they could eat first or do *other things* and then eat. She was flexible.

She glanced down at her attire, a British flag T-shirt and jeans, and laughed quietly to herself, not that the pizza guy would get her joke. Or maybe it was trick-or-treaters.

"Coming!" she called toward the door, grabbing the bowl of candy from the small table and, miscalculating the turn around the wall before the entryway, stubbing her toe on the baseboard. "Shit!" she yelped, hopping the last two steps and throwing the door open to see Will standing there, thirty minutes early, pizza box in his hand.

"Here I thought you fancied pizza," he said, eyebrows raised, "yet you're yelling profanities as if Lou Malnati himself has disappointed you by delivering this very hot, deep-dish pie."

He shifted the box from one palm to another, shaking his free hand as if to ward off the heat. "Trick or treat?" he asked, a devilish smirk spreading across that gorgeous, clean-shaven face.

Holly lowered the candy bowl to the ground outside her door and grabbed the pizza from him, hobbling back a few steps to the kitchen counter.

"You're hurt," he said, observing her awkward gait as she spun back to face him, but she shook her head.

"Stubbed my toe rushing for the door."

He nodded. "And I, perhaps, should have thought twice before paying the delivery chap and palming the pizza box fresh from its heat-preserving sleeve. I'm not sure, but I may have just lost all my fingerprints. Should we go commit a crime and test out my theory?"

Holly's hand flew to her mouth, and she tried to suppress her giggles, but it was a worthless effort.

"We're ridiculous," she said.

"Pathetic," he added.

"You're early." Holly crossed her arms in mock annoyance, but really she was trying to direct his attention anywhere but at her shirt. Yes, she'd worn it for him, but she hadn't anticipated how seeing him just thirty minutes before he was supposed to arrive would affect her—or more specifically, affect her heart. If he looked too closely, would he see it beating beneath the thin cotton of the garment? Would he hear the thunder of activity beneath her rib cage? Funny, she'd always thought of the heart as that necessary organ that kept her alive and stuff, but its current behavior had nothing to do with maintaining her health. And it wasn't as if today was anything out of the ordinary. This was a regular occurrence for them. Will went to England. Will returned from England. Holly and Will had sex. Repeat. Tonight he'd caught her off guard, before she was fully prepared. That was the logical explanation for what felt to her like an illogical reaction. Everything would go back to normal soon.

"Good tailwinds, I guess," he said, shrugging.

Will Evans and his…his stupid nonchalance. What fazed him? Seriously, Holly wanted to know. He was always so even and unruffled. Sure, he could be surly and reserved, but she hadn't seen that side of him in months. And what about him saying he missed her last night like it was nothing, like it was the most natural thing for him to do? They didn't say things like that, things that involved that blood-pumping, keep-you-alive organ thingy.

This was Brynn's fault. *She* made Holly think about things she didn't want to think about. Fine. She liked Will. A lot. But that didn't matter. How she felt now was nothing when she knew it would ebb, fading away like it always did.

The fading just hadn't begun, yet. But it was on its way. She was sure of it.

Will skimmed his teeth across his bottom lip.

"I like your shirt," he said, his gaze intent on hers.

She nodded. She'd prepared something naughty to say about it, something along the lines of wanting to climb his tower of London to hoist her flag, but she couldn't seem to get beyond the nod.

"May I take it off you?" he asked, stepping forward.

Holly was keenly aware that he'd been in her apartment for several minutes now, and she still hadn't kissed him. She also knew that the Lou's pizza sitting on the counter was best eaten fresh from the box, that if she didn't get it in the oven to keep warm, she would compromise the integrity of some of the best deep dish Chicago had to offer.

Sorry, Lou. But you're going to have to take one for the team.

She nodded again and held her arms up in the air, watching Will hang on to the last of his restraint as he lifted the shirt over her head and let out a soft growl.

"*Holly.*" His voice was hoarse.

Right. She'd decided that if they weren't leaving the apartment tonight, a bra was too much of a formality.

His palm was already on her left breast, and he dipped his head, swirling his tongue around her peaked nipple. She let out a moan. Her belly tightened, and she squeezed her legs together, trying to ease the ache building between them.

"The pizza?" she squeaked, a last-ditch effort to stick to how the evening's plan was supposed to go.

"That's not what I'm hungry for," he said, and she arched her back, needing him closer.

He lifted her, and she yelped with laughter, wrapping her legs around his waist as he piloted them to her room and deposited her on the bed. He looked at her, his blue eyes so intense, and the words just tumbled from her lips.

"I missed you, too," she said, eyes wide at the way she sounded to herself—how she must have sounded to him. Like she only now realized that she was happier when he was here.

Maybe there was more to be said, but Will didn't give her the chance, because as soon as she'd spoken, he was kissing her, feverish and hungry, and she couldn't get enough, needed him closer, wanted to taste only him.

He'd had a coffee on the plane, the flavor still on his tongue, and she knew he must be exhausted, the jet lag something he never seemed to get used to. Yet he was awake and full of need and *here*. And Holly hated that this past weekend he wasn't.

He was unbuttoning her jeans and she his. They spoke only through urgent kisses and frenzied clothing removal so they could explore and touch what both seemed starved for. Will took her other nipple into his mouth while simultaneously reaching for the box of condoms in her nightstand drawer. Holly gasped and reached for his erection, bare and hard against her thigh. She spread his wetness over the tip, and Will groaned, leaving her breasts so he could tear the small package open with his teeth.

She wasn't sure who rolled the condom down his length, her or him, because it happened so fast. All she knew was that he was up on his knees, spreading her wide and lowering himself so he could tease her clit with his tip and then nudge the warm, wet opening where she ached, so ready for him to plunge inside.

And that's exactly what Will Evans did. He sank deep, with zero resistance, not that she was surprised. Her sharp intake of breath had nothing to do with how ready she was with zero foreplay. It was because something about tonight was different, something she couldn't articulate.

"God, Holly," he whispered between kisses, pulling out slowly and thrusting back in.

All she could say in return was, "I know." Because aside from the sweet agony of her need to take him deeper, harder, something squeezed in her chest, and she was afraid if she said anything else, she might burst into tears.

What the hell was the matter with her?

She squeezed her eyes shut and hooked her legs around his, hands firm on his hips. She pulled him deep, thrust her pelvis into his, increasing the speed of her movements until a growl tore from his throat.

"Christ, Holly. I'm not going to last."

"Don't hold back," she eked out between gasps, but he stilled inside her.

"Open your eyes, then. I want you to see what you're doing to me."

He pulled out, rubbing her wetness against her swollen center, and her eyes flew open. She *wanted* to see, even if it meant the reverse was true, that he would be witness to what was happening to her. She'd never say it out loud, because that's not what they were in this for. It wasn't part of the agreement. But somewhere in between several pints of green ale and Brynn's visit and Will's early arrival, Holly Chandler had fallen in love.

She got it. She finally freaking got it, and it was the best worst feeling she'd ever had. And the only way she was able to watch that same realization spread over Will's face as he rocked inside her, making sure she came inside and out while he came harder than he ever had with her before, was to remind herself it would all pass by the time he left in January.

It had to, or Holly wasn't sure she'd survive the fallout.

They never ate the pizza. After they'd made love—that's what it was this time—Will had fallen asleep so fast and so soundly, Holly didn't bother trying to feed him. She had showered and put the pizza in the fridge, saving it for lunch the next day. On her own, of course. In the morning when he woke, she felt the weight of him leave the bed but feigned sleep, not ready to put words to what had happened the night before.

"Holly, love. Are you awake?"

He'd sat down again beside her after she listened to him dress. She said nothing.

"I'm an arse for saying it like this, when you won't even hear me, but I think maybe it's better."

She listened as he let out a breath, silently pleading with each thrum of her heart for him not to say any more. But he didn't hear. He was going to say what she already knew, what she felt deep in her core. And as much as she wanted confirmation that he was in as much trouble as she was, she couldn't stop the shudder in her breath. Nothing had ever scared her more than lying in her bed with a man she loved—because Holly had never known love before.

"It wasn't supposed to happen like this. *I'm* not supposed to want for myself anymore, not now that I've got Sophie. *Shite.*" That last word was under his breath. "But I want you, Holly. And I know this wasn't part of the arrangement, but I love you."

He kissed her on the back of her head, and Holly held her breath. She wouldn't be able to hide the tremors otherwise. She didn't exhale until she heard the door close behind him. Then she sniffed, swallowed back the tears, and told the absence of him, "I love you, too."

NOVEMBER

Chapter Twenty

Will slammed his laptop shut and collapsed onto the couch in his office. He loosened his tie and then rubbed at his eyes with the heels of his hands. It was only Monday, but the Monday of Thanksgiving week, and he'd learned the hard way that the city basically shut down for the holiday by noon when he'd received a mountain of out-of-office email replies to contacts he'd just messaged that morning.

He'd scrambled to track down the reporter from the *Sun-Times* who would be covering the fashion show. He'd luckily caught her on the phone and solidified details of how and when she'd interview Tallulah Chan and made sure she would be accompanied by the photographer he had hand-picked from their staff. He was able to cram in a breakfast meeting with the jeweler and sunglasses designer who'd be contributing to the gift packages they'd be doling out to the representatives from Macy's, Nordstrom, and Neiman Marcus who'd be attending the show as well as those from the smaller, independent boutiques. With the industry basically going on hiatus completely in the next two weeks until after the holidays, he'd planned to nail down as many of the final details as he could before Thanksgiving. He'd just thought Thanksgiving happened closer to Thursday—the day of the holiday—but Monday it was.

"You're the last one here," Holly said, and he looked up to see her leaning against his open door. Even in jeans and an oversize sweater, she still took his breath away. Not that she knew how he really felt. Since the crap move he'd pulled a month ago, professing his love to her while she was asleep, he hadn't brought up the subject again. What would be the point? He was in love with a woman who didn't do relationships, who put work first, and who lived thousands of miles away from him. And she didn't seem to be banging down his door to sign up for moving overseas and becoming a stepmother.

Yes, Will Evans. You are a right handful.

"You're here, too," he informed her.

He'd wondered since showing up at her door on Halloween if she'd felt the same shift he had that night. He'd already crossed some unspoken boundary telling her he missed her when he was in London, one she'd balked at, just as he knew she would. But when he'd laid her down on her bed the next day, and she'd admitted to missing him, too, he could have sworn there was something bigger in those words.

And when they had sex? His chest tightened now just as it did every time he thought of that night, because he couldn't remember feeling that way about anyone before her. Yes, he had loved Tara, Sophie's mum, but he'd been young and stupid and way more in love with being William Evans, rising star in the world of publicity for the most high-profile clients in England. She was his first love, but the younger version of himself hadn't known the first thing about what that meant or how to be a proper boyfriend. Now that he was older, though, had anything changed? Did it matter if he loved Holly if he still couldn't give her what she deserved?

"Yeah," she said. "But it's…" She hissed in an exaggerated breath. "It's twelve thirty. Even the cafeteria is closed, and I'm starved. Buy you lunch? I know this great place that has beer—or lager, if you want to get all British on me—and really great pub fare." She finally stepped into the room, making herself comfortable in one of the ergonomic chairs and swiveling to face him. "In fact, I know the owner. We could probably get the lager for free."

She gave him an exaggerated wink, and he chuckled. Yet he couldn't help noticing how in the past four weeks, Holly had chosen a chair rather than the spot next to him—or *on* him—like she used to do when she swore they wouldn't get caught. Hell, she'd pleasured him on that couch enough to make him sentimental about the thought of leaving it, since it was the location of some of the best oral sex he'd ever received.

Whatever happened between them on Halloween night, spoken or not, had elicited small changes like this in Holly's behavior. They still spent two to three nights together each week, and the sex was phenomenal, but she was holding something back, and Will was too much of a coward to ask what and risk messing up whatever it was they had for the final weeks they would have it. Holly claimed her feelings never lasted past six months with anyone before, and he wasn't ready to hear her say her feelings for him were already waning. Things *would* end four weeks from now, but he wanted to believe they still had four stellar weeks left to enjoy.

"Yes," he said. "One of Jamie's pints and a burger sounds absolutely brilliant right now."

He put his laptop in his leather case and stood, slinging it over his shoulder and then extending a hand for Holly. She accepted and stood, letting him pull her to her feet. When she went to let go of his hand, he tugged her closer and leaned in for a quick kiss. She melted into him, parting her lips and inviting him to take more, and he breathed against her.

"What?" she asked, and he could feel her grin.

But he didn't answer, kissing her again instead. She didn't ask another question, and because neither of them liked to waste opportunity, especially when they were the only souls left at Trousseau until after the holiday, they added a bit more sentimental value to the conference room couch before heading to Kingston Ale House.

Will had thought today would be like the day Holly made her six-month proposition—the two of them enjoying an intimate lunch laced with tension they released soon after sealing the deal. But Brynn sat to his right and their friend Annie to his left. Holly was across from him flanked by Jamie and Annie's boyfriend, Brett, and after depositing another pitcher at the table, Jeremy had taken up residence as well. There was nothing intimate about this gathering.

"Does no one work the week of Thanksgiving?" Will asked, reaching for the pitcher to refill his pint.

"Not if they can help it," Annie said, passing a plate of fried pickles across to Holly.

Jamie leaned back in his chair and took a sip of beer, his other arm stretched across the back of Holly's chair. "Speak for yourself," he told her. "Kingston's is open every day this week *except* Thursday. I only get to sit with you slackers because business is slower this week."

"Hey," Annie said with a fake pout. "The bookshop is still open. I'm just taking a long lunch. I've gotta conserve my strength for Black Friday. Plus, that's what employees are for—to hold down the fort while I spend extra time with you lovely humans."

Jamie lifted his pint glass in Jeremy's direction. "I can usually get this one to do my bidding, but he's got the balls to take vacation time to go visit a buddy in L.A."

Jeremy nodded. "You're just jealous I'm heading to your little love nest while you and Brynn are stuck here in the cold."

Brynn raised her brows. "While L.A. might be the place where Jamie *finally* realized I was the one for him, I think we'll find a way to stay warm here, Jer."

Jeremy rolled his eyes, and Jamie grinned as he sipped his beer.

Annie cleared her throat. "What are you doing for the holiday, Will? Spending it with the Chandlers?"

Will coughed, a dribble of lager leaking from his lip to his chin. Bloody charming.

Holly had assumed he'd be heading back to London this weekend, and he hadn't corrected her. If they couldn't have a conversation about how they felt, *if* they felt, or what to do with any feelings that didn't make sense or were, at best, inconvenient for their situation, he certainly wasn't going to insert himself into her family's Thanksgiving dinner.

"He's going home to London for the weekend," Holly said, a strained smile on her face.

Will shook his head and then cleared his throat.

"I'm not, actually," he said.

"Not what?" Holly asked.

"Going home. To London."

Holly crossed her arms and gave him a pointed look.

"You're *not* going back to London when the work portion of this week has already ended at"—she examined the nonexistent watch on her wrist—"half past one in the afternoon?"

He shook his head, enjoying watching her get a little flustered—knowing *he* was flustering her.

"We don't celebrate Thanksgiving in England." He sipped his pint. "Sophie has school all week long. If I was home I'd just be sitting there, waiting to have a quick meal with her after dance class or before her football game."

"She plays football?" Brynn asked, eyes wide.

Holly closed her eyes and shook her head. Will's eyebrows drew together until the lightbulb went on.

"Soccer," he explained, laughing. "We call it football."

Brynn's face went red as everyone laughed, but she didn't join in.

"What?" she asked. "Why couldn't a little girl play football if she wanted to? *American* football?"

"I don't know, Chandler," Jeremy said. "But you're the one who seemed so bent out of shape if that's what she *was* doing."

She pushed back her chair and stood.

"Aw, come on, B," Jamie pleaded. "Don't be mad."

She huffed out a breath and then focused her gaze on Holly.

"I'm not mad," she insisted. "But I do have one more question for Will."

His brows rose as he focused his attention on Holly's sister.

"Do you like turkey?" she asked.

"Sorry. What?" he asked, lowering his own pint back to the table.

"I know Thanksgiving is far from a British holiday, but if you actually *like* turkey, gravy, mashed potatoes, and maybe even pumpkin pie—it wouldn't be a total loss, right?"

Will mustered the last of his resolve. He knew where this was going, and he also knew what his answer would be. "Yes, of course. I enjoy turkey, but—"

Brynn slapped a palm down on the table. "Well, then it's settled. Of course you'll be having Thanksgiving with the

Chandlers."

Holly gasped, then coughed, and he wasn't sure, but a bit of lager might have leaked from her nose.

"Brynn," Jamie said but didn't follow up with anything else.

She looked at him, wide-eyed and innocent. "What? He's here in the city alone on one of the biggest holidays of the season. We're just going to leave him in a hotel?" Her gaze fell on Will again. "Our parents live right by a Metra station. You wouldn't even have to worry about transportation. What do you say?"

Holly sat there, mouth half open, but she said nothing.

Saying yes, of course, was a terrible idea. Holly was a temporary part of his life. He already felt like an interloper here with her sister and friends. It didn't matter that they'd welcomed him into their fold. The closer he got to Holly—to the people who were permanent fixtures in her life—the more he felt like they were heading in a direction they simply couldn't go.

This was why he'd kept Sophie—everything from photos to text messages to Skyping Holly when Sophie wasn't around—independent from his life in Chicago. He didn't mix the temporary with the permanent. Never mind that she and Holly would adore each other if they ever met. He was protecting them both by keeping them separate, which was quite noble if he did say so himself.

But maintaining the wall between him and everything that rooted Holly to Chicago? He couldn't put a selfless spin on that. He was protecting himself as much as he was them, not that he cared to admit it. When it came down to it, the more he infiltrated Holly's inner circle, the more difficult it would be to extract himself.

The whole table was staring at him expectantly, and Holly, despite the whole lager-out-the-nose reaction, wasn't protesting.

"I'd love to," he said. Because as much as he told himself that *no* was the correct answer, he couldn't form the word. Not when it meant more time with Holly.

Holly's eyes widened, and she smiled nervously.

"That's a great idea, B," she said, her voice a bit uneven. Then her eyes fell on his. "Of course you shouldn't be alone on the holiday."

Brynn clapped her hands together while the rest of the table stayed silent.

"Well, now that that's settled, I'm going to run to the restroom. Holly?"

Holly turned to her sister. "What?"

"You wanted to go, too, right?"

He watched as Holly's brow furrowed. "Oh, yeah. Right."

She pushed her chair back and stood. "Excuse me," she said, the waver in her voice still present. "I guess we're heading to the restroom." And with that the two women were gone.

Will couldn't help but laugh. His nerves were getting the best of him, and he was sure the same held true for Holly. But he'd said yes. And just like that, he'd stepped far over the line of safe into the most dangerous territory yet—the Chandler family.

Chapter Twenty-One

Gemini: Today could be your game changer, but only if you want it to be—and only if you let it happen. Look past your boundaries, especially if you are the one who put them there in the first place. Self-imposed walls are easily torn down if you weaken the foundation.

Holly groaned. Brynn glanced at her from her peripheral vision, keeping her eyes on the road, and grinned. A self-satisfied, I-told-you-so, shit-eating grin.

"What?" her sister asked, her inflection rising with feigned innocence.

"*You,*" Holly said, wagging a finger at her sister. "You did this."

Brynn pulled into the suburban train station nearest their parents' new condo, parking her mom's car in a spot facing the track. They were ten minutes early, so Holly could enjoy the cold sweat and clammy hands awhile longer.

They'd spent the night with their parents, a tradition since both had moved out, cooking and preparing and then watching their dad's favorite movie of the season, *Planes, Trains, and Automobiles*. Maybe it was a silly comedy, but it was also a movie about being with the people you loved most for the holidays. Holly knew what the cold sweat and clammy hands were for, but she'd be damned if she was going to give her sister the satisfaction.

With the car in park, Brynn could turn to face her sister now, and Holly thought she might choke on the smugness.

"Fine," Brynn said, arms crossed. "Just admit you're in love with him, and we'll call the whole thing off."

Holly whacked her head against the back of her seat, groaning once more.

"He's going to be here any minute," she said. "It's not like we can just leave him stranded at the train station." Plus, her parents knew her out-of-town *friend* from work would be joining them tonight. It would look odd if they came home empty-handed.

Brynn shrugged. "Suit yourself. You're just not woman enough to own up to your *feelings*."

Holly shook her head and closed her eyes, replaying their restroom visit from Monday afternoon. She never should have told her sister about Will professing his love for her when he thought she was asleep.

"Of course he loves you," Brynn had said. "I knew he was falling for you the night he took you to file the police report for the break-in and then cared for you while you were sick. Duh, honey. That's when I fell for Jamie in high school." She'd let out a wistful sigh. "Took us another decade to get our shit together, but look at us now."

Holly knew where the conversation was going. She just wasn't expecting the challenge.

"You love him, too, right? Tell me that finally my baby sister has fallen in love."

But Holly held her tongue. What would have been the

point, then or now, admitting to Brynn that she maybe, possibly thought she loved Will? That didn't mean she'd still have those same feelings come New Year's Eve.

"What are you going to tell Mom?" Brynn asked. God, Holly swore if there was a table in front of her sister instead of a steering wheel, she'd be steepling her fingers right about now.

"About what?" she asked.

"About the way he's going to look at you all afternoon and evening. About the way you're going to look back at him when your eyes meet across the table. About—"

But Holly was saved by the bell that warned of the approaching train.

Shit. Will was on the approaching train.

She reached for the door handle but didn't make it out of the car fast enough to miss Brynn saying, "If you're not in love with him, why do you need me as a buffer for a ten-minute car ride?"

Holly didn't look back at her sister, just huffed out a breath into the crisp November air, watching as it formed a small cloud, and then made her way to the platform as the train came to a halt.

"Happy Thanksgiving, Ms. Chandler."

Goose bumps peppered the skin on Holly's neck, but they had nothing to do with the chill in the air. She spun to her right to see Will standing there. She'd been looking for him in the wrong direction.

For the first time in five months, she wasn't sure how to greet him, and Will seemed to be waiting for her to make the first move. What she wanted to do was grab the lapels of his double-breasted wool coat and tug his head down to hers. Though he'd accepted Brynn's invitation to come to Thanksgiving dinner, they hadn't been alone since—no opportunity to discuss what they were getting themselves into.

He'd had a late-night overseas conference call on Monday, and Holly and Brynn had a preholiday get-together with out-of-town relatives on Tuesday. Whatever happened at dinner tonight, she was determined to have Will ride the train home with her, to her place, where she planned all sorts of ways for the two of them to work off the Thanksgiving eat-fest. But right now, she didn't know whether to kiss him or shake his hand.

"Holly? Is everything all right?"

She shook herself from her daze and stared up at him. Finally he closed the distance, leaning down to kiss her on the cheek.

"Hi," she said. "I mean yes, everything's all right. I just—you startled me, is all."

His mouth was still by her ear, and as she pulled away he whispered, "I do like to keep you on your toes, Ms. Chandler."

Brynn honked the horn, and Holly stifled her gasp and instead rolled her eyes as she took a step away from Will.

"My sister's a little impatient today," she said and tugged on the strap of the leather messenger bag slung across his torso. "We should go."

Holly offered him the front seat of her mom's SUV, but Will shook his head, climbing into the back before she could protest. So she climbed in next to her sister in time to see Will lean forward and plant a kiss on Brynn's cheek.

"Happy Thanksgiving, Brynn. Thanks for the lift."

"My pleasure," she said, then gave Holly a knowing grin. "Quite the charmer, isn't he?"

Holly didn't respond. She just fastened her seat belt and sat back, going over in her mind how Will had greeted her sister the same way he had greeted her. What was up with that?

The quick ride to the condo was a quiet one, and when the three of them walked in, they were greeted by Holly's dad,

Jamie, and Jamie's dad parked on the couch in front of the TV with beers in hand, already shouting at the first of three football games that would be on throughout the day. Guests weren't officially arriving until three, but the Kingstons had come early, wanting to spend as much time with Jamie and Brynn before the two of them ate their fill and headed to Jamie's mom's house for round two. Holly could see Jamie's stepmom in the kitchen with Holly's own mother, no doubt gossiping about when Jamie would pop the question.

"There are my girls!" her dad called, waving them over to the living room. "Introduce your friend and get him a beer, sweetheart!"

On instinct, Holly threaded her fingers through Will's before they approached, and he squeezed her hand as she did. She'd spent all morning worrying about herself, and she hadn't thought about what this must be like for him, that he would be every bit as nervous as she was, if not more.

"Dad, Mr. Kingston, this is Will," she said, then glanced at her sister's soon-to-be fiancé, who was already standing and greeting Brynn with a kiss. "You already know Jamie," Holly added. "Will is the publicist on the big account I'm working on."

Holly's dad stood and extended a hand.

"Ed Chandler," he said as he and Will shook.

"Pleasure, sir," Will responded. "Thank you for having me."

"George Kingston," Jamie's dad said, all of them standing now. "Been trying to get your girl here to call me George ever since she graduated high school, but you know what they say about old habits."

Will's grin was broad. "I'd love to hear more about Holly's high school years," he said. "I'm afraid I don't know much about her life outside Trousseau."

Holly's dad laughed. "What life outside Trousseau?" he

asked, and Holly winced. Will smiled politely at the joke, but it seemed he didn't find it as funny as good old Ed.

Will let her hand go, and their small moment of connection was severed as he reached into his bag and produced a bottle of red wine.

"Jamie, always a pleasure," he said. "I hope you don't mind that I brought this for the Chandlers."

Jamie chuckled. "Are you kidding? It's not a requirement to drink beer in my presence—though I'm working on it. Actually, I think Deb and Shelly are almost out of red already. They'll be thrilled."

"I'll introduce you," Holly said, and Jamie headed back to watch the game while she and Will made their way to the kitchen. Before Holly could say a word, her mom had wrapped Will into a welcoming hug.

"Look at this tall drink of British water, Deb," her mom said to Jamie's stepmother. "I'm so glad Holly didn't let you spend the holiday alone."

Will grinned and handed her the bottle of wine. "Happy Thanksgiving, Mrs. Chandler," he said, but she waved him off.

"Please," she said. "It's Shelly. And Holly, sweetheart, can you go and grab the wine opener? I think your father left it in the other room."

Holly looked at Will expectantly, and he gave her a confident grin. He'd be okay for a few seconds on his own. But when she returned with the wine opener, it was as if she'd never been there at all. Her mom and Deb were hovering over each of Will's shoulders as he showed them something on his phone.

"Holl!" her mom called when she noticed her standing there. "Have you seen William's daughter, Sophie? He's showing us pictures on his phone. Gorgeous, just *gorgeous*!"

She took one step into the kitchen and dropped the bottle opener on the kitchen island, avoiding eye contact with Will before retreating back to the living room and collapsing into a recliner.

No. She hadn't seen pictures of Sophie. In all the months she'd known him, all Will had ever shared about Sophie was her name and age. He didn't offer up photographs or videos, so she didn't ask. She realized that in addition to him knowing only Trousseau Holly, *she* only knew Trousseau Will. Yet three minutes in her parents' home and he was showing complete strangers what he'd never shown her.

Will met her in the living room several minutes later, after what must have been a slide show titled The Part of Will's Life Holly Doesn't Get to See. Will's coat and bag were deposited in the spare room, and he relaxed in the recliner next to hers. She figured all he had to worry about now was staying awake in the ridiculously comfortable chair. All *she* had to do was obsess for the rest of the afternoon and evening over what it meant that Will was opening up to her family about parts of his life he'd kept private from her.

How could he say he loved her yet not share the most important aspect of his life? Maybe today was all Brynn's doing, but he was here, with Holly's *family*, and she'd never even seen a photo of Sophie.

Her throat tightened. What if he saw her avoidance of the subject as indifference? She'd always assumed if he didn't bring up the whole fatherhood thing, it wasn't her place to do so. Like an unwritten part of their rules.

But the rules were changing. It didn't matter that he'd thought she was asleep. Will had said what he said, and she'd heard what she heard, and now there were expectations. And feelings she wouldn't admit to her sister and was terrified to admit to herself. Because it was just physical chemistry. And that *bloody* English accent.

She sat silent, thankful for the white noise of the football game on TV. Her dad and Jamie filled Will in on who was playing and whom to root for. Just like that he'd infiltrated her life outside of Trousseau, one that she would argue *did* exist, and he fit in seamlessly. The question was, where did she fit in all of this?

She hadn't realized her sister was still standing next to her. "Game with the boys or wine with the ladies?" Brynn asked, appearing behind her chair.

Holly blinked, looking from the living room to the kitchen and back again.

"Wine with the ladies," she croaked, her throat suddenly dry. She had been the one, initially, to insist they were just playing at this. A game that would end when their arrangement ran its six-month course.

So why did her chest ache as Brynn led her toward the kitchen and away from Will? Why did a lump rise in her throat to know he had this whole life an ocean away that didn't include her? And why, for the love of Häagen-Dazs, did it feel so right to have him here with everyone else she loved?

Oh.

Oh, no.

This wasn't a game anymore.

A turkey, stuffing, two kinds of potatoes, homemade cranberry sauce, green bean casserole, and pumpkin pie later, the Chandler friends and extended family were scattered throughout the kitchen, dining room, and living room. Holly stood outside under the pretense of making sure the grill was turned off when really she just wanted a few minutes to herself.

Will had fit in so seamlessly. Her mom and Deb took to him immediately, but then again, who could resist that charm? When Will turned it on, anyone within a ten-mile radius was helpless against it. But then he'd sat with her dad and let him go on about the two teams playing, even though she was sure Will took no interest in American football before tonight. Seeing him through their eyes only made her wonder about things she didn't have the luxury to wonder about—like permanency or what it meant that she *wanted* him to share with her the parts of him he kept locked up so tight.

A knock sounded on the glass slider, and she turned to see Will holding two glasses of wine and motioning for her to open the door.

She blew into her hands and rubbed them together, then slid the door open so Will could join her.

"Thirsty?" he asked, a lazy grin on his face.

She reached for one of the glasses and took a sip of what she assumed was the merlot she'd last seen open on the kitchen island. The liquid warmed her throat and belly, and she relaxed into a smile.

"I'm getting a little jealous of these stars," he said. "They seem to keep your attention more than me tonight."

He leaned forward to kiss her, and she backed away after a quick peck, realizing the door was still open. She reached around him and pushed it shut, heart thumping in her chest. True, she loved her stars, but they didn't make her pulse race like this.

"Are you tipsy, Mr. Evans? Because you seem to have an alarming lack of propriety for being at the home of your girlfriend's parents."

Her hand flew to her mouth, and Will's brows rose.

"I *am* tipsy," he said with a crooked grin. "Your mum hasn't let my glass go empty all night." He pulled her hand free from where it still covered her lips. "Am I your boyfriend, Ms. Chandler? I don't remember our arrangement specifying labels."

That was the problem. Will was mildly drunk and teasing

her, but this didn't feel like an arrangement anymore. He'd told her he loved her when he thought she wasn't listening, but he'd never let her in on the part of his life he kept separate. And the crazy part was, Holly understood. It made sense, maintaining some level of disconnect. So why was she suddenly looking for things like labels that made their setup all too real?

His smile fell.

"Right. I get it. I've made an arse out of myself in front of your family. I will tell Shelly I am cut off from here on out— *just* as soon as I finish this glass."

He swirled the wine in the goblet, and dammit, he was irresistible like this—funny, relaxed, his guard down. Holly thought the only time he really let everything else fall away was during sex. That was when she saw him, or as much of him as he'd let her see. Right now he wasn't the man with one foot out the door, always feeling like he should be somewhere else. He was just a guy who'd had a little too much to drink and made goofy jokes and laughed at them even if she didn't.

"I've never seen a picture of Sophie," she said.

Will's expression sobered.

"What?" he asked, but she could tell from his eyes, from the way they tried to focus anywhere but on hers, that he knew it was true. Will Evans had a shit poker face when he was buzzed.

"Will…come on. What kind of a *girlfriend* doesn't know what her boyfriend's daughter looks like? You're right. We never discussed labels, and we probably shouldn't start now. I'm Holly. You're Will. We have a good time together—and some really great sex. We don't have to call it anything when it's almost over."

She gulped down her wine and moved to step past him and back into the house. She knew it was cold outside, but all she could feel was the heat of the wine traveling to her belly and the knot in her throat warning her not to say any more.

Will stopped her with a gentle hand on her shoulder, but she didn't meet his gaze.

"She'd adore you, you know. Sophie."

This got her attention, forcing her to look up at him.

"She would?"

He nodded.

"You're brilliant, successful, beautiful. You've got legs that go on for miles when you wear your damn stilettos."

Holly narrowed her gaze.

"I thought we were talking about why Sophie would adore me."

He laughed quietly.

"I don't— *No* one I date meets Sophie, not unless I think she's the one. Because until that point, both my daughter and whoever I'm dating have the potential to get hurt. I know what it's like to be parted from someone I love more than my own life, and I don't want anyone else to feel a fraction of that, not if I can help it."

She reached a hand to his cheek, his skin warming her chilled palm as it rested against his light beard.

"I don't think I've ever told you what a great dad you are," Holly said, and Will breathed in, a slight hitch in his breath. "I know I've never actually seen you in action, but I see how much you love her. I see what you do for her with the beard and the photos and the shaving when you go home. Everything you do is in her best interest, and I love y—" She stopped before she revealed herself too much. "I love the way you worry about her. I do. But god, Will. The weight you put on yourself, worrying about everyone else's happiness? What about yours?"

He shook his head. "My what?"

Holly groaned. "Your happiness."

"Ah," he said, nodding. "I'll worry about that when

Sophie's eighteen. Maybe thirty. Not sure yet."

Something in her heart sank, because he was 100 percent serious. As good of a father as he tried to be, he was putting his needs on the back burner for his daughter.

So she slid her hand to his neck and urged his head down toward hers. She kissed him, and he kissed her back with such sweetness, it made her heart break just a little, not that she'd ever had a broken heart before.

"How about"—she whispered against him—"you let me worry about it tonight?" She bit his earlobe, just a light nibble. "Come home with me," she said. "And I promise I'll put a smile on your face."

Will hummed, the vibration of the noise pulsing through her.

"Is that a yes?" she asked, her voice hoarse now.

He laughed. "I'm not sure," he said. "You didn't say *May I.*"

Chapter Twenty-Two

Holly rolled to face Will, her naked body flecked with sunlight as it filtered through the leaves of the tree outside her window. God, he loved how comfortable she was with him, that she didn't cover herself up to sleep next to him, even after they'd made love. And now, as morning brought everything from last night into focus—being welcomed by her family, realizing that Sophie would love her like he did—it made his heart swell even more to see her bared to him like this, a groggy smile on her face.

And…it also made him hard.

"I did it. Didn't I?" she asked, the words coming out with a yawn.

"Did what?" He traced lazy circles around her belly button. He watched her nipples grow firm and grinned, though he knew he didn't have time to do something about it. It would have to be quick or not at all, and he was nothing if not a man who liked to take his time. Plus, if he wasn't back at the hotel within the hour…

"Will? Hello? Anyone home?"

Shite.

"Sorry, what?" he asked.

Holly's eyes narrowed at him, and he felt the warmth of her palm on his upper thigh—a palm that must have been there for several seconds while she was, no doubt, speaking to him without getting any sort of answer. Christ, he knew his focus was crap if he didn't notice her touching him...

"Your happiness," she said, voice firm. "I thought that's why you came home with me last night, to let me worry about your happiness. Which, by the way, I think I *did*, splendidly. But you're somewhere else right now, and it's freaking me out a bit."

So many things were left unsaid last night. He'd thought he'd have more time to let the alcohol wear off, to tell her properly how he felt or maybe for her to do the same. But they barely spoke a word on the train back from the suburbs, and when they made it through her front door, well, they'd both been at a loss for words. Not that anyone was complaining.

And now? Now there was no time to talk, because his worlds were about to collide.

"I...have to be...somewhere else," he said. Then he kissed her, fighting the urge to linger, before climbing out of her bed.

"Wait," she said, and he turned to see her pull the sheet up to cover herself. Something in that gesture tore at him. It was clear she knew he was keeping something from her, and she wasn't wrong. "You're kidding, right? I know our usual drill, Mr. Evans. On workdays you go back to your room to regroup, show up at the office alone, so no one suspects a thing. I can't even bring you coffee because it's too familiar. Maybe it was silly to assume today would be any different." She raised her brows. "And for the record, I make a delicious cup of coffee. It's no quadruple shot of espresso, but it's *good*."

His eyes widened.

"Really?" she went on. "You're surprised that I know you

so well?"

She let out a long breath, room enough for him to speak, but he didn't. He hung on to the anticipation of what came next, because either it all came crashing down right now, without him having to hurt her, or he'd bought himself a few more days.

"But I don't really know you at all. Do I? You're a fixture in my professional life. My personal life. And now you've filtered into my family life. You've seen it all, and you've shown me nothing."

Will climbed into his jeans and let out a sigh.

"That's not true," he said, and she opened her mouth to argue. But he would have none of that. She didn't get to play this card. "Yes, we're brilliant as business partners. And we have done things in that conference room that would get us both fired, and I don't even work for Trousseau." He couldn't help but smile at that last remark, but Holly's expression remained impassive. "I've had dinner with you and your sister and friends, and it's been lovely. And it was equally lovely to meet your parents. But come on, Holly. That's hardly me seeing it all. It's me seeing snapshots of you through other people's eyes, a distorted view. And do you want to know what a distorted view is?"

She closed her eyes and shook her head.

"It's safe, Holly. Bloody safe. It's no different than the way I compartmentalize for you. It's just your own particular method."

God. If he could just explain that it was *because* he loved her that he was pulling back now—but he was shite with articulation when she was arguing with him naked. He wasn't supposed to find anything to make him happy in Chicago, yet here was this woman who was as brilliant as she was maddening. A woman he loved more every second he was with her. And a woman who believed she couldn't love him back—not for the long haul.

The thought hit him like a tidal wave, and he staggered as he gathered his clothes. Did she notice the wind being knocked from his lungs?

His shirt was on now, and he was searching for his missing sock, choosing to abandon it for the sake of getting a cab back to the hotel.

"I have to go," he said, wriggling a bare foot into his shoe.

"Back to your own safety?"

Her question wasn't angry, only matter-of-fact. She did know him. Too well. Which was why he had to leave before he did something crazy, like asking her to come with him. To *stay* with him. But this was just a game to her. Wasn't it? She wasn't fighting for *him* to stay. Only challenging why he had to leave.

"I guess you could call it that," he said. *Or*, he thought, *straight into the danger zone*. Either way, the clock was ticking.

"I'll call you this evening," he told her. "It's probably a good time to have a chat."

When she nodded, agreeing to his call rather than telling him he was daft and should come by tonight to say whatever needed saying in person, he wondered if this was the beginning of the end. He knew people in relationships argued. It's not like this was out of the ordinary. But what were they fighting for in the long run if there wasn't a long run to begin with? He thought he'd be okay with it, because, dammit, he and Holly Chandler did not make sense. But the facts did nothing to cull his emotional reaction. Whatever happened from here on out, Will was in Chicago for four more weeks and then back to England. For good.

His steps were leaden, those that carried him from her bedroom to the front door. And the short ride back to the hotel was excruciating because she didn't even try to stop him. She let him go—like she'd said she would, like he'd believed she would, but right now, like he wished she hadn't.

"Cash or credit, sir?"

Will rubbed his eyes with his thumb and forefinger. He pulled his bank card from his pocket and slid it through the credit card machine.

"Credit, thanks," he said. Then he stepped out of the cab just as a door in the cab in front of him opened as well, a small pair of red trainers hitting the pavement before the passenger hopped out and made eye contact with him.

"Daddy!" she yelled and barreled into his arms as he dropped to a squat so she wouldn't have to reach.

"Soph!" He buried his face in her dark curls, his voice cracking before he could utter her full name. He stood, her hands still hooked around his neck, and spun her in a circle, his heart leaping into his throat. He didn't know how he did it, stayed away from her so long and survived. Every reunion between the two of them made each parting that much more difficult.

He kissed her cheeks through her peals of giggles and hugged her tight again. *This*, he thought. *This is why my happiness is on hold.* Nothing he could want for himself could make up for the father he should have been in Sophie's early years, the one he was still learning how to be now.

"I missed you so much," he told her. "Shite, I missed you so much."

She laughed again then whispered in his ear. "Daddy…no cursing or Mummy will be cross with you."

Will laughed at this, too. Tara was cross with him more often than not. A slip of the tongue was the least of his worries.

"William…" His back was to the taxi line, but he didn't need to turn to match the look on Tara's face with the tone in her voice. He didn't *need* to turn, but it would probably be rude to speak to her like this. So he lowered Sophie. As soon as her feet hit the ground, she laced her fingers with his, both spinning to face her mum—his ex.

"Hi, Tara." He bent to kiss her on the cheek.

"I see you're just getting home," she observed. "Some things never change."

He closed his eyes and shook his head, jaw clenched. But he would not engage her with Sophie here. There was no argument between him and Tara anymore, only the one she wanted to perpetuate despite her being the one to leave *him*.

"William, mate. How's our man about town?"

Phillip, Tara's husband, was the last to emerge from the taxi. Oddly enough, Phillip was often his ally in awkward meetings with his ex, probably the whole keep-your-enemies-closer deal. But Will wasn't a threat to them, never had been. Someday Phillip would realize that.

He shook Phillip's hand, his other still in Sophie's.

"Morning, Phillip. Flight okay? I did offer to send a car for you all."

Phillip stepped around to the back of the taxi where the driver unloaded their luggage.

"Nonsense, William. Everything went swimmingly. Sophie slept quite a bit on the plane, and Tara enjoyed a few cocktails while I got some work done. Can't complain."

Will guessed Tara had a thing or two to say about Phillip working on the plane, but then again, Thanksgiving certainly wasn't a bank holiday in Britain. This was just another weekend for Phillip.

"Daddy, whatever will we do today?" Sophie asked, and Will let out a long breath. That was his Sophie, always interrupting just in time to ease the tension. Would it always be like that? Would she always have to bear that burden even when she didn't realize she was? God, he hoped not.

He picked her up again, rested her on his hip, and smacked a loud kiss on her cheek, causing her to burst into giggles again. That was more like it. He opened his mouth to tell her about his plan for the day, to bring her to the Shedd Aquarium while Tara and Phillip slept off their jet lag—that was the deal—but was cut off by the sound of tires screeching and someone wailing on their car's horn.

His head jerked in the direction of the commotion, and that's when he saw Holly picking herself up from the curb across the street, an angry driver yelling at her from his window.

"Sorry," Will said, placing Sophie's hand in Tara's. "I just need to…" He trailed off as he stepped out into the street, holding up his hand for oncoming cars as he jogged to where Holly now stood, one palm braced against the pillar of a streetlamp, the other on her heaving chest.

"What the hell are you doing, lady?" the driver was yelling. "If there had been black ice there, I wouldn't have been able to stop!"

"Fucking hell!" Will yelled once he made it to the other side of the street. He had one hand on the man's door where the window was open. The other reached for Holly, who grabbed it and squeezed it tight. "Maybe she slipped on some ice herself, you bloody arsehole. How about asking the lady if she's okay?"

"Fuck you," the driver said, closing his window and forcing Will to pull his hand away. Will jammed the heel of his hand into the top of the door before the guy sped off, a whole string of curses spilling from his lips that he hoped weren't loud enough for Sophie to hear—or worse, Tara.

He shook his free hand, having hit the car harder than he'd intended, and turned to face Holly.

"Christ, Holly! What the hell were you doing?" Both hands were on her cheeks now. "Are you okay? Are you hurt? What are you doing here?" He glanced down the length of her body as he yelled his barrage of questions, his eyes stopping where her jeans were torn at the knee, the skin scraped and bloodied underneath.

"You *are* hurt," he said, but she wasn't looking at him. Her eyes were focused past his shoulder and across the street to where he knew Tara, Phillip, and Sophie stood.

She pulled away from him. "I'm fine. I shouldn't have—Shit. What *am* I doing here?" She limped as she took a couple of steps back, and he grabbed her hand again.

"You can't leave like this," he said. "Come upstairs and let me make sure you're okay. Let me at least explain—"

He didn't know *how* he would explain, but he couldn't let her go without ensuring she was all right, and he didn't just mean her knee. He had to trust that the right words would come, that she'd understand. Then he'd give her an earful about traffic signals and crosswalks and— Bloody hell, he'd swear his heart was banging louder than a drum.

She opened her mouth to protest, but he cut her off.

"I'm not letting you leave before I fix up your knee, so you might as well come with me. Does anything else hurt?"

Holly blew out a breath.

"Just my nonexistent pride," she said, rolling her eyes but letting her hand relax in his.

"Should I call an ambulance?" he teased, relieved to see Holly being Holly.

She groaned. "This isn't something we can laugh our way out of, Will." And he nodded as she let him lead her to the traffic light, where there was a crosswalk.

"I know," he admitted.

"As long as we're clear on that," she said. They waited for the walk signal. "Also, I'm so sorry. I have no right to be here, to interfere. I know if you wanted me to meet her you would have told me, and I didn't mean to undermine that. I really didn't." She paused, chewing on her lip. "This morning was so weird, and I'm not used to weird. I've never been in a situation with a guy where things got—weird."

He nodded. "I get it. Weird."

"And I didn't like it—leaving things like that."

"No," he said. "Neither did I."

"I don't usually chase men across the city."

He smiled at this. "But you chased me." Maybe she was going to fight for them. He had no clue how it would work, only that he was finally admitting to himself that he wanted to try.

"It felt like the right thing to do—in a crazy sort of way. I just didn't like leaving things so—"

"Weird?"

She let out a nervous laugh. "Yeah."

The light changed, and the signal for them to walk lit up. "And I do want you to meet her," he added, realizing right then that he meant the words. He'd introduce Holly as his friend, not caring that Tara would know it was a lie. He could still protect Sophie the best way he knew how, but he wanted his daughter to at least meet the woman he'd fallen for, even if Sophie would never know he loved Holly as he did.

They crossed the street, and despite the chill—it couldn't be more than twenty-five degrees outside—Will could feel the perspiration on the back of his neck. He'd kept his life neat and tidy for so long. He wasn't sure how to proceed with a situation as muddled as this one was, but he guessed introductions were a start.

When they reached the opposite side of the street, Holly let go of his hand. She was limping still, but steady on her own, so he let her shove her hands into her coat pockets as they approached Tara, Phillip, and Sophie, still watching from where they stood.

Sophie let go of Tara's hand and ran to him once he was only a few feet away.

"That was so heroic, Daddy!" she squealed as he bent

to hug her. "Mummy said you were daft, but I said it was lovely what you did, and Phillip thinks Americans are terrible drivers, but you saved that lady." Sophie took a breath and backed up a step to look at Holly. "Do you know the lady?" she asked and then gasped. "She needs a plaster. Are you going to put a plaster on her knee?"

Will couldn't help it. He laughed at his inquisitive little girl, and when he looked at Holly, she was smiling, too.

"Sophie, love," he said. "This is my friend Holly. Holly, this is my daughter, Sophie."

The two girls shook hands.

"Pleased to meet you," Sophie said.

"I'm very happy to meet you," Holly told her. "You're just as lovely as your daddy told me you were."

Sophie beamed, and Will couldn't help but smile, too.

His daughter led them the last few feet to where Tara and Phillip stood.

"Mummy, Phillip, this is Daddy's friend Holly. She's lovely, isn't she? Daddy's going to get a plaster for her knee, aren't you?"

Will nodded.

"Holly manages Tallulah Chan's account at Trousseau. We…work together."

Phillip shook Holly's hand enthusiastically while Tara kept her arms crossed as she nodded.

"Pleasure," Phillip said.

"It's nice to meet you both," Holly told them, even as Tara sized her up.

Will knew what went through her head—that no woman was worthy of Sophie's praise. Hell, she didn't even think *he* was worthy of it. But that's why he was working so tirelessly to do right by his daughter—not just because he loved her but to prove to Tara that he was the father he should have been from the start.

"I'm sure you all need to check in and get situated," he said. "Ring me in an hour to let me know when I can pick Sophie up for our trip?"

Tara finally opened her mouth to speak.

"Is your *friend* going to be joining you, William? Because we never discussed—"

Sophie bounced where she stood. "Oh, yes," she said. "Can you come, Holly? Mummy and Phillip need to rest, and I do like how Daddy smiles with you."

"Sophie," Tara said, "I'm sure Holly has plenty she needs to do today."

"Aw, come on, Tar," Phillip said. "It's just a museum. She's not asking Sophie to call her Mum."

Holly gasped. "Oh, no, I wasn't—I mean, it's Black Friday. I've got shopping." She nodded to herself. "Yes, I'm going to go shopping."

Will met Tara's stare. It was her call. He wouldn't go against her will. He knew the worry. It was the same one he had every day, that Phillip would cease to be Phillip and eventually turn into *Dad*. He had to remind himself that while Phillip was a good guy, a great stepfather, in fact, that *he* was Dad, and he always would be. Just as Tara would always be Mum.

"Tara?" he asked, and she sighed.

"You want Holly to join you?" she asked Sophie, and their daughter nodded.

"Right then," Tara said. "I'll ring you in an hour, and the three of you can head to the museum."

"Aquarium," Sophie corrected. "With the dolphins."

Will chuckled. "So you'll join us," he said to Holly, careful not to phrase it as a question, knowing she could still decline. "That is, if you can postpone your shopping."

Holly's lips pressed into a small smile. "I guess I could find some good deals online as well," she told him.

Will grinned. This was good. It would all work out. It was actually better than he could have hoped, and as he kissed Sophie good-bye for the hour and helped them all inside, Tara and Phillip with the luggage and Holly with her injured knee, he looked forward to the day, his guilt all but vanished.

Then he and Holly were in the lift alone, heading to his room where he would tend to her knee. He laid a palm on her cheek, bending to kiss her, but she backed away.

"You're going to explain why you didn't tell me they were coming to Chicago, right?"

Oh. Right. There was still *that*.

Chapter Twenty-Three

Gemini: Be careful what you wish for. Today has the power to be exactly what you want, but don't bite off more than you can chew. Don't be afraid of needing someone else's care, but do be sure you offer that same care in return, even if it isn't well received.

Holly slid out of her jeans, albeit reluctantly. Ha, there was a first, her *not* wanting to drop her pants for Will Evans. She knew he saw the sulk on her face, the clenched teeth and furrowed brow, but she didn't care. She wanted him to know there'd be *nothing* but wound cleaning going on today.

"Do I at least get to be angry, too?" he asked as he sat her down on the couch. "You did follow me like Inspector Clouseau. A really *bad* Inspector Clouseau."

She huffed out a breath. "Maybe I came to talk," she said. "Clear the air after, you know…"

"The weirdness you keep speaking of?"

She nodded. "Right. The weirdness."

He raised a brow.

"Okay, fine. I followed you—*because* of the weirdness—but you lied first," she said. She knew she was right. She also knew she had sort of stalked him, and she was so not proud of that.

"I omitted information that would have informed you of Sophie's visit. Not exactly a lie."

She pursed her lips, her eyes narrowing to slits. Yeah, he was not getting off on a technicality here. No freaking way.

"It's called a lie of omission for a reason, William. Because it's a *lie*. And you didn't just leave out that Sophie was visiting. What about your ex-wife?"

He shook his head. "We were never married."

It didn't matter. Seeing Tara, the woman he'd made a baby with? Holly wasn't prepared for the punch to the gut that would be. Will wasn't just a father. He was a father with another woman, one he'd probably loved at some point. And no matter how he felt about Holly right now, he'd shared something infinitely bigger with another woman, something she couldn't compete with—not that she thought she wanted to.

She hissed as he brought a wet cotton ball to her knee.

"Sorry," he said. "You made a right mess of yourself. I need to clean it." She nodded. "Also, I'm sorry for not telling you. About Sophie and Tara and—I didn't know how to do it." He paused for a breath. "I didn't know what came next after I told you," he added.

This she understood. Holly was never supposed to be a part of Will's life in England. But now his English life was here, and she'd thrown herself into the thick of it without giving him time to process. She got that, too.

He narrowed his eyes at her as he held up a box of Band-Aids. "I bought these to prepare for Sophie's visit. Looks like I was worried about the wrong girl." Then he got back to work at fixing her up from her fall.

Holly blew out a breath. There was no point in arguing because he was right. Maybe she did need looking after now and then. But what would it mean if she wanted Will to be the one to do it?

"I'm sorry, too," Holly said softly. "I had no right to follow you. I swear I've never done anything like this before. I don't know what's wrong with me. I always have things under control."

He grinned as he finished cleaning the blood from her knee, kissing it just above the wound before he covered it with one of those giant Band-Aids that always went unused whenever she bought the variety pack. Looked like there *were* wounds big enough for such a bandage, yet the thought only made her sigh. Would this thing with Will—these *feelings*—really dissipate when he left? Or would there be an ache too big for the myriad of remedies in her medicine cabinet?

"Are you saying I make you lose control?" he asked, looking up at her through dark lashes, and suddenly his hand on the back of her calf felt hot, the spot where his lips had just been—utterly molten.

Her anger melting away, Holly was acutely aware that she was sitting in front of him pantless, so she reached for her torn jeans on the floor and wriggled back into them, somehow without leaving the couch.

"You know you do, Evans," she admitted, leaning back to button her pants. "I guess I wasn't expecting things to be different with you," she added, blaming her verbal fountain of honesty on her near-death experience. But the truth was, she'd stepped into the street because her eyes and thoughts were on what she saw on the other side, Will and his daughter and everyone—and she'd already forfeited control.

"But it is different with me?" he asked, and she nodded. "It's different with you, too," he said.

So, there it was. Saying it without saying it. Holly still

felt guilty about feigning sleep earlier that month, hearing his profession of love yet never letting him know she felt the same. At least she thought she did, but how could she know for sure? She didn't think she'd actually loved anyone before, and until she was 100 percent certain that her feelings for Will were the real deal, she wouldn't do that to him, say something she couldn't back up with definitive proof.

"So what do we do now?" he asked.

She wanted to tell him to kiss her, to take her pants off again, but this time so he *could* do more than tend to a wounded knee. She wanted to say with their bodies what she couldn't yet put into words, but where would that get them other than late to pick up Sophie?

"We go to a museum," Holly said.

"Aquarium," he corrected, "with the dolphins."

Holly laughed, a nervous kind of sound, then leaned forward to where he still knelt in front of her and pressed a soft kiss to his lips.

"Thank you for taking care of me," she said, and he didn't hesitate to respond.

"Always," he said. An unrecognizable warmth coursed through her veins, and she wondered what it would mean if that word were true.

Sophie gripped Holly's hand in hers, forcing her to a slow jog as she took off down a ramp.

"Look here!" Sophie yelled. "Otters!" She pulled Holly farther until they were in a near gallop down the stairs. "Sea lions!" She couldn't contain herself. "And the dolphin tank!"

When they were flush against the large salt-water tank, Sophie let Holly go so she could belly up to the glass, palms and nose pressed as close as they could get without injury.

Will caught up to them, too cool to run alongside Holly and Sophie as they nearly bulldozed everyone in their path. Actually, Holly enjoyed the few minutes alone with Sophie after they'd all watched the dolphin show together.

He stood at her side, sandwiching Holly between Sophie and himself.

"I told you she'd adore you," he said quietly, and Holly grinned.

"Why didn't you warn me how much I'd adore *her*?" she asked. "Did you know she has an English accent? You could warn a girl how irresistible an English accent is on a six-year-old. I may have to keep her forever and ever."

As soon as the words left her mouth, Holly wanted to suck them back in. She knew a day at the aquarium equated to nothing in the grand scheme of mothering. She wasn't an idiot. But she was learning something that day, something that was becoming easier to articulate. Because these feelings she had for Will—they grew even stronger in Sophie's presence. Before, Holly had guessed he was a wonderful father. But seeing him in action was something she hadn't been prepared for.

"What if that was a possibility?" he asked, eyes still aimed at the tank just as hers were. "What if after our six months are up—"

He spun slowly to face her, and Holly's heart leaped. His hand rested lightly on her cheek, and then his lips were on hers. There it was. That inexplicable warmth, but Holly knew what it meant now. It meant this was *real*. What she felt wasn't fading, and instead of relying on the fact that it would, she let those words loop over and over again along with the rhythm of the kiss.

What if after our six months are up—

Will pulled away with a start, and his eyes went wide, the blue of his irises so dark they nearly looked black. She took a step back, furthering the distance between them.

"Will, what—" But then she realized what that look in his eyes was for, and she was sure hers now mirrored it. Because when she backed up, she should have stumbled into a six-year-old girl.

"Where is she? Fuck, Holly. Where the hell is Sophie?"

She spun to her left, and the precocious six-year-old with the British accent wasn't there.

"Oh my god, Will. Oh my god, I don't know. She was right there!"

"Sophie!" Will was searching the lower level where they were, his gait wild and unsteady as he bumped into patrons, his hands tearing at his hair. "Sophie!"

Tears pricked at Holly's eyes, and she didn't try to sniff them back. Not this time. She'd messed up, somehow. Hadn't she? Sophie was standing next to her, so she should have noticed her wander off—or worse, if someone had…

She shook her head. *No.* Sophie was fine, and they were going to find her, and the big thing that Will was about to say—he'd say it again. This wasn't how the day was going to end.

Holly caught up to him and grabbed his forearm. But he shook it free, looking at her like he didn't know her.

"We need to find security," she said, trying to keep her voice calm even though she was anything but. Will was terrified enough as it was, and he didn't need her adding to that. She took his hand in hers, and he let her lead him around the whale tank where they found someone wearing a museum polo shirt and name tag. *Lia.* She wasn't exactly security, but she had a walkie-talkie holstered on her belt. She could help.

"My daughter," Will said, his breathing labored. "I've lost my daughter."

Holly squeezed his hand, trying to offer whatever reassurance she could.

"We were watching the dolphins," Holly added, pointing to where they'd just come from.

"Okay," said the woman, doing a way better job with the whole calm thing than she and Will were, which was good. Calm was good. If she wasn't worried, then everything was going to be all right. "I'm going to radio security."

Within seconds of her doing so, a uniformed security officer came jogging down the staircase and into the lower level.

"Sir, can you give me a description of your daughter?" the man asked, and Will fumbled for his phone, pulling up a photo, where Sophie's beautiful smile filled the screen.

"Take it," Will said, thrusting the device at him. "The longer we stand here, the worse our chances are of something…"

He didn't finish, and Holly guessed he both couldn't and *wouldn't*, as if stating what the possibilities were made them—possible.

"We're on it, Mister…" the man said.

"Evans," Holly told him. "Will Evans, and her name is Sophie."

"Sophie Montgomery," Will added and then mumbled under his breath. "She doesn't even have my name."

The man nodded and spoke briefly into his walkie-talkie, then listened to the response. "We've got someone on every level, sir, and at every exit. We're going to make an announcement—"

As soon as he said the word, they heard it.

"Attention, Shedd Aquarium patrons. Sophie Montgomery, please find the nearest aquarium employee. Your parents are looking for you."

Will shook his head. "Just me. I'm the parent."

Holly's stomach sank. Of course she wasn't the parent, but Will's need to clarify hurt in a way she wasn't expecting. But this wasn't about her. *He* was hurting. *He* was on the brink of losing his mind with worry.

"Will, listen to me," she pleaded, putting a hand on his shoulder. "I came to this place all the time as a kid. I practically grew up here. Let security do their thing, and we'll do ours. We can divide and conquer."

He nodded, and Holly didn't waste any time.

"Okay, it goes off in two directions down here. I'll go left toward the area where you can pet the sea stars. You go right, toward the penguin play area. If she wandered off, either one of these places would catch her interest."

He nodded again.

"I need to find my daughter. Please. I don't know what I'd do if…" He trailed off, and she reached for his hand, giving it a quick squeeze.

"We'll find her," she said, and he pulled his hand from hers and walked swiftly away. Holly did the same.

Maybe Sophie had moved slowly along the glass with the dolphins, as Holly was doing now. They were Sophie's favorites, after all. Maybe she didn't even realize she'd strayed from their spot. Sophie didn't seem like the type to get distracted and wander off, yet that's what Holly wished for. If it was nighttime and she could see the stars, she'd take back every single wish she'd ever made and trade them all for the one she had right now, to find Sophie safe. To take that look of horror from Will's eyes. She'd give anything not to see that again.

"Holly, look! I'm touching a sea star!"

She heard her before she saw her, but tears were already leaking down her cheeks at the sound of Sophie's voice. And when she rounded the shallow pool of starfish, she found the little wanderer, sleeves rolled up and arms plunged elbow deep in the shallow, reef-like environment.

"Sophie, thank goodness!" she yelled, scooping the girl into a hug and pulling her up onto her hip. "Did you hear them calling your name?" Holly didn't care that she was getting soaked by Sophie's dripping arms. She just knew she had to make it to Will as soon as possible.

"They called my name?" Sophie asked, then added, "Are you crying, Holly?" Holly choked out a laugh. "I told you and Daddy I was going to explore." She giggled. "You were kissing, and no one said *not* to. Explore."

She lowered Sophie to the ground, then swiped at her tearstained cheeks.

"It's okay," Holly said. "We were a bit distracted." She grabbed Sophie's hand. "Come on, though. We have to find your dad. He's very worried."

Sophie frowned. "Will he be cross at me?"

She shook her head, laughing again through still-falling tears.

"No, sweetie. He won't be cross. He loves you so much. Do you know that? Your dad could never be cross at you."

The corners of Sophie's mouth turned up into a grin.

"Okay," she said. "I believe you."

And Holly was right. When they found Will by the penguin habitat, the first thing he did when he saw Sophie was drop to his knees and hug her as he held in what she could tell was a much-needed sob.

"I'll tell security we found her and get your phone back," Holly said, giving him a few minutes alone with his daughter. When she returned, he was still on the ground with Sophie in his arms. Holly wasn't sure if he'd be able to let go, and her heart broke to see him in such a state.

After several long moments, he stood, and they all walked until they found a family bathroom where Sophie could wash up after her sea-star adventure.

"I'd like some privacy," Sophie said. "I have to do a wee as well."

Will laughed and nodded, allowing her to go in unattended

since it was a solo bathroom.

"We'll be right outside," he said, as Sophie pulled the door shut behind her.

Will's head fell against the wall. His arms crossed over his torso, and he closed his eyes and took a few shaky breaths.

"She said she told us where she was going," Holly said softly. "And when we didn't answer, she took that as permission. Will, I'm so sorry." She reached for his face, but before her palm could make it to his cheek, his eyes shot open and he wrapped a hand around her wrist, lowering her arm to her side.

"It's not your fault," he said. "It's mine. *I* was supposed to take her out today. On my own, no distractions. I lost my focus and bloody lost my daughter."

He ran a hand through his hair, and she noticed the sheen of sweat at his temples.

"Will, don't do this to yourself," she pleaded. "You didn't lose her. She wandered off. It could have happened if you were alone just as easily."

He shook his head.

"You know that's not true," he said. "Our eyes were bloody closed, Holly."

Despite the words, there was no anger in his tone. It was simply matter-of-fact.

The bathroom door opened, and Sophie stepped out, her smile dropping as soon as she looked between the two of them.

"You *are* cross, aren't you?" she asked Will, and he shook his head.

"Just tired, sweetheart. Promise."

Holly believed him, the weariness in his voice dripping off every word.

"Can we get an ice lolly?" Sophie asked, and Will let out a strangled laugh.

"What's an ice lolly?" Holly asked.

Sophie beamed. "Ice cream on a stick," she said then crossed her arms, waiting for a response.

Will picked up his daughter, hoisting her onto his hip and painting on one of his patented Will Evans smiles, the kind that didn't reach his eyes. Hopefully Sophie wouldn't notice.

"If my girl wants an ice lolly, then my girl gets an ice lolly," he told her and then kissed her on the cheek. "Holly," he said, addressing her for the first time since Sophie came out of the bathroom, "do you know a place we can go?"

It was Holly's first time at Shooting Star Café when she didn't have an appetite for ice cream. She and Will sat in silence as Sophie devoured not an ice lolly but a dipped vanilla soft serve cone. With rainbow sprinkles. Holly's mouth watered. Who was she kidding? She *always* had a taste for ice cream, but somehow indulging didn't seem right.

"I love Chicago," Sophie said, trying to lick at a sprinkle stuck just below her bottom lip, her chocolate-covered tongue turning the sprinkle into a soul patch.

Holly snorted, and Sophie laughed with her. But Will? He looked a million miles away.

"Did you know they have a game shelf, just over there?" Holly pointed to a small bookshelf perpendicular to the pastry counter. "Bet you can't beat me at Connect Four!"

Sophie bounced in her chair. "Can I look at the games, Daddy? I promise not to run off."

Will nodded but didn't say anything, so Sophie hopped up, half-eaten cone in her hand, and strode to the shelf full of board games.

"Hey," Holly said, resting a tentative hand on Will's knee. His eyes finally lost that far-off look, and he focused his gaze on her.

"Hey," he said softly.

"Are you…okay? I know today was awful, but we found her. She's okay. Everything's okay." That was three okays, yet saying the word didn't seem to make it so.

He shook his head.

"I'm not okay," he said, his voice rough as gravel. "I'm selfish," he added. "Seems I've always been good at that." He ran a hand over his jaw. "I thought I could start wanting for me. I *thought* I was done making up for not putting her first in the past. But that was foolish. Thinking this could work?" He motioned between them. "It was foolish," he said again.

She raised a palm to his cheek, this man who never gave himself any credit but shouldered all the blame, and he turned away from her touch.

"No," she said, this time succeeding as she brought her hand back to his face. "It wasn't foolish. I don't believe you really think that."

He didn't push her away, but he didn't lean into her touch like he'd done so many times before. He just sat there, so she continued speaking.

"I heard you," she said, and Holly knew there was no going back from here. So she soldiered on. "I heard you the morning after Halloween. You said you loved me, and I'm pretty sure I might love you, too, and I know if this hadn't happened we'd be talking about possibilities beyond six months, and for the first time in my life, I want to see what comes next. With *you*."

Now he did pull away, his expression unreadable, but Holly's heart sank just the same. This was it.

"This is what I've figured out," he said, and Holly braced herself for what came next. Because she could tell by his tone, by the finality in it, that he believed every word he was about to say.

"It doesn't matter how I feel. Being with you is a

distraction. Wanting you kept me from being a good father today, just like Andrea thinks I'll distract you from doing your utmost on the Chan account."

Holly leaned back.

"A distraction? I'm a distraction? And when did Andrea talk to you about my performance? What business is it of yours, anyway?" Fear was morphing quickly to anger.

He laughed, but somehow he wasn't smiling.

"It became my business when we started fucking in the conference room, Holly."

She flinched at this, and his jaw clenched.

"Christ, Holly. I'm sorry. I didn't mean it like that."

"Yeah," she told him. "You did." Then she turned to Sophie, who'd just returned to the table, Connect Four in hand and a chocolate mustache above her adorable little mouth, and dropped to a squat. "I'm gonna need to take a rain check," Holly said, trying to swallow back the lump in her throat. "It was so lovely to meet you, Sophie. But I have to go now."

She pulled the girl into a hug, and Sophie whispered in her ear, "I like how Daddy smiles when he's with you. You make me smile, too."

At that, Holly kissed her on the top of the head then stood, not bothering to wipe away the few tears that began to fall. She gave Will one last glance, but no more words passed between them.

And then, like every relationship that came before, Holly walked away.

Chapter Twenty-Four

Will avoided the elevator on Monday. The cafeteria, too. It didn't matter that he'd begun to break a sweat by the time he made it to the tenth floor. He wouldn't be there long.

He burst through the stairwell door and into the reception area and checked his watch. It wasn't quite nine o'clock, and the office was just starting to buzz with the electricity of a staff that had reenergized over a holiday weekend. To the left was where he knew Holly would be, latte in hand and head buried in her digital in-box. He felt the corner of his mouth turn up into the hint of a grin until he remembered what he'd said on Friday.

Being with you is a distraction.

Jesus, he hadn't meant to blame her, but he also believed his own words. If he hadn't been so wrapped up in falling for Holly, he would have been more focused. Right? What other explanation was there?

So he ignored the sickening ache in his chest and turned right, past the reception desk and toward Andrea's office. She was already at her desk, thank goodness, so Will could be quick.

He knocked on the door frame, and she looked up from her computer screen and motioned for him to come in.

"Did you have a nice Thanksgiving, Mr. Evans?" she asked.

Will cleared his throat, trying not to remember how good it was—how welcomed he was by the Chandlers and how he'd even pictured himself at future family events. With Holly. But that was all a fantasy. What had happened the next day—that was reality.

"I was thinking," he said. "Now that everything's in place, I won't be needing much office time here. At Trousseau. I can manage the rest of the publicity from the hotel, which is convenient because I'm staying there—"

"You're leaving Trousseau?"

It wasn't Andrea's question, but he recognized the voice that came from behind. Not only that, he heard the hurt in those words, and it nearly leveled him. When he turned to face her, though, that's when the rug was pulled out from under him.

She was beautiful as always, her dark hair hanging loose over her shoulders. She stood in a simple gray shift dress, complemented by a pair of knockout knee-high boots, but what he'd always remember was the way her eyes shone with tears she seemed to barely be holding back.

He could feel Andrea watching him, waiting for his response.

"Yes," he said, before he lost his nerve. "Our jobs are separate from here on out. Not much more use for collaboration. Just seems to make sense I tie up my end of the deal from there and you from here."

God, he was an arse, reducing their time to *collaboration*. But what else was there to do? Holly deserved better. And he deserved—well, he'd already been given more than he thought himself worthy of.

"I'm with Will on this," Andrea said, and when he turned to face her, he recognized her knowing look. She'd warned him that his relationship with Holly would come with pitfalls. He'd just been too blind to see it. "I've got a meeting off-site," she said after that, rising from her desk. "Mr. Evans, I'm sure you'll call if you need anything more from Trousseau? Otherwise we'll see you at the show."

He straightened his tie and nodded at Andrea. "I'll clear my things out of the conference room."

Andrea brushed past him and out of the office. He knew what she was doing—giving him a chance for a proper good-bye.

He turned to face Holly, who still hadn't moved from the doorway.

"I guess this is it, then?" she asked, her tone even. But her eyes betrayed her as a lone tear fell, which she quickly swiped away.

"Holly," he said, but any other words got lost in his throat. Instead he stood there, staring at her, loving her and losing her all at once. His jaw clenched, and his hands fisted at his sides. He just wanted to do right by his daughter. Holly had to know that.

"It's okay," she said, forcing a smile. "This was always the plan, right?" She laughed, but the sound was bitter. "It was *my* plan. You just agreed to go along for the ride. The ride's just ending a few weeks early. That's all."

He opened his mouth to speak again, but she shook her head.

"We got in over our heads." She gave him a sad shrug. "Sophie's okay?" she asked, and his heart sank. After everything he'd said, she still cared about Sophie.

He nodded. "Yes. Thank you. She made it home safely yesterday afternoon."

She smiled—a real, genuine smile, and he tried to lock

this image of her permanently into his mind. This was how he wanted to remember her.

"She's an amazing little girl, Will. No matter what you think, you've done a wonderful job raising her."

Holly moved as if she was going to step toward him, but she must have changed her mind, because she was backing away from the door now.

"I guess I'll see you in a few weeks," she said. "It's been a pleasure working with you."

And before he could respond, she spun on her heel and vanished quickly from his sight. She left him standing there, heart in his throat, and not a chance to tell her what he should have said three days ago.

I'm sorry.

• • •

Gemini: Throw everything you thought you knew out the window. Life will throw you for a loop some days, and guess what? Today is that day. What will you do with the loop, Gemini? You can either let it make you dizzy until you fall down, or you can right yourself and roll in a new direction.

Holly beelined it for the other side of the office, but when she reached the reception area opted for the elevator instead. She furiously pressed the button, wishing for once this tactic actually worked. Maybe it did, because after several seconds an empty elevator welcomed her with open doors.

She stepped over the threshold and kept her back to the lobby as she waited for the doors to close. And when they did, she slumped against the back wall and let out a shuddering breath.

That's when it happened—the profuse eye leakage.

As much as she tried, she couldn't wipe the tears away fast enough. They just kept falling.

It wasn't as if Holly had never cried before. But, good gracious, she'd never had such a reaction to the end of a relationship, had never felt such a gut-wrenching ache. She took a few hiccupping breaths, not noticing that the elevator started moving. *Or* that it stopped and opened again on the fourth floor.

"Holly?"

She froze at the sound of her name, swallowing back another wave of sadness, but she didn't dare turn around.

"Holly. Come on. I know it's you."

She felt Charlie's voice get closer as he approached, but she remained with her arm resting on the elevator wall and her head buried beneath it.

The elevator started moving, but seconds later they jolted to a halt.

"Hey," he said softly, his hand on her shoulder. "It's just me. Tell me what's going on. Do I need to call someone for help? Just turn around and show me you're okay. Okay? Because I'm getting a little freaked out."

She let out a long breath, then attempted to suck in any bodily fluids that were still leaking from her face, and turned toward Charlie.

He flinched, but then his gaze softened.

"That bad?" she asked.

He pulled out his blue pocket square and handed it to her with a nod.

"Maybe waterproof mascara next time?" he said with a reassuring grin.

She wiped the soft material across one cheek then recoiled when she saw it streaked with her eye makeup.

"No worries," he said. "Consider it a gift."

She didn't argue but instead continued to try to clean

herself up without a mirror.

"Why aren't we moving?" she asked, her voice far from even.

He crossed his arms. "Emergency stop button. You seemed like you were in a state of—emergency."

She let her head fall back against the elevator wall with a soft thud.

"Is stupidity an emergency?" she asked. "Because then yes. I guess that's what I've got."

He rested a palm on her soaked cheek, urging her eyes to meet his.

"Does this have anything to do with that British publicity guy?" he asked.

Holly rolled her eyes. "Were we really that obvious?" she asked.

Charlie laughed. "As obvious as it is that your six-month rule seems to have finally bitten the dust."

She blew her nose into his pocket square, narrowing her eyes at him as she did.

"You fell in love, Chandler. It happens."

She crossed her arms.

"Why didn't *we* fall in love, Charlie? It worked with us. It worked with everyone else I ever dated even before I realized it."

He laughed, then licked his thumb and streaked it under her eye.

"You missed a spot," he said. "And why didn't we fall in love? I don't know. We knew each other already. We were both looking for the same thing, which did *not* include commitment. I think we knew we were safe before it ever started. But here's the secret no one ever tells you."

Her brows furrowed. "What's that?"

"You can't choose it. Or plan it—the person you fall for. It just happens, like a slap upside the head. A wake-up call," he said.

She pursed her lips into a pout. "I didn't even see it coming."

He patted his shoulder, urging her toward him, and because she really, *really* needed someone's arms around her right now, she let Charlie hold her, his hand rubbing her back in long, soothing strokes.

"I don't think anyone ever does," he told her. "So why the tears?"

She let out a shaky breath against him. "Because we messed it up. We messed it up, and now he's leaving to work on his part of the show alone. And after New Year's Eve, that's it. He's going back to England for good, and I'll never see him again."

The finality of what she'd just said hit her like a freaking anvil.

She'd fallen in love *and* gotten her heart broken before they'd even made it to six months.

The new year would come and go, yet it would return in twelve months' time. But Will Evans was leaving for good. That was *always* the plan. And she'd been fool enough to think that would somehow change.

She tilted her head up until her eyes met Charlie's.

"It's really over," she said, and then she buried her head in his shoulder once more. She let him hold her until there were no tears left to stain his jacket, until his poor pocket square could take no more.

And then, because Holly Chandler wasn't the type to cry in public over a broken heart, she left the building before she saw Will Evans leave Trousseau for good.

After that she hopped in the first cab she found and kept her composure until she'd made it safely through her front door, where she would continue her emotional outpouring in the privacy of her own home.

With a pint of Häagen-Dazs and a spoon.

DECEMBER

Chapter Twenty-Five

Sophie's little fingers tickled Will's jaw, and he chuckled, delighting in her touch. She'd grown so much these past six months. He'd hardly recognized her when his mum had shown up at the airport with her to greet him when he arrived.

"Who is this young lady?" he'd asked, pretending as if he'd never met her, which made Sophie laugh until tears ran down her face.

"It's *me*, Daddy. Your Sophie!"

But oh, how she'd changed since Thanksgiving weekend. It had been three weeks since he'd sent his daughter back to England, which meant right now his beard was rivaling Santa's.

"Can I take it off tonight?" he asked as Sophie studied him, the two of them snuggled in the back of his mum's Mini Cooper. After the incident at the aquarium, he was relieved Tara was still giving him Christmas weekend. Sophie had tried to take the responsibility when Will had explained what happened, but Tara wouldn't hear it. He *and* Phillip had had to talk her out of heading straight back to O'Hare and hopping the next flight back to London.

"I quite like it when it's this long," she said. "Does Holly like it, too?"

Will swallowed hard but kept his composure for Sophie's sake.

"Darling, I told you. Holly is just a friend from work, and we don't even work together anymore. Not really."

He'd hated what he'd done that Monday after Thanksgiving at Trousseau, leaving as he had, but it was the only answer he saw fit.

Andrea hadn't argued, not that he thought she would. He knew her real loyalties were with Holly, that she wanted the best for her almost partner, and Will being out of the picture was what was best—for everyone. Never mind that he'd never be able to erase the hurt he saw in Holly's eyes the last time they'd seen each other. He'd have to find some way to live with that—with knowing that he'd extinguished their light.

"Tara told me about the aquarium," his mum piped up from the front seat. "I'd be surprised if she doesn't have Sophie microchipped by now, from the sound of how traumatic it was for her to lose Sophie."

Will's skin grew hot, and his eyes burned.

"Traumatic for *her*? I'm sorry, what? Tara wasn't even there when Sophie went missing. Christ."

His mom chuckled, and Sophie grabbed his forearm.

"I wasn't lost, Daddy. I knew where I was going. I read a sign that said sea stars, and I wanted to see the sea stars."

He shook his head.

"You were lost to me," he said.

Will closed his eyes, rubbing them with his thumb and forefinger. Even weeks after the incident, his stomach sank at the mere mention of it. It was like thinking he'd lost Sophie all over again—then reminding himself he'd lost Holly for good. They rode in silence for the next several minutes, and he tried to bury any further thoughts of Chicago. He was *home*. England was home. All he needed was here.

"Do you want to know what I asked Santa to bring me for Christmas?" Sophie asked, and he opened his eyes.

"Whatever it is, love, I'll make sure you get it."

She grinned at this just as the car came to a stop in front of his house.

"I asked for you to marry Holly because she makes you smile."

Will coughed, and his mum laughed as she exited the front seat.

He opened his door and stepped out onto the snow-dusted curb, then reached his hand for his presumptuous daughter.

"Sophie, *you* make me smile. I don't need to marry — "

She cut him off once she was standing in front of him.

"Daddy, I'm nearly seven now, so I know how things work." He nodded and smiled, and she went on. "And I do love you and Mummy and Phillip, and I know *I* make you smile. But who makes you smile when I'm not there?"

Just then his mum put a hand on his shoulder.

"You're a good man, William."

He shook his head, refusing to believe such rubbish. "No, Mum. I'm really not. I've been trying to be a good father, but I'm a long way off from being a good man."

His mum huffed out a breath. "William. I am your mother, and as such you will not only listen to what I have to say, but you will take care to believe it."

He responded with a raised brow, but he didn't dare interrupt.

"As I was saying, you are my son *and* a good man who became a father before he was prepared for what that entailed, but you did the best you could then, and you're doing even better today. Just look at that beautiful girl you helped create."

He glanced down at Sophie, who preened at her grandmum's compliment.

"Plus," she continued, "you've got your wits about you now. And you've got a damn smart little girl who finds happiness in seeing others happy. You could learn something from her, you know. If you care for this woman, then you owe it to yourself to do right by her." She sighed and placed a hand over his. "Oh, William. You owe it to yourself to do right by *you.*"

"It's not that easy, Mum," he finally said.

"Nothing ever is," she said. "If life and love were so bloody easy, how would we ever know what was worth fighting for if there was nothing worthy of a fight?"

Sophie giggled. "Grandmum cursed," she said.

Will couldn't help laughing, too. "When did the women in my life get so smart?"

His mum shook her head. "Oh, darling, you know we've always been. It's just taken you ages to hear what we have to say."

"I bet Holly is quite smart," Sophie said, and Will bent to kiss his daughter's nose.

"She is, sweetheart."

I, on the other hand, am a total and complete wanker.

Will tucked Sophie into bed, grabbed a bottle of ale from the refrigerator, and found his parents in the lounge watching an old episode of *Fawlty Towers* on the telly. They were staying in the spare room so they could all wake on Christmas morning together, which he knew would be at the crack of dawn if his daughter had anything to say about it.

His mum was sipping a cup of tea while his dad opted for

a bottle of Newcastle. Like father, like son.

"Thanks for stocking the fridge, Dad."

His mum huffed out a breath.

"Sure, thank your father for the ale but not your mum for all the food—for looking after the place while you're gone."

He stepped around to the chair where she sat and kissed her on the cheek, then sat on the sofa next to his father.

"Thank you, Mum. For *everything*."

She raised her brows at this, and he could tell she was waiting for what came next. Because something absolutely did come next.

"I think I need to make a phone call," he told her, then took a swig of his ale. His mother grinned.

"Sophie likes her? The American?"

He nodded. "Holly." He even missed saying her name.

"And *you* like her," she added. It wasn't a question. She was his mum. She could read him even when he tried to keep the pages of his book sealed shut.

This apparently piqued his dad's interest, because his eyes left the telly and were now on Will. Guess he had a full audience now.

"I love her." At this his mum's hand flew to her heart as her smile grew wider than before, but Will shook his head. "I love her, and I messed up. I said some terrible things, practically blamed her for losing Sophie, and we haven't spoken since. I don't think she'll forgive me."

His dad's hand was on Will's knee now. Then he stood, wiggling his empty bottle.

"Just say you're sorry, son. Even if it's not your fault—which this time it absolutely is—say you're sorry. Women love that, you being wrong and owning up to it."

"Oh, Edward!"

His mother reached across him and swatted his father on the arse. His father simply chuckled and ambled out of the room.

"Apologies are nice," she admitted, "but I swear if your father wasn't such an excellent lover—"

"Mum!" With that Will was off the sofa and making his way to his small study.

"Oh, William, we aren't prudes," his mother called after him, and he shuddered but didn't look back.

He could call her. He could apologize and ask for a second chance. But there was still the whole geography situation. He couldn't leave England, and she wouldn't leave Chicago. That was the part he hadn't yet figured out. And if her crazy six-month rule really was true, he wouldn't have to, because she wouldn't want him anyway. Christ, even if her feelings hadn't fizzled, he'd made a right mess of everything. Maybe she loved him, but he'd hurt her. He just wasn't sure if the damage was irreparable.

When he was inside the study, he pulled out his phone and checked the time. It was eleven, which meant it was only five in Chicago. Maybe she'd answer, and maybe she wouldn't, but he'd been the one to push her away. It was up to him to try to get her back. So he brought up her number and was ready to hit send.

"Daddy!" Sophie cried. "Daddy!"

He dropped the phone and ran to his daughter's room, his parents right behind him. Will knelt next to her bed where she lay with her eyes still closed, yet her cheeks were streaked with tears and she was still calling his name.

He laid a palm on her forehead and sucked in a breath.

"She's burning up," he said. "Sophie, darling. It's Daddy. Wake up so we can give you some medicine." But she just kept whimpering and saying his name.

"I'll warm up the car," his father said, and Will nodded.

"Mum, call Tara. Tell her we're heading to the urgent care."

His mum left the room, and Will scooped his daughter into his arms. She was a furnace against him. She would be okay. He told this to himself again and again. But that didn't stop him from shaking as she cried into his shoulder. Then he realized it wasn't him who was shaking. It was Sophie.

Her arms and legs convulsed, and her eyes rolled back into her head. He had to find purchase up against a wall before she knocked him over. He couldn't drive with her like this.

"Mum!" he yelled. He slid down the wall before he dropped his daughter altogether. "Mum, call an ambulance!"

His mother ran to him, phone in hand. He was on the floor with his daughter seizing in his arms. His vision blurred as tears streaked his cheeks.

"It's all right, William," she said as she dialed. "It's all right. It will be all right." But her voice shook. She couldn't protect him from her fear.

He wasn't a religious man, but it didn't stop him from silently begging any higher power that might exist to make his daughter all right. He loved Sophie more than his own life, and as he carried his daughter out to the car, the same thought repeated in his head like a mantra. *Take me instead.*

"It was a febrile seizure," the doctor said after Sophie was sleeping peacefully. The seizure hadn't even lasted as long as it took the ambulance to arrive, but to Will it felt endless. "Quite scary, but we've reduced the fever. We'll do some tests in the morning, but not to worry. All her vitals look good. These things are more common than you think."

For the rest of the night, he and Tara sat vigilant at his daughter's bedside. He stayed awake as nurses came in every few hours to monitor Sophie's temperature—to check the intravenous medication that flowed through a tiny tube into her small, limp arm. And when her fever finally broke the next morning, he thanked God or the stars or whoever listened and gave him what he wanted.

"Mummy. Daddy," Sophie said quietly as she woke. "Why do you look so sad?"

Tara burst into tears, peppering their daughter's forehead with kisses. Will swallowed back his own emotion. At least he thought he had until his daughter reached her hand to his face and swiped a rogue tear away.

"It's okay," Sophie said to them both, and Will laughed at the severity of his love for his daughter—and her unwavering love for him. Maybe he hadn't done as badly in the parenting department as he'd thought.

Phillip walked up behind Tara, resting his hands on his wife's shoulders and leaning down to kiss her teary cheek. "Happy Christmas, love," he said softly before leaning over her to kiss Sophie as well. Tara reached for one of his hands and gripped it firmly. Will looked over his shoulder to where his parents sat on a small couch—their makeshift bed for the night. His mum blew him a kiss, and he grinned.

Maybe he'd had it all wrong. He'd believed for so long that he wasn't allowed to want. That he didn't deserve anything that was for his own selfish gain. But that's not what loving someone meant. It wasn't one-sided. Love was a give and take. And if you were lucky enough to earn the love of someone wonderful, you'd be willing to give more than you got—just for a tiny taste of that love.

He had that with his daughter. He knew that now. Christ, it had taken him years, but he finally got it. Loving Holly wasn't selfish, not when all he wanted was the privilege to *give* his love to her. What he got in return, he'd never take for granted.

That was, if she'd take him back.

Chapter Twenty-Six

Gemini: Your single-minded nature is often your strength, but when you focus on only one aspect of your life, others get neglected. Feed your ambition. Feed your soul. Rinse and repeat. There's a recipe for balance, Gemini, but only you know the ingredients.

Holly knocked on Andrea's office door even though it was wide open. She glanced toward the empty conference room, and her heart sank a little, just like it had every day this last month when she walked past to find Will not there.

"Burning the holiday oil as well?" Andrea asked, motioning for her to come in.

It was December 29, and Holly was pretty sure she had all she needed for the final site survey at the W, except for her partner in her biggest professional endeavor. The Tallulah Chan show was supposed to be her grand event—her starring role that would prove to Andrea that she truly was up for the task of partner. But now New Year's Eve was like one of those cartoon rain clouds that followed one unlucky schlub.

She was the schlub, unable to get out from beyond the gloom. Now all she wanted was closure—to end the incessant rain and get to see sunny skies again.

"Yeah," Holly said. "Just wanted to make sure I had all the paperwork for Ms. Chan to sign, releases for the VIP ticket winners so we can take photos for the paper, all that fun stuff."

She sat in one of the chairs, knees bouncing, not sure which question she wanted to ask first. Her eyes drifted toward the wall that connected Andrea's office with the conference room.

"You seem a little distracted," Andrea said, and Holly's head snapped back, her eyes locking on the other woman's.

"Did you really think that?" she asked. Guess this would be question number one. "Did you really think that Mr. Evans…" She groaned. There was zero point in pretense right now. "Did you think Will was a distraction for me?"

Andrea laughed. "Oh, honey. I think he still is, though I admit I thought you two were just sleeping together. I didn't realize you really liked him. And yes, I was worried what it meant to put you on our most high-profile event only to see your attention divided between the job itself and the man you were working with. Maybe it wasn't your most professional decision, but it was wrong of me to judge." Holly's brows rose. She'd expected a lecture, but instead she was getting… understanding? "I don't think I've ever seen you do more than smile pleasantly at a man you brought to a party or a show," she continued. "But right now you're mooning over drywall."

Holly winced. Was she that obvious? She guessed so, but she couldn't help it. She was way out of her element here, and she was still holding on to that whole six-month idea, that any day now—any minute, hopefully—she'd be back to her old self. She didn't *want* to moon over drywall. She didn't want to be angry that he hadn't called or texted to even wish her a merry Christmas. Then again, neither had she. But she wasn't the one who'd called him a distraction. She wasn't the one who'd blamed her for the terrible scare of losing Sophie.

She was just the one who proposed a bit of fun and ended up falling in love with a guy whose life didn't seem to have room in it for her. Not that she'd truly told him how she felt—*I might love you, too*? Ugh. She was the worst. Not that it mattered, because Will Evans only had room in his life for his daughter.

Sophie. Even after one day, she adored that little girl. But Will was a father, with fatherly responsibilities. In *London.* And Holly was no stranger to putting a relationship at the bottom of her priority list. She found it unfortunate that she'd finally realized she wanted to put the work in with Will, *outside* the office, just as he decided he couldn't. But she still understood.

She leaned forward, rested her arms on Andrea's desk, then let her forehead fall with a soft thud against the wood. Again. And then one more time after that.

"What is happening to me?"

She groaned. Andrea laughed.

"They're called *feelings*, Holly. Are you not enjoying them?"

She looked up and met Andrea's gaze.

"Are you going to make me partner, or am I too distracted for the job?"

Andrea leaned back in her chair and sighed.

"How badly do you want it?" she asked.

Holly rolled her eyes—*at her boss*. But screw it. She was an open book at this point, and there was no reason to hold back.

"I've been with you from the beginning," she said. "I've been loyal, hardworking, and you *know* I can hold my own directing a show." Her eyes were getting misty, and it had to be from lack of sleep. She'd never had trouble sleeping alone, but now her body had the sense memory of what it was like to sleep with someone else molded to her own shape, warm arms wrapped around her naked body. As tired as she'd been—and the last few weeks before the show had been the busiest—she wasn't getting more than three to four hours of sleep a night.

"I love what I do, Andrea. And I'm good at it, and I know you don't want to run this ship on your own forever. You built Trousseau from the ground up, and you've done an amazing job. With me next door you can do even better."

If she knew that her future was set—if Andrea gave the word that she'd start the new year as Trousseau's new partner—then that would be enough. This was everything she'd always wanted. How could it not be?

Andrea pulled a file folder from her desk drawer and slid it across the desk.

"I agree," she said. "Maybe you can sign these, then?"

Holly opened the folder, and inside she found a contract.

"I trust you'll want a lawyer to take a look at the paperwork before you sign on the dotted line, but I think you'll be happy with my terms and the location clause."

Holly's hand shook as she flipped through the pages. Brynn could read it for her. She'd taken a couple contracts classes in law school before going the CPA route. Everything was lining up. This was exactly what she wanted, and suddenly it terrified her to get it.

"Location clause?"

Andrea shrugged. "You're about to solidify us in the international market," she said. "I may need you to scout some international talent from time to time. Maybe even for extended periods of time."

Her boss and—she guessed—soon-to-be partner winked.

"Andrea, I don't understand. You already have the contract? B-but the show hasn't even happened yet. What if something goes wrong? What if I mess up? What if you change your mind?"

Andrea laughed, though Holly couldn't imagine what was

so funny. Did this woman know what she was doing, giving half her company to someone who had her priorities all jumbled up?

"What if work isn't the only number one on my list anymore?" Holly added, not realizing she knew the answer to the question until she asked it. "What if I don't live and breathe *just* for Trousseau?"

Because she finally got what had changed. Just like she put her theater roles first when she was in high school and college, she put her career above every other connection in her life. Being good at something and having others recognize it was an intoxicating feeling. And those feelings were always on her terms—under her control. A performance ran from Wednesday through Sunday? She'd be adored for those four days and then move on to whatever came next. She could be a star, shine bright until her time was up, and know that feeling would come again with the next role, the next show, the next time she saw her name in the paper.

But having Will in her life? That had filled those spaces in between, the ones she didn't know needed filling. He'd seen her pull off reconstructing a lost presentation in little more than twenty-four hours. And he'd seen her helpless and sick, afraid of failure, unwilling to admit she even missed him let alone was falling for him. Even if he wasn't here, Will made her understand what Andrea was offering, what it really meant to put that kind of trust in someone else.

"Do you know what it means to me to have you sitting next door—or *wherever* you set up your home base?" Andrea asked. "It means *I* don't have to live and breathe *just* Trousseau anymore. I never asked that of you, Holly. That was all your doing. But now I'll have your back and you'll have mine, and no one needs to carry the weight alone. No one needs to sacrifice one aspect of her life for another."

Holly nodded. "I get it," she said. "I finally get it."

Chapter Twenty-Seven

The taxi pulled up in front of the W at half past six, and the fashion show began at seven. In the world of professionalism, he had never cut it this close. But in all her six years, Sophie had never been so sick. He'd almost missed the show altogether until her fever finally broke yesterday morning, and he'd been lucky enough to get a flight in just enough time.

According to Will's internal clock, it was already after midnight, and he was running on fumes. He handed the driver a wad of cash and grabbed his small weekend bag. He'd only be here for two nights before heading back to England for good. Well, he guessed that all depended on Holly.

This was *not* supposed to be how their reunion went. There was going to be coffee or beer or wine. And a quiet space, like a corner booth at Kingston's. Her kitchen. His hotel room. After missing his chance to ring her on Christmas Eve, he decided the only way to do this was in person. They would have a chance to sort *them* out, if there was still a them, before a perfectly amazing event that would earn Holly an office with a door and Will his year to leave everything behind to focus on his daughter.

He found Tallulah in a lounge just next to the ballroom, one that would serve as the dressing area for the models. She was putting finishing touches on her pieces now that the women were wearing them, and there was Holly, lining them up in the order they would enter the room and take the stage.

His breath caught in his throat, and his first instinct was to go to her, but he wouldn't interrupt her moment. This evening belonged to Holly, not him. So he watched her from a distance, heart pounding in his chest.

"There he is!" Tallulah called, her long black hair swishing across her shoulders as she strode toward him. "This is sound, Billy. Really sound. I mean, I loved the photos you and Holly had in your presentation, but seeing this place in the flesh? Just brilliant."

Holly looked up, her eyes meeting his. He smiled, because how could he not? She was the woman he loved, and no matter what came of this evening, he couldn't react to her in any other way. Holly's eyes widened for only a second, and then she returned the gesture.

Marisa burst through the door, grinning from ear to ear.

"We need to get everyone backstage," she said. "It's just about go time!"

Holly tore her gaze from his and nodded in Marisa's direction. "Here we go!" she said, and led the line of Tallulah Chan–clad women out the door.

He let out a breath as he watched her exit, his eyes finally registering the dress—black lace hugging her skin at the bodice, long bell sleeves, and an asymmetrical skirt that hit just below midthigh. Her *bare* midthigh. A Tallulah Chan original. But it was what came next that nearly drove him to madness, his eyes raking down her legs that were covered from knee to toe in ruby-red suede.

"Your lass is quite a stunner, yeah?" Tallulah said, sidling up to him.

"She's not my…I mean, we aren't…"

She nudged his hip with her own.

"Bollocks, Billy. Pick your chin up off the floor and come watch my show. Then she's all yours."

He opened his mouth to protest, but he was obviously an open book.

"Maybe you could refrain from the whole *Billy* thing at least."

She laughed. "Is that what your…" She cleared her throat. "Is that what *Holly* calls you?"

Will closed his eyes and shook his head.

"I'd actually welcome that at the moment. But no. I think she has a larger vocabulary of words to describe me these days. *Arsehole. Wanker. Bloody prick.*"

"Ah." She grinned. "It's worse than I thought. She's quite a talent, too. The whole package. Well, don't let my little show get in the way of your love story." She winked at him and then sauntered toward the door, graceful and poised as if she was about to take the runway herself. "I saw the way she looked at you, *William*," she called back to him. "You've still got a shot. Don't blow it this time."

He loved Holly. A month hadn't changed that, but his timing was shite. And the distance that had grown between them since he'd blamed her for his own insecurity as a parent? He had to hope one evening would be enough time to get from one end to the other.

He stood at the back of the ballroom and watched as Holly Chandler and Tallulah Chan took the stage hand in hand as the DJ played Fleetwood Mac's "Go Your Own Way." The industry professionals stood for the women, applauding as they took a lap down the runway together. Holly had gotten what she wanted. She was a star, and he only hoped she knew how brightly she shone. He clapped, too, hidden behind the crowd that was already transitioning to New Year's Eve party mode.

When designer and director exited the stage, he hurried back to the dressing area to catch up with them, to grab a few precious minutes to tell Holly everything he should have said weeks ago. But as soon as she entered the room, Andrea was already there doling out champagne. Someone from the *Sun-Times* walked past, flashing a press pass and asking to speak to the two women, and he watched as Holly beamed, nodding yes but asking the guy to wait a moment while she grabbed a bag from a nearby dressing station and pulled out a folder and a pen. She opened it on the table and bent to sign a page before handing it to Andrea.

So she'd made partner, not that he doubted she would. He realized this was *her* night, though. And he had no business making it about him. So he backed out of the room, letting her have her moment.

Even if it meant he might not get his.

Chapter Twenty-Eight

Gemini: Just because you make the rules doesn't mean you can break them. Or does it?

After the W had gone from fashion show to fashionable New Year's Eve festivities, Holly headed back to Kingston's. She'd originally planned to stay at the W long after the show had ended, but when it had sunk in after Christmas that she'd be staying alone—well, that had altered her plans. Jamie had offered up the bar for anyone who wanted a more intimate celebration.

Once Holly arrived, though, she wasn't quite ready to put her party hat on. She stood at the foot of the stairs. Annie's boyfriend, Brett, was on the upper level playing DJ for the after-party, spinning a perfect sixties- and seventies-inspired set that continued the boho vibe from the fashion show. "Benny and the Jets" had Jeremy dancing behind the downstairs bar while Jamie stayed composed as he filled pint glasses for those who'd taken the shuttle from the W. Everything was—dare she say it?—perfect.

Everything except that sinking feeling in her stomach, the one she'd felt when she saw Will leave the hotel without so much as a congratulations.

"I've already seen pictures online, Holl. You were amazing tonight," Brynn said, sidling up beside her. "So what's with the frowny face?"

Holly eyed her sister, taking her in from head to toe, pausing at her feet.

"When did I lend you those boots?" she asked, and Brynn laughed.

"I might have snuck them out when you were putting the finishing touches on your hair."

Holly let out a sigh.

"Do *not* walk in the snow with those. You took a cab here tonight, right? Please tell me you took a cab."

Brynn gripped her sister's shoulders.

"It's a wind chill of negative eleven out there. I took a cab from the bathroom to this end of the bar."

Holly rolled her eyes.

"Relax, honey," Brynn continued. "You did it. And, um, you look gorgeous."

She curtsied and smiled. "Thanks."

"Is he here yet?" her sister asked, and Holly knew she meant that certain Brit.

She shook her head. "I'm guessing he's not even coming. He was at the show, but he left without really saying a word to me. I think this might have been it, B. I think it's really over."

"Then you guessed wrong," Brynn said, nodding to the door.

There were times Holly wished she could conjure a thought and just as quickly have that thought become reality. Like when she ran out of ice cream. If she could think about Häagen-Dazs salted caramel and make a pint appear on her counter, that would be fantastic. *This* season's Jimmy Choos?

If she could think those into existence, she'd have Carrie Bradshaw's closet in no time, and she'd probably live in it—happy and fulfilled with all the shoes. Or Choos. Either way.

But as much as she'd been thinking about Will, she couldn't conjure the right words, especially if the words included *good-bye*.

"Oh, shit, honey," Brynn said. "*Look* at him."

He was taking off his coat and handing it to one of Kingston's servers who was acting as coat check. Holly knew Brynn wasn't referring to the fitted red sweater or the shirt and tie underneath. Yes, he was gorgeous. But he looked how she felt—bone weary and dejected, and she wasn't sure she could handle more.

"I know he said hurtful things, Holl. But I can also tell that man is hurting himself."

Holly shrugged.

"Our six months are up," she said. "That's probably all he has to say."

"Your six months are bullshit," Brynn countered.

Holly had no argument left in her, so she just watched him as he scanned the crowd, his eyes finding hers. Jeez, the two of them were dressed like they were ready to pose for their own couple's Christmas card. But they weren't a couple. Not anymore. And not ever, if they were going to get technical about things.

Holly turned toward her sister to argue, but Brynn was already behind the bar helping Jamie and Jeremy.

Traitor, she thought. And then she heard the voice she'd longed for since that awful day after Thanksgiving.

"Everything all right?" he asked, and she nodded, then shook her head.

A small smile broke through his morose, Eeyore-like expression, and Holly realized that's what she must have looked like for the past few weeks.

"I don't mope," she said, and Will's brows drew together.

"Okay—" he began, but she wasn't going to let him. The floodgates were open, and she suddenly had everything to say.

"I don't mope, not over relationships. I walk away unscathed. I dust off my sleeves and go back to life as it was before. No harm, no foul."

He crossed his arms and nodded. They stood off to the side in a quiet nook of unused tables, a stream of figures striding up and down the stairs behind them.

"And I get that you have Sophie and that your life is in England and that you said some really awful things because you were in a really awful situation. And as much as it hurt for you to blame your insecurities on me—because that's what they are, Will, *your* issues that *you* need to straighten out—I should be over it by now. I should be over *you*."

He grinned. Dammit, he freaking *grinned*, and he looked so good doing it she almost forgot she was giving him hell for making her fall in love.

"May I have permission to speak, Ms. Chandler?"

Holly huffed out a breath and tried to think of something else to say just to spite him, but she couldn't. She'd just about said it all.

"Fine," she told him. "Permission granted."

He took a step closer, enough that she had to back up against the underside of the stairway, enough that she could smell him, and she had to fight not to let her familiar urges win out over logical thought.

"I am an arse," he said, and she nodded. He laughed, and again it took effort not to smile back. "Thank you for agreeing." He scrubbed a hand over his face, and she ached to do the same, to run her fingers over the world-weary lines at the corner of his eyes. She had to remind herself what had weighed on him from the start—how they'd ended up where they were now.

"Shite," he said. "I don't even know where to begin. I probably should have planned this better."

Holly rolled her eyes.

"Maybe that's part of the problem," she said. "Trying to fit everything into a plan." She knew she wasn't only talking about him, but he had the floor. "Why don't you try just saying whatever it is you want me to know without worrying about the right words or the plan or—"

He placed two fingers gingerly over her lips, and she stopped talking.

"Fine," he said. "No plan. Just me telling you that I've been a mess since Thanksgiving. That I never should have let the past month go by without speaking to you. That my behavior was inexcusable. But I didn't know how to fix what I thought couldn't be fixed." He took a breath, ran a hand through his hair. "I don't blame you for what happened at the museum, Holly."

"Aquarium," she corrected. Then her own hand flew to her mouth. "My bad," she said, the sound muffled through her hand. "You sound like you're gearing up to something good, so I'll just zip it."

Sure, zip it and hope she didn't let out a sob or some other sort of ridiculous noise that would be the culmination of a heartbreaking month, an amazing show, and the man she loved hopefully realizing he was lost without her.

Dramatic? Of *course* she was being dramatic. What came next meant *everything*.

He wasn't smiling. Not yet, but God, she hoped there was a yet.

"I'm so sorry, Holly. I'll never forgive myself for speaking to you like that, for not calling on Christmas Eve when I meant to because I had to take Sophie to hospital and I just have not been myself and—"

Holly's hand slid from her mouth.

"Will, what happened to Sophie?"

Her heart sank. Here she'd been thinking of only herself, of how Will would win her back if he was, in fact, trying to do so. She still hoped he was. But she hadn't once thought about what had been going on with him.

"It's all right," he said. "Sophie's okay now. But she was quite ill, and I was bloody terrified, and do you want to know what I kept thinking for the past week as I waited for her to get well?"

She shook her head, afraid that this was the closure she was seeking. But it was hard to want closure when he was standing there being so—so *Will*.

"I kept thinking that if *you* were there, you'd have been strong for me like you were at the aquarium. You would have touched my cheek, my arm, or my hand and told me I'd get through it. You'd have sat next to me in the hospital overnight while they administered fluids and brought Sophie's fever down. And when she went home with Tara and Phillip after we missed having a proper Christmas, I wouldn't have had to go home alone. I wouldn't have faced the past week alone— the whole time wishing you were by my side. And it's not just because of the holidays or Sophie getting ill. London, Chicago—it doesn't matter where. Your touch is home, Holly."

She couldn't help it. Holly lifted her hand and rested it on his cheek.

"Yes," he said softly, leaning into her touch. "Just like that." He reached for her hand, threading their fingers together. "I know Sophie comes first for me and Trousseau for you, but I think there's room at the top for more than one *first*. I don't deserve it, but I'm hoping there's some ridiculous reason you'll forgive me."

She bit her lip because it was trembling, and she sniffed hard to keep the tears at bay because she didn't mope over relationships. She didn't mope over a guy. And she wouldn't mope over Will Evans begging her to forgive him and then leaving for good.

But after that, how could she not let him off the hook? She wouldn't let this beautiful man punish himself any longer.

"I have one," she said. "A ridiculous reason to forgive you."

Will bent down, resting his forehead against hers.

"Tell me," he pleaded.

He tucked her hair behind her ear, and she didn't shy away from his touch.

"I'm in love with you, Billy."

Well, dammit. The first tear fell, which meant the floodgates were open.

He barked out a laugh. "I hate that bloody name," he said. "But I've been going mad, I'm so in love with you," he added.

She let out something like a laugh, but the tears made it sound more like a sob. He swiped his thumb across her wet cheek.

"What do we do now?" Holly asked. "You're leaving."

He nodded. "And you're staying."

She threw up her hands. "Then what are we... *Why* are we having this conversation?"

He smiled.

Why? Why was he freaking smiling?

"Tara and I had lots of time to chat while Sophie was ill. She and I are splitting our time with Sophie next year. Fifty-fifty. For the first two weeks of the month she'll live with me, and for the second two she'll live with Tara and Phillip. I was hoping for the time that I don't have her—when she doesn't have any obligations I wouldn't want to miss—that I'd come here. To Chicago. To be with you. Even with the sabbatical, I've racked up enough of those damned frequent flyer miles, so we won't have to be apart for long stretches. Not if we don't want to." He cleared his throat. "I mean, if *you* don't want to."

Holly sniffed again. Although this time it was because her nose was running. She reached around him to an unused place setting at the table and stole the napkin so she could dry her leaking face.

"You're going to come to Chicago every month? For me? But I thought you hated being away from Sophie."

He nodded. "I do, but I think it will be different now that I get to be more than a weekend dad. And if I don't make things right with you, Sophie might disown me anyway." He laughed. "We need to wait out this six-month rule of yours first, though. You never know. Your timing could be off, and you might be hit with a wave of indifference by tomorrow."

Enough of this. She grabbed his sweater and pulled him to her, but he stopped short just as their lips were about to meet.

"You didn't say *may I*, Ms. Chandler."

She couldn't help but laugh. "May I...break the rules, Mr. Evans?"

He dipped his head and brushed her nose with his own.

"I thought you'd never ask."

Holly kissed him, even though she couldn't stop simultaneously smiling and crying. His hands were in her hair and hers fisted in his sweater. Cashmere.

She loosened her grip.

"What's wrong?" he asked, and she shook her head.

"I'm not going to ruin a beautiful knit," she admitted, and this only made his smile broaden.

"I guess you're going to have to find somewhere more suitable to place your hands."

She giggled, letting her hands slide down his torso to the top of his jeans, sneaking his sweater up and pulling his button-down free, her finger teasing the small patch of exposed skin. He sucked in a breath.

"I guess I am."

FEBRUARY

Chapter Twenty-Nine

Sophie bounced on Will's lap while Holly snuggled under his arm. He listened as Holly pointed out the different constellations to his daughter. She showed them Castor and Pollux, the twins of her own sign, Gemini.

"And that's Taurus," she said, drawing with her finger in the sky. "Some see him as a raging bull, which means angry, but I don't agree."

Sophie giggled. "Because Daddy is a Taurus?"

Holly nodded. "He's too loving and gentle for that. Don't you think?"

Will groaned. "I can be cross if you girls want me to." But it was no use. Because Will couldn't imagine himself happier than he was in this very moment. It didn't matter that it was unseasonably cold, Holly having brought the tail end of Chicago's winter with her to London. He'd stay out on his front steps all night and long into the morning if it meant not interrupting this moment. The two people he loved most in the world were in his arms, and to top it off, they loved him right back.

A car slowed in front of his place, and when it came to a stop, Tara exited the driver's side.

"Mummy!" Sophie said and sprang from Will's lap so she could welcome her mum with a hug. Tara lifted their daughter up and onto her hip, but the seven-year-old girl barely fit there anymore.

"She's growing up so quickly," he said softly, and Holly wrapped her arms around his torso and squeezed.

"You made that, you know," she told him. "You made that perfect little girl, and she'll grow up to be a lovely woman because of how you and Tara raised her."

He sighed. He had never given himself much of the credit before, but he could see it better now—his own subtle influences on his daughter.

She came bounding back up the steps and wrapped him and Holly both in a hug.

"You can snog as soon as I leave," she whispered to them both, and Will choked on a laugh.

Like that, he thought. *Speaking before thinking.* He could take credit for that.

"Good night, Soph," he said. "I love you."

"Good night, Sophie," Holly added. "See you in a couple weeks."

Tara, still standing by the car, waved to them both.

"Nice to see you, Holly," she said, and it nearly sounded sincere. "Good night, William."

He waved back, as did Holly, and they watched her get Sophie situated in her seat before climbing back in and pulling away.

Holly picked up her mug and sipped. She licked the foam off her upper lip and grinned.

"I didn't know what I'd signed up for coming over to your side of the pond," she said. "I mean, I was expecting a tall, dark, and sexy Brit who's also a wonderful father." She sipped again, this time letting the foam remain so that she was now looking at him with a hazelnut soy mustache. "But a barista? Well, that's just icing on the cake. Or—foam on the latte, I guess."

He leaned over and kissed her, long and slow and sweet. Any remaining foam he swiped away with his thumb and then licked it clean.

"You had a little something," he said, and she laughed. He'd never get tired of that sound. Or the fact that she was here—and not just on a visit. As Trousseau's new partner and international scout, she was setting up shop in London for at least the next six months, if not indefinitely. After the success of the Tallulah Chan show, Andrea hadn't wanted to take a step back. She wanted to expand.

Holly was running a hand through his hair now, and Will thought he'd never get tired of her touch, either.

"What about your sister?" he asked, and she shrugged.

"She and Jamie are applying for passports as we speak. As soon as I have my own place, they'll be on the first plane to jolly old England. Jamie's already planning a pub tour."

Will nodded in approval, but this all still felt so surreal.

"What if you *don't* find your own place?" he asked, a grin teasing at the corners of his mouth. "It's not easy to find a place to let for less than a year."

His heart was racing. He knew it was too much. They'd only just gotten back together six weeks ago, and Holly had been in London for less than twelve hours.

"I'm sorry," he said. "I'm going to give you your space. First thing tomorrow we shop for a flat, just like we planned."

She nudged his shoulder with her hers, biting that bottom lip like she did, driving him mad with the thought of her mouth and teeth—other places.

He shook his head. This was an important conversation. It was *not* the time to let his mind wander.

"My current visa is only for six months, enough time for

me to scout the area and see if this is where the first satellite office should be. Andrea said it's up to me, my call," she said, grinning. "For some renters it's a short time, but for *others*— it's a big commitment. A lot can happen in six months, you know. Are you sure you want to commit to that?"

He pulled her closer, that heart of his doing ridiculous things in his chest as it realized what she was saying, that she was *staying*. Right here. With him. There was only one problem.

He kissed the cold tip of her nose and then each cheek, but he paused just centimeters from her lips.

"I have this rule," he said, his voice low and soft, and he could hear Holly's breath hitch. "Do you want to know what it is?"

She nodded.

"Just let me love you for as long as you'll have me. Six months. Six years. Six decades. I'm a goner, Holly Chandler. You had me at last season's Jimmy Choos."

She pulled back and huffed out a breath.

"The shoes? Seriously, Will, you're going to bring up the shoes? Honestly, you can be so—"

But she didn't get to finish because he was kissing her again, and she was kissing him back, melting into his touch.

"Did you hear the part about me loving you for as long as you'll let me?" he asked, lips still against hers.

"I did," she said.

"Will you stay with me, in my home?" He hadn't known he'd be asking her this. It wasn't part of the plan. But now that he'd said it, he couldn't imagine it any other way. "I don't want to wake up without you for another morning, Holly. Not if I don't have to."

She nodded. "I will."

He pulled away and stood, reaching a hand down for hers, but her hand was already on her phone, swiping open the screen.

"Gonna see what the astrologists have to say about my proposal—for you to *stay* here? Christ, I'm really not trying to rush you, Holly."

It was bloody cold out, but his palms began to sweat. She still made him nervous, and he loved every second of it.

She shoved the phone into her pocket and picked up her mug before standing to meet him.

"I was. But...no," she answered. "You're living proof that I make my own magic now."

His brows furrowed, but she didn't say anything else, only grabbed his outstretched hand.

"*May I* escort you inside, Ms. Chandler?"

She squeezed his hand. Good sign. He hadn't scared her off yet.

"You may," she answered, smiling at him like she saw no one else. "And one other thing."

"Anything," he said.

"I'll take six decades. Six decades of loving Will Evans. Where do I sign?"

He opened the door and led her inside, setting her mug on the side table by the door so he could wrap his arms around her hips and pull her close.

"I don't have any official papers, but I'm sure we can think of some way to seal this deal."

She laughed. "I'm sure we can."

And they left a trail of clothing and shoes from the front door to Will's room, to *their* room. Some of the items were this season, some last. But it didn't matter, not when he had Holly winter, spring, summer, and autumn. She loved him, forgave him, and breathed new life into one that had forgotten how to breathe on its own.

She could wear any damn shoes she wanted, and he'd never say another word.

Well...as long as they were red.

Acknowledgments

Thank you to my agent, Courtney Miller-Callihan, for encouraging my *Sherlock* fandom—and also for your support of this series. When I said I wanted to try my hand at lighthearted adult romance, you told me to go for it. Now here we are.

Thanks to my fabulous editor, Karen Grove, for not only falling for Holly and Will and making their story oh so sparkly, but for your love of Lou Malnati's and ice cream as well. I knew we were a good fit.

Lia Riley, Megan Erickson, Natalie Blitt, and Jennifer Blackwood, you are lifesavers day in and day out, as critique partners, as sanity preservers, and as my friends. I love you all.

S and C, I love you times infinity to the infinity power. There. I win.

And always, thank you to my wonderful readers who have shown me it's never too late to chase a dream. Your support means the world.

About the Author

A. J. Pine writes stories to break readers' hearts, but don't worry—she'll mend them with a happily ever after. As an English teacher and a librarian, A. J. has always surrounded herself with books. All her favorites have one big commonality—romance. Naturally, the books she writes have the same. When she's not writing, she's of course reading. Then there's online shopping (everything from groceries to shoes). And a tiny bit of TV where she nourishes her undying love of vampires, superheroes, and a certain high-functioning sociopath detective. You'll also find her hanging with her family in the Chicago 'burbs.

Discover more Entangled Select Contemporary titles...

HEALING LOVE
a *Love to the Extreme* novel by Abby Niles

Doctor Ella Watts wants her old life back. Desperately. Personal trainer Lance Black is the man to help her gain confidence in her MMA abilities. Not only is he toned, muscular, and gorgeous, he's patient, a great teacher, and willing to treat her like a worthy opponent. Except his size makes her freeze whenever he gets too close. There's more to the mysterious blonde ninja than a beautiful woman determined to improve her MMA skills, and underground fighter Lance Black plans on finding that out. If he can get to know her outside the gym, all the better. As long as she never learns his secrets.

HOW TO FALL
a novel by Rebecca Brooks

Julia Evans puts everyone else first—but all that is about to change, starting with a spontaneous trip to Brazil. Now Julia can be anyone she wants. Like someone who's willing to have a wickedly hot hook-up with the sexy Aussie at her hotel. Except, Blake Williams may not be what he seems. Julia and Blake will have to decide if they're jumping into the biggest adventure of all or playing it safe.

A Friendly Flirtation
a *Friends First* novel by Christine Warner

Allison Hall is fed up with being the invisible nerdy girl. She needs confidence—and that requires a makeover and dating tips. Jared Esterly says no when his business partner and best friend Nick's little sister comes to him for advice. But when Al's attempt to make changes on her own fails spectacularly, he's there to pick up the pieces. As lessons move from the salon to the bedroom, Allison discovers change can come at a very high price.

Snowbound Seduction
a novella by Melissa Schroeder

Trevor MacMillian is the tart and incredibly sexy executive chef who's made pastry chef Elaine Masterson's life a living hell. But when she catches him in nothing but a tiny little towel, it's almost enough to make her forget they're stranded in a luxurious mountain cabin together—or that she hates him almost as much as she craves him like a sinfully forbidden dessert. Then an intense and unexpected kiss turns their hostility into insatiable hunger. And with this much heat, the snowstorm outside doesn't stand a chance...